THE GRAIN KINGS

THE GRAIN KINGS

Keith Roberts

THE GRAIN KINGS

Published by:

Wildside Press
PO Box 45
Gillette, NJ 07933-0045

www.wildsidepress.com
ISBN 1-880448-84-X

For Anthony Whittome and
Giles Gordon, who do the
really hard part.

Contents

Weihnachtsabend

I

The big car moved slowly, nosing its way along narrowing lanes. Here, beyond the little market town of Wilton, the snow lay thicker. Trees and bushes loomed in the headlights, coated with driven white. The tail of the Mercedes wagged slightly, steadied. Mainwaring heard the chauffeur swear under his breath. The link had been left live.

Dials let into the seatback recorded the vehicle's mechanical wellbeing: oil pressure, temperature, revs, k.p.h. Lights from the repeater glowed softly on his companion's face. She moved, restlessly; he saw the swing of yellow hair. He turned slightly. She was wearing a neat, brief kilt, heavy boots. Her legs were excellent.

He clicked the dial lights off. He said, 'Not much farther.'

He wondered if she was aware of the open link. He said, 'First time down?'

She nodded in the dark. She said, 'I was a bit overwhelmed.'

Wilton Great House sprawled across a hilltop five miles or more beyond the town. The car drove for some distance beside the wall that fringed the estate. The perimeter defences had been strengthened since Mainwaring's last visit. Watchtowers reared at intervals; the wall itself had been topped by multiple strands of wire.

The lodge gates were commanded by two new stone pillboxes. The Merc edged between them, stopped. On the road from London the snow had eased; now big flakes drifted again, lit by the headlights. Somewhere, orders were barked.

A man stepped forward, tapped at the window. Mainwaring buttoned it open. He saw a GFP armband, a hip holster with the flap tucked back. He said, 'Good evening, Captain.'

'*Guten Abend, mein Herr. Ihre Ausweiskarte?*'

Cold air gusted against Mainwaring's cheek. He passed across his identity card and security clearance, He said, *'Richard Mainwaring. Die rechte Hand des Gesandten. Fräulein Hunter, von meiner Abteilung.'*

A torch flashed over the papers, dazzled into his eyes, moved to examine the girl. She sat stiffly, staring ahead. Beyond the security officer Mainwaring made out two steel-helmeted troopers, automatics slung. In front of him the wipers clicked steadily.

The GFP man stepped back. He said, *'Ihre Ausweis wird in einer Woche ablaufen. Erneuen Sie Ihre Karte.'*

Mainwaring said, *'Vielen Dank, Herr Hauptmann. Frohe Weihnachten.'*

The man saluted stiffly, unclipped a walkie-talkie from his belt. A pause, and the gates swung back. The Merc creamed through. Mainwaring said, *'Bastard . . .'*

She said, 'Is it always like this?'

He said, 'They're tightening up all round.'

She pulled her coat round her shoulders. She said, 'Frankly, I find it a bit scary.'

He said, 'Just the Minister taking care of his guests.'

Wilton stood in open downland set with great trees. Hans negotiated a bend, carefully, drove beneath half-seen branches. The wind moaned, zipping round a quarterlight. It was as if the car butted into a black tunnel, full of swirling pale flakes. He thought he saw her shiver. He said, 'Soon be there.'

The headlamps lit a rolling expanse of snow. Posts, buried nearly to their tops, marked the drive. Another bend, and the house showed ahead. The car lights swept across a façade of mullioned windows, crenellated towers. Hard for the uninitiated to guess, staring at the skilfully weathered stone, that the shell of the place was of reinforced concrete. The car swung right with a crunching of unseen gravel, and stopped. The ignition repeater glowed on the seatback.

Mainwaring said, 'Thank you, Hans. Nice drive.'

Hans said, 'My pleasure, sir.'

She flicked her hair free, picked up her handbag. He held the door for her. He said, 'OK, Diane?'

She shrugged. She said, 'Yes. I'm a bit silly sometimes.' She squeezed his hand, briefly. She said, 'I'm glad you'll be here. Somebody to rely on.'

Mainwaring lay back on the bed and stared at the ceiling. Inside as well as out, Wilton was a triumph of art over nature. Here, in the Tudor wing where most of the guests were housed, walls and ceilings were of wavy plaster framed by heavy oak beams. He turned his head. The room was dominated by a fireplace of yellow Ham stone; on the overmantel, carved in bold relief, the *Hakenkreuz* was flanked by the lion and eagle emblems of the Two Empires. A fire burned in the wrought-iron basket; the logs glowed cheerfully, casting wavering warm reflections across the ceiling. Beside the bed a bookshelf offered required reading: the Fuehrer's official biography, Shirer's *Rise of the Third Reich*, Cummings' monumental *Churchill: the Trial of Decadence*. There were a nicely bound set of Buchan novels, some Kiplings, a Shakespeare, a complete Wilde. A side table carried a stack of current magazines: *Connoisseur, The Field, Der Spiegel, Paris Match*. There was a washstand, its rail hung with dark blue towels; in the corner of the room were the doors to the bathroom and wardrobe, in which a servant had already neatly disposed his clothes.

He stubbed his cigarette, lit another. He swung his legs off the bed, poured himself a whisky. From the grounds, faintly, came voices, snatches of laughter. He heard the crash of a pistol, the rattle of an automatic. He walked to the window, pushed the curtain aside. Snow was still falling, drifting silently from the black sky; but the firing pits beside the big house were brightly lit. He watched the figures move and bunch for a while, let the curtain fall. He sat by the fire, shoulders hunched, staring into the flames. He was remembering the trip through London; the flags hanging limp over Whitehall, slow, jerking movement of traffic, the light tanks drawn up outside St James's. The Kensington road had been crowded, traffic edging and hooting; the vast frontage of Harrods looked grim and oriental against the louring sky. He frowned, remembering the call he had had before leaving the Ministry.

Kosowicz had been the name. From *Time International*; or so he had claimed. He'd refused twice to speak to him; but Kosowicz had been insistent. In the end, he'd asked his secretary to put him through.

Kosowicz had sounded very American. He said, 'Mr Mainwaring, I'd like to arrange a personal interview with your Minister.'

'I'm afraid that's out of the question. I must also point out that this communication is extremely irregular.'

Kosowicz said, 'What do I take that as, sir? A warning, or a threat?'

Mainwaring said carefully, 'It was neither. I merely observed that proper channels of approach do exist.'

Kosowicz said, 'Uh-huh. Mr Mainwaring, what's the truth behind this rumour that Action Groups are being moved into Moscow?'

Mainwaring said, 'Deputy Fuehrer Hess has already issued a statement on the situation. I can see that you're supplied with a copy.'

The phone said, 'I have it before me. Mr Mainwaring, what are you people trying to set up? Another Warsaw?'

Mainwaring said, 'I'm afraid I can't comment further, Mr Kosowicz. The Deputy Fuehrer deplored the necessity of force. The *Einsatzgruppen* have been alerted; at this time, that is all. They will be used if necessary to disperse militants. As of this moment, the need has not arisen.'

Kosowicz shifted his ground. 'You mentioned the Deputy Fuehrer, sir. I hear there was another bomb attempt two nights ago, can you comment on this?'

Mainwaring tightened his knuckles on the handset. He said, 'I'm afraid you've been misinformed. We know nothing of any such incident.'

The phone was silent for a moment. Then it said, 'Can I take your denial as official?'

Mainwaring said, 'This is not an official conversation. I'm not empowered to issue statements in any respect.'

The phone said, 'Yeah, channels do exist. Mr Mainwaring, thanks for your time.'

Mainwaring said, 'Goodbye.' He put the handset down, sat staring at it. After a while he lit a cigarette.

Outside the windows of the Ministry the snow still fell, a dark whirl and dance against the sky. His tea, when he came to drink it, was half cold.

The fire crackled and shifted. He poured himself another whisky, sat back. Before leaving for Wilton, he'd lunched with Winsby-Walker from Productivity. Winsby-Walker made it his business to know everything; but he had known nothing of a correspondent called Kosowicz. He thought, 'I should have checked with Security.' But then, Security would have checked with him.

He sat up, looked at his watch. The noise from the ranges had diminished. He turned his mind with a deliberate effort into another channel. The new thoughts brought no more comfort. Last Christmas he had spent with his mother; now, that couldn't happen again. He remembered other Christmases, back across the years. Once, to the child unknowing, they had been gay affairs of crackers and toys. He remembered the scent and texture of pine branches, closeness of candlelight; and books read by torchlight under the sheets, the hard angles of the filled pillowslip, heavy at the foot of the bed. Then, he had been complete; only later, slowly, had come the knowledge of failure. And with it, loneliness. He thought, 'She wanted to see me settled. It didn't seem much to ask.'

The Scotch was making him maudlin. He drained the glass, walked through to the bathroom. He stripped, and showered. Towelling himself, he thought, 'Richard Mainwaring, Personal Assistant to the British Minister of Liaison.' Aloud he said, 'One must remember the compensations.'

He dressed, lathered his face and began to shave. He thought, 'Thirty-five is the exact middle of one's life.' He was re-membering another time with the girl Diane when just for a little while some magic had interposed. Now, the affair was never mentioned between them. Because of James. Always, of course, there is a James.

He towelled his face, applied aftershave. Despite himself, his mind had drifted back to the phone call. One fact was certain:

there had been a major security spillage. Somebody somewhere had supplied Kosowicz with closely guarded information. That same someone, presumably, had supplied a list of ex-directory lines. He frowned, grappling with the problem. One country, and one only, opposed the Two Empires with gigantic, latent strength. To that country had shifted the focus of Semitic nationalism. And Kosowicz had been an American.

He thought, 'Freedom, schmeedom. Democracy is Jew-shaped.' He frowned again, fingering his face. It didn't alter the salient fact. The tip-off had come from the Freedom Front; and he had been contacted, however obliquely. Now, he had become an accessory; the thought had been nagging at the back of his brain all day.

He wondered what they could want of him. There was a rumour – a nasty rumour – that you never found out. Not till the end, till you'd done whatever was required from you. They were untiring, deadly and subtle. He hadn't run squalling to Security at the first hint of danger; but that would have been allowed for. Every turn and twist would have been allowed for.

Every squirm on the hook.

He grunted, angry with himself. Fear was half their strength. He buttoned his shirt, remembering the guards at the gates, the wire and pillboxes. Here, of all places, nothing could reach him. For a few days he could forget the whole affair. He said aloud, 'Anyway, I don't even matter. I'm not important.' The thought cheered him, nearly.

He clicked the light off, walked through to his room, closed the door behind him. He crossed to the bed and stood quite still, staring at the bookshelf. Between Shirer and the Churchill tome there rested a third slim volume. He reached to touch the spine, delicately; read the author's name, Geissler, and the title, *Toward Humanity*. Below the title, like a topless Cross of Lorraine, were the twin linked 'F's' of the Freedom Front.

Ten minutes ago the book hadn't been there.

He walked to the door. The corridor beyond was deserted. From somewhere in the house, faintly, came music: *Till Eulenspiegel*. There were no nearer sounds. He closed the door again, locked it. Turned back and saw the wardrobe stood slightly ajar.

His case still lay on the side table. He crossed to it, took out the Lüger. The feel of the heavy pistol was comforting. He pushed the clip home, thumbed the safety forward, chambered a round. The breech closed with a hard snap. He walked to the wardrobe, shoved the door wide with his foot.

Nothing there.

He let his held breath escape with a little hiss. He pressed the clip release, ejected the cartridge, laid the gun on the bed. He stood again looking at the shelf. He thought, 'I must have been mistaken.'

He took the book down, carefully. Geissler had been banned since publication in every province of the Two Empires; Mainwaring himself had never even seen a copy. He squatted on the edge of the bed, opened it at random.

The doctrine of Aryan co-ancestry, seized on so eagerly by the English middle classes, had the superficial reasonableness of most theories ultimately traceable to Rosenberg. Churchill's answer, in one sense, had already been made; but Chamberlain, and the country, turned to Hess. . . .

The Cologne settlement, though seeming to offer hope of security to Jews already domiciled in Britain, in fact paved the way for campaigns of intimidation and extortion similar to those already undertaken in history, notably by King John. The comparison is not unapt; for the English bourgeoisie, anxious to construct a rationale, discovered many unassailable precedents. A true Sign of the Times, almost certainly, was the resurgence of interest in the novels of Sir Walter Scott. By 1942 the lesson had been learned on both sides; and the Star of David was a common sight on the streets of most British cities.

The wind rose momentarily in a long wail, shaking the window casement. Mainwaring glanced up, turned his attention back to the book. He leafed through several pages.

In 1940, her Expeditionary Force shattered, her allies quiescent or defeated, the island truly stood alone. Her pro-

*letariat, bedevilled by bad leadership, weakened by a gigantic
depression, was effectively without a voice. Her aristocracy,
like their* Junker *counterparts, embraced coldly what could no
longer be ignored; while after the Whitehall* Putsch *the Cabinet
was reduced to the status of an Executive Council. . . .*

The knock at the door made him start, guiltily. He pushed
the book away. He said, 'Who's that?'

She said, 'Me. Richard, aren't you ready?'

He said, 'Just a minute.' He stared at the book, then placed it
back on the shelf. He thought, 'That at least wouldn't be
expected.' He slipped the Lüger into his case and closed it.
Then he went to the door.

She was wearing a lacy black dress. Her shoulders were bare;
her hair, worn loose, had been brushed till it gleamed. He
stared at her a moment, stupidly. Then he said, 'Please come in.'

She said, 'I was starting to wonder. . . . Are you all right?'

'Yes. Yes, of course.'

She said, 'You look as if you've seen a ghost.'

He smiled. He said, 'I expect I was taken aback. Those Aryan
good looks.'

She grinned at him. She said, 'I'm half Irish, half English,
half Scandinavian. If you have to know.'

'That doesn't add up.'

She said, 'Neither do I, most of the time.'

'Drink?'

'Just a little one. We shall be late.'

He said, 'It's not very formal tonight.' He turned away,
fiddling with his tie.

She sipped her drink, pointed her foot, scuffed her toe on the
carpet. She said, 'I expect you've been to a lot of house parties.'

He said, 'One or two.'

She said, 'Richard, are they . . .?'

'Are they what?'

She said, 'I don't know. You can't help hearing things.'

He said, 'You'll be all right. One's very much like the next.'

She said, 'Are you honestly OK?'

'Sure.'

She said, 'You're all thumbs. Here, let me.' She reached up, knotted deftly. Her eyes searched his face for a moment, moving in little shifts and changes of direction. She said, 'There. I think you just need looking after.'

He said carefully, 'How's James?'

She stared a moment longer. She said, 'I don't know. He's in Nairobi. I haven't seen him for months.'

He said, 'I am a bit nervous, actually.'

'Why?'

He said, 'Escorting a rather lovely blonde.'

She tossed her head, and laughed. She said, 'You need a drink as well then.'

He poured whisky, said, 'Cheers.' The book, now, seemed to be burning into his shoulderblades.

She said, 'As a matter of fact, you're looking rather fetching yourself.'

He thought, 'This is the night when all things come together. There should be a word for it.' Then he remembered about *Till Eulenspiegel*.

She said, 'We'd honestly better go down.'

Lights gleamed in the Great Hall, reflecting from polished boards, dark linenfold panelling. At the nearer end of the chamber a huge fire burned. Beneath the minstrels' gallery long tables had been set. Informal or not, they shone with glass and silverware. Candles glowed amid wreaths of dark evergreen; beside each place was a rolled crimson napkin.

In the middle of the Hall, its tip brushing the coffered ceiling, stood a Christmas tree. Its branches were hung with apples, baskets of sweets, red paper roses; at its base were piled gifts in gay-striped wrappers. Round the tree folk stood in groups, chatting and laughing. Richard saw Müller, the Defence Minister, with a striking-looking blonde he took to be his wife; beside them was a tall, monocled man who was something or other in Security. There was a group of GSP officers in their dark, neat uniforms, beyond them half a dozen Liaison people. He saw Hans the chauffeur standing head bent, nodding intently, smiling at some remark; and thought as he had thought before, how he looked like a big, handsome ox.

Diane had paused in the doorway, and linked her arm through his. But the Minister had already seen them. He came weaving through the crowd, a glass in his hand. He was wearing tight black trews, a dark blue roll-neck shirt. He looked happy and relaxed. He said, 'Richard. And my dear Miss Hunter. We'd nearly given you up for lost. After all, Hans Trapp is about. Now, some drinks. And come, do come; please join my friends. Over here, where it is warm.'

She said, 'Who's Hans Trapp?'

Mainwaring said, 'You'll find out in a bit.'

A little later the Minister said, 'Ladies and gentlemen, I think we may be seated.'

The meal was superb, the wine abundant. By the time the brandy was served Richard found himself talking more easily, and the Geissler copy pushed nearly to the back of his mind. The traditional toasts – King and Fuehrer, the provinces, the Two Empires – were drunk; then the Minister clapped his hands for quiet. 'My friends,' he said, 'tonight, this special night when we can all mix so freely, is *Weihnachtsabend*. It means, I suppose, many things to the many of us here. But let us remember, first and foremost, that this is the night of the children. Your children, who have come with you to share part at least of this very special Christmas.'

He paused. 'Already,' he said, 'they have been called from their crèche; soon, they will be with us. Let me show them to you.' He nodded; at the gesture servants wheeled forward a heavy, ornate box. A drape was twitched aside, revealing the grey surface of a big TV screen. Simultaneously, the lamps that lit the Hall began to dim. Diane turned to Mainwaring, frowning; he touched her hand, gently, and shook his head.

Save for the firelight, the Hall was now nearly dark. The candles guttered in their wreaths, flames stirring in some draught; in the hush, the droning of the wind round the great façade of the place was once more audible. The lights would be out, now, all over the house.

'For some of you,' said the Minister, 'this is your first visit here. For you, I will explain.

'On *Weihnachtsabend* all ghosts and goblins walk. The demon

Hans Trapp is abroad; his face is black and terrible, his clothing the skins of bears. Against him comes the Lightbringer, the Spirit of Christmas. Some call her Lucia Queen, some *Das Christkind*. See her now.'

The screen lit up.

She moved slowly, like a sleepwalker. She was slender, and robed in white. Her ashen hair tumbled round her shoulders; above her head glowed a diadem of burning tapers. Behind her trod the Star Boys with their wands and tinsel robes; behind again came a little group of children. They ranged in age from eight- and nine-year-olds to toddlers. They gripped each other's hands, apprehensively, setting feet in line like cats, darting terrified glances at the shadows to either side.

'They lie in darkness, waiting,' said the Minister softly. 'Their nurses have left them. If they cry out, there is none to hear. So they do not cry out. And one by one she has called them. They see her light pass beneath the door; and they must rise and follow. Here, where we sit, is warmth. Here is safety. Their gifts are waiting; to reach them they must run the gauntlet of the dark.'

The camera angle changed. Now they were watching the procession from above. The Lucia Queen stepped steadily; the shadows she cast leaped and flickered on panelled walls.

'They are in the Long Gallery now,' said the Minister, 'almost directly above us. They must not falter, they must not look back. Somewhere, Hans Trapp is hiding. From Hans, only *Das Christkind* can protect them. See how close they bunch behind her light!'

A howling began, like the crying of a wolf. In part it seemed to come from the screen, in part to echo through the Hall itself. The *Christkind* turned, raising her arms; the howling split into a many-voiced cadence, died to a mutter. In its place came a distant huge thudding, like the beating of a drum.

Diane said abruptly, 'I don't find this particularly funny.'

Mainwaring said, 'It isn't supposed to be. Shh.'

The Minister said evenly, 'The Aryan child must know, from earliest years, the darkness that surrounds him. He must learn to fear, and to overcome that fear. He must learn to be strong. The Two Empires were not built by weakness; weakness will not sustain them. There is no place for it. This in part your children already know. The house is big, and dark; but they will win through to the light. They fight as the Empires once fought. For their birthright.'

The shot changed again, showed a wide, sweeping staircase. The head of the little procession appeared, began to descend. 'Now, where is our friend Hans?' said the Minister. '*Ah* . . .'

Her grip tightened convulsively on Mainwaring's arm. A black-smeared face loomed at the screen. The bogey snarled, clawing at the camera; then turned, loped swiftly towards the staircase. The children shrieked, and bunched; instantly the air was wild with din. Grotesque figures capered and leaped; hands grabbed, clutching. The column was buffeted and swirled; Mainwaring saw a child bowled completely over. The screaming reached a high pitch of terror; and the *Christkind* turned, arms once more raised. The goblins and were-things backed away, growling, into shadow; the slow march was resumed.

The Minister said, 'They are nearly here. And they are good children, worthy of their race. Prepare the tree.'

Servants ran forward with tapers to light the many candles. The tree sprang from gloom, glinting, black-green; and Mainwaring thought for the first time what a dark thing it was, although it blazed with light.

The big doors at the end of the Hall were flung back; and the children came tumbling through. Tear-stained and sobbing they were, some bruised; but all, before they ran to the tree, stopped, made obeisance to the strange creature who had brought them through the dark. Then the crown was lifted, the tapers extinguished; and Lucia Queen became a child like the rest, a slim, barefooted girl in a gauzy white dress.

The Minister rose, laughing. 'Now,' he said, 'music, and some more wine. Hans Trapp is dead. My friends, one and all, and children; *frohe Weihnachten!*'

Diane said, 'Excuse me a moment.'

Mainwaring turned. He said, 'Are you all right?'

She said, 'I'm just going to get rid of a certain taste.'

He watched her go, concernedly; and the Minister had his

arm, was talking. 'Excellent, Richard,' he said. 'It has gone excellently so far, don't you think?'

Richard said, 'Excellently, sir.'

'Good, good. Eh, Heidi, Erna . . . and Frederick, is it Frederick? What have you got there? Oh, very fine. . . .' He steered Mainwaring away, still with his fingers tucked beneath his elbow. Squeals of joy sounded; somebody had discovered a sled, tucked away behind the tree. The Minister said, 'Look at them; how happy they are now. I would like children, Richard. Children of my own. Sometimes I think I have given too much. . . . Still, the opportunity remains. I am younger than you, do you realize that? This is the Age of Youth.'

Mainwaring said, 'I wish the Minister every happiness.'

'Richard, Richard, you must learn not to be so very correct at all times. Unbend a little, you are too aware of dignity. You are my friend. I trust you; above all others, I trust you. Do you realize this?'

Richard said, 'Thank you, sir. I do.'

The Minister seemed bubbling over with some inner pleasure. He said, 'Richard, come with me. Just for a moment. I have prepared a special gift for you. I won't keep you from the party very long.'

Mainwaring followed, drawn as ever by the curious dynamism of the man. The Minister ducked through an arched doorway, turned right and left, descended a narrow flight of stairs. At the bottom the way was barred by a door of plain grey steel. The Minister pressed his palm flat to a sensor plate; a click, the whine of some mechanism, and the door swung inward. Beyond was a further flight of concrete steps, lit by a single lamp in a heavy well-glass. Chilly air blew upward. Mainwaring realized, with something approaching a shock, that they had entered part of the bunker system that honeycombed the ground beneath Wilton.

The Minister hurried ahead of him, palmed a further door. He said, 'Toys, Richard. All toys. But they amuse me.' Then, catching sight of Mainwaring's face, 'Come, man, come! You are more nervous than the children, frightened of poor old Hans!'

The door gave on to a darkened space. There was a heavy, sweetish smell that Mainwaring, for a whirling moment, couldn't place. His companion propelled him forward, gently. He resisted, pressing back; and the Minister's arm shot by him. A click, and the place was flooded with light. He saw a wide, low area, also concrete-built. To one side, already polished and gleaming, stood the Mercedes, next to it the Minister's private Porsche. There were a couple of Volkswagens, a Ford Executive; and in the farthest corner a vision in glinting white. A Lamborghini. They had emerged in the garage underneath the house.

The Minister said, 'My private short cut.' He walked forward to the Lamborghini, stood running his fingers across the low, broad bonnet. He said, 'Look at her, Richard. Here, sit in. Isn't she a beauty? Isn't she fine?'

Mainwaring said, 'She certainly is.'

'You like her?'

Mainwaring smiled. He said, 'Very much, sir. Who wouldn't?'

The Minister said, 'Good, I'm so pleased. Richard, I'm upgrading you. She's yours. Enjoy her.'

Mainwaring stared.

The Minister said, 'Here, man. Don't look like that, like a fish. Here, see. Logbook, your keys. All entered up, finished.' He gripped Mainwaring's shoulders, swung him round laughing. He said, 'You've worked well for me. The Two Empires don't forget; their good friends, their servants.'

Mainwaring said, 'I'm deeply honoured, sir.'

'Don't be honoured. You're still being formal. Richard . . .'

'Sir?'

The Minister said, 'Stay be me. Stay by me. Up there . . . they don't understand. But we understand . . . eh? These are difficult times. We must be together, always together. Kingdom and Reich. Apart . . . we could be destroyed!' He turned away, placed clenched hands on the roof of the car. He said, 'Here, all this. Jewry, the Americans . . . Capitalism. They must stay afraid. Nobody fears an Empire divided. It would fall!'

Mainwaring said, 'I'll do my best, sir. We all will.'

The Minister said, 'I know, I know. But, Richard, this afternoon. I was playing with swords. Silly little swords.'

Mainwaring thought, 'I know how he keeps me. I can see the mechanism. But I mustn't imagine I know the entire truth.'

The Minister turned back, as if in pain. He said, 'Strength is Right. It has to be. But Hess . . .'

Mainwaring said slowly, 'We've tried before, sir . . .'

The Minister slammed his fist on to metal. He said, 'Richard, don't you see? It wasn't us. Not this time. It was his own people. Baumann, von Thaden . . . I can't tell. He's an old man, he doesn't matter any more. It's an idea they want to kill, Hess is an idea. Do you understand? It's *Lebensraum*. Again. . . . Half the world isn't enough.'

He straightened. He said, 'The worm, in the apple. It gnaws, gnaws. . . . But we are Liaison. We matter, so much. Richard, be my eyes. Be my ears.'

Mainwaring stayed silent, thinking about the book in his room; and the Minister once more took his arm. He said, 'The shadows, Richard. They were never closer. Well might we teach our children to fear the dark. But . . . not in our time. Eh? Not for us. There is life, and hope. So much we can do. . . .'

Mainwaring thought, 'Maybe it's the wine I drank. I'm being pressed too hard.' A dull, queer mood, almost of indifference, had fallen on him. He followed his Minister without complaint, back through the bunker complex, up to where the great fire and the tapers on the tree burned low. He heard the singing mixed with the wind-voice, watched the children rock heavy-eyed, carolling sleep. The house seemed winding down, to rest; and she had gone, of course. He sat in a corner and drank wine and brooded, watched the Minister move from group to group until he too was gone, the Hall nearly empty and the servants clearing away.

He found his own self, his inner self, dozing at last as it dozed at each day's end. Tiredness, as ever, had come like a benison. He rose carefully, walked to the door. He thought, 'I shan't be missed here.' Shutters closed, in his head.

He found his key, unlocked his room. He thought, 'Now, she will be waiting. Like all the letters that never came, the phones that never rang.' He opened the door.

She said, 'What kept you?'

He closed the door behind him, quietly. The fire crackled in the little room, the curtains were drawn against the night. She sat by the hearth, barefooted, still in her party dress. Beside her on the carpet were glasses, an ashtray with half-smoked stubs. One lamp was burning; in the warm light her eyes were huge and dark.

He looked across to the bookshelf. The Geissler stood where he had left it. He said, 'How did you get in?'

She chuckled. She said, 'There was a spare key on the back of the door. Didn't you see me steal it?'

He walked toward her, stood looking down. He thought, 'Adding another fragment to the puzzle. Too much, too complicated.'

She said, 'Are you angry?'

He said, 'No.'

She patted the floor. She said gently, 'Please, Richard. Don't be cross.'

He sat, slowly, watching her.

She said, 'Drink?' He didn't answer. She poured one anyway. She said, 'What were you doing all this time? I thought you'd be up hours ago.'

He said, 'I was talking to the Minister.'

She traced a pattern on the rug with her forefinger. Her hair fell forward, golden and heavy, baring the nape of her neck. She said, 'I'm sorry about earlier on. I was stupid. I think I was a bit scared too.'

He drank, slowly. He felt like a run-down machine. Hell to have to start thinking again at this time of night. He said, 'What were you doing?'

She watched up at him. Her eyes were candid. She said, 'Sitting here. Listening to the wind.'

He said, 'That couldn't have been much fun.'

She shook her head, slowly, eyes fixed on his face. She said softly, 'You don't know me at all.'

He was quiet again. She said, 'You don't believe in me, do you?'

He thought, 'You need understanding. You're different from the rest; and I'm selling myself short.' Aloud he said, 'No.'

She put the glass down, smiled, took his glass away. She hotched towards him across the rug, slid her arm round his neck. She said, 'I was thinking about you. Making my mind up.' She kissed him. He felt her tongue pushing, opened his lips. She said, '*Mmm . . .*' She sat back a little, smiling. She said, 'Do you mind?'

'No.'

She pressed a strand of hair across her mouth, parted her teeth, kissed again. He felt himself react, involuntarily; and felt her touch and squeeze.

She said, 'This is a silly dress. It gets in the way.' She reached behind her. The fabric parted; she pushed it down, to the waist. She said, 'Now it's like last time.'

He said slowly, 'Nothing's ever like last time.'

She rolled across his lap, lay looking up. She whispered, 'I've put the clock back.'

Later in the dream she said, 'I was so silly.'

'What do you mean?'

She said, 'I was shy. That was all. You weren't really supposed to go away.'

He said, 'What about James?'

'He's got somebody else. I didn't know what I was missing.'

He let his hand stray over her; and present and immediate past became confused so that as he held her he still saw her kneeling, firelight dancing on her body. He reached for her and she was ready again; she fought, chuckling, taking it bareback, staying all the way.

Much later he said, 'The Minister gave me a Lamborghini.'

She rolled on to her belly, lay chin in hands watching under a tangle of hair. She said, 'And now you've got yourself a blonde. What are you going to do with us?'

He said, 'None of it's real.'

She said, '*Oh . . .*' She punched him. She said, 'Richard, you make me cross. It's happened, you idiot. That's all. It happens to everybody.' She scratched again with a finger on the carpet. She said, 'I hope you've made me pregnant. Then you'd have to marry me.'

He narrowed his eyes; and the wine began again, singing in his head.

She nuzzled him. She said, 'You asked me once. Say it again.'

'I don't remember.'

She said, 'Richard, please . . .' So he said, 'Diane, will you marry me?' And she said, 'Yes, yes, yes,' then afterwards awareness came and though it wasn't possible he took her again and that time was finest of all, tight and sweet as honey. He'd fetched pillows from the bed and the counterpane, they curled close and he found himself talking, talking, how it wasn't the sex, it was shopping in Marlborough and having tea and seeing the sun set from White Horse Hill and being together, together; then she pressed fingers to his mouth and he fell with her in sleep past cold and loneliness and fear, past deserts and unlit places, down maybe to where spires reared gold and tree leaves moved and dazzled and white cars sang on roads and suns burned inwardly, lighting new worlds.

He woke, and the fire was low. He sat up, dazed. She was watching him. He stroked her hair a while, smiling; then she pushed away. She said, 'Richard, I have to go now.'

'Not yet.'

'It's the middle of the night.'

He said, 'It doesn't matter.'

She said, 'It does. He mustn't know.'

'Who?'

She said, 'You know who. You know why I was asked here.'

He said, 'He's not like that. Honestly.'

She shivered. She said, 'Richard, please. Don't get me in trouble.' She smiled. She said, 'It's only till tomorrow. Only a little while.'

He stood, awkwardly, and held her, pressing her warmth close. Shoeless, she was tiny; her shoulder fitted beneath his armpit.

Halfway through dressing she stopped and laughed, leaned a hand against the wall. She said, 'I'm all woozy.'

Later he said, 'I'll see you to your room.'

She said, 'No, please. I'm all right.' She was holding her

handbag, and her hair was combed. She looked, again, as if she had been to a party.

At the door she turned. She said, 'I love you, Richard. Truly.' She kissed again, quickly; and was gone.

He closed the door, dropped the latch. He stood a while looking round the room. In the fire a burned-through log broke with a snap, sending up a little whirl of sparks. He walked to the washstand, bathed his face and hands. He shook the counterpane out on the bed, rearranged the pillows. Her scent still clung to him; he remembered how she had felt, and what she had said.

He crossed to the window, pushed it ajar. Outside, the snow lay in deep swaths and drifts. Starlight gleamed from it, ghost-white; and the whole great house was mute. He stood feeling the chill move against his skin; and in all the silence a voice drifted far-off and clear. It came maybe from the guardhouses, full of distance and peace.

> *'Stille Nacht, heilige Nacht,*
> *alles schläft, einsam wacht . . .'*

He walked to the bed, pulled back the covers. The sheets were crisp and spotless, fresh-smelling. He smiled, and turned off the lamp.

> *'Nur das traute, hochheilige Paar.*
> *Holder Knabe mit lochigem Haar. . . .'*

In the wall of the room, an inch behind the plasterwork, a complex little machine hummed. A spool of delicate golden wire shook slightly; but the creak of the opening window had been the last thing to interest the recorder, the singing alone couldn't activate its relays. A micro-switch tripped, inaudibly; valve filaments faded, and died. Mainwaring lay back in the last of the firelight, and closed his eyes.

> *'Schlaf' in himmlischer Ruh,*
> *'Schlaf' in himmlischer Ruh. . . .'*

2

Beyond drawn curtains, brightness flicks on.

The sky is a hard, clear blue; icy, full of sunlight. The light dazzles back from the brilliant land. Far things – copses, hills, solitary trees – stand sharp-etched. Roofs and eaves carry hummocks of whiteness, twigs a three-inch crest. In the stillness, here and there, the snow cracks and falls, powdering.

The shadows of the riders jerk and undulate. The quiet is interrupted. Hooves ring on swept courtyards or stamp muffled, churning the snow. It seems the air itself has been rendered crystalline by cold; through it the voices break and shatter, brittle as glass.

'*Guten Morgen, Hans . . .*'

'*Verflucht kalt!*'

'*Der Hundenmeister sagt, sehr gefahrlich!*'

'*Macht nichts! Wir erwischen es bevor dem Wald!*'

A rider plunges beneath an arch. The horse snorts and curvets.

'*Ich wette dir fünfzig amerikanische Dollar!*'

'*Einverstanden! Heute, habe ich Glück!*'

The noise, the jangling and stamping, rings back on itself. Cheeks flush, perception is heightened; for more than one of the riders, the early courtyard reels. Beside the house door trestles have been set up. A great bowl is carried, steaming. The cups are raised, the toasts given; the responses ring again, crashing.

'*The Two Empires . . .!*'

'*The Hunt . . .!*'

Now, time is like a tight-wound spring. The dogs plunge forward, six to a handler, leashes straining, choke links creaking and snapping. Behind them jostle the riders. The bobbing scarlet coats splash across the snow. In the house drive an officer salutes; another strikes gloved palms together, nods. The gates whine open.

And across the country for miles around doors slam, bolts are shot, shutters closed, children scurried indoors. Village streets, muffled with snow, wait dumbly. Somewhere a dog barks, is silenced. The houses squat sullen, blind-eyed. The word has gone out, faster than horses could gallop. Today the Hunt will run; on snow.

The riders fan out, across a speckled waste of fields. A check, a questing; and the horns begin to yelp. Ahead the dogs bound and leap, black spots against whiteness. The horns cry again; but these hounds run mute. The riders sweep forward, on to the line.

Now, for the hunters, time and vision are fragmented. Twigs and snow merge in a racing blur; and tree-boles, ditches, gates. The tide reaches a crest of land, pours down the opposing slope. Hedges rear, mantled with white; and muffled thunder is interrupted by sailing silence, the smash and crackle of landing. The View sounds, harsh and high; and frenzy, and the racing blood, discharge intelligence. A horse goes down, in a gigantic flailing; another rolls, crushing its rider into the snow. A mount runs riderless. The Hunt, destroying, destroys itself unaware.

There are cottages, a paling fence. The fence goes over, unnoticed. A chicken house erupts in a cloud of flung crystals; birds run squawking, under the hooves. Caps are lost, flung away; hair flogs wild. Whips flail, spurs rake streaming flanks; and the woods are close. Twigs lash, and branches; snow falls, thudding. The crackling, now, is all around.

At the end, it is always the same. The handlers close in, yodelling, waist-high in trampled brush; the riders force close and closer, mounts sidling and shaking; and silence falls. Only the quarry, reddened, flops and twists; the thin high noise it makes is the noise of anything in pain.

Now, if he chooses, the *Jagdmeister* may end the suffering. The crash of the pistol rings hollow; and birds erupt, high from frozen twigs, wheel with the echoes and cry. The pistol fires again; and the quarry lies still. In time, the shaking stops; and a dog creeps forward, begins to lick.

Now a slow movement begins; a spreading-out, away from the place. There are mutterings, a laugh that chokes to silence. The fever passes. Somebody begins to shiver; and a girl, blood glittering on cheek and neck, puts a glove to her forehead and moans. The Need has come and gone; for a little while, the Two Empires have purged themselves.

The riders straggle back on tired mounts, shamble in through the gates. As the last enters, a closed black van starts up, drives away. In an hour, quietly, it returns; and the gates swing shut behind it.

Surfacing from deepest sleep was like rising, slowly, through a warm sea. For a time, as Mainwaring lay eyes closed, memory and awareness were confused so that she was with him and the room a recollected, childhood place. He rubbed his face, yawned, shook his head; and the knocking that had roused him came again. He said, 'Yes?'

The voice said, 'Last breakfast in fifteen minutes, sir.'

He called, 'Thank you,' heard the footsteps pad away.

He pushed himself up, groped on the side table for his watch, held it close to his eyes. It read ten-forty-five.

He swung the bedclothes back, felt air tingle on his skin. She had been with him, certainly, in the dawn; his body remembered the succubus, with nearly painful strength. He looked down smiling, walked to the bathroom. He showered, towelled himself, shaved and dressed. He closed his door and locked it, walked to the breakfast room. A few couples still sat over their coffee; he smiled a good morning, took a window seat. Beyond the double panes the snow piled thickly; its reflection lit the room with a white, inverted brilliance. He ate slowly, hearing distant shouts. On the long slope behind the house, groups of children pelted each other vigorously. Once a toboggan came into sight, vanished behind a rising swell of ground.

He had hoped he might see her, but she didn't come. He drank coffee, smoked a cigarette. He walked to the television lounge. The big colour screen showed a children's party taking place in a Berlin hospital. He watched for a while. The door behind him clicked a couple of times, but it wasn't Diane.

There was a second guests' lounge, not usually much frequented at this time of the year; and a reading room and library.

He wandered through them, but there was no sign of her. It occurred to him she might not yet be up; at Wilton there were few hard-and-fast rules for Christmas Day. He thought, 'I should have checked her room number.' He wasn't even sure in which of the guest wings she had been placed.

The house was quiet; it seemed most of the visitors had taken to their rooms. He wondered if she could have ridden with the Hunt; he'd heard it vaguely, leaving and returning. He doubted if the affair would have held much appeal.

He strolled back to the TV lounge, watched for an hour or more. By lunchtime he was feeling vaguely piqued; and sensing too the rise of a curious unease. He went back to his room, wondering if by any chance she had gone there; but the miracle was not repeated. The room was empty.

The fire was burning, and the bed had been remade. He had forgotten the servants' pass keys. The Geissler copy still stood on the shelf. He took it down, stood weighing it in his hand and frowning. It was, in a sense, madness to leave it there.

He shrugged, put the thing back. He thought, 'So who reads bookshelves anyway?' The plot, if plot there had been, seemed absurd now in the clearer light of day. He stepped into the corridor, closed the door and locked it behind him. He tried as far as possible to put the book from his mind. It represented a problem; and problems, as yet, he wasn't prepared to cope with. Too much else was going on in his brain.

He lunched alone, now with a very definite pang; the process was disquietingly like that of other years. Once he thought he caught sight of her in the corridor. His heart thumped; but it was the other blonde, Müller's wife. The gestures, the fall of the hair, were similar; but this woman was taller.

He let himself drift into a reverie. Images of her, it seemed, were engraved on his mind; each to be selected now, studied, placed lovingly aside. He saw the firelit texture of her hair and skin, her lashes brushing her cheek as she lay in his arms and slept. Other memories, sharper, more immediate still, throbbed like little shocks in the mind. She tossed her head, smiling; her hair swung, touched the point of a breast.

He pushed his cup away, rose. At fifteen hundred, patriotism required her presence in the TV lounge. As it required the presence of every other guest. Then, if not before, he would see her. He reflected, wryly, that he had waited half a lifetime for her; a little longer now would do no harm.

He took to prowling the house again; the Great Hall, the Long Gallery where the *Christkind* had walked. Below the windows that lined it was a snow-covered roof. The tart, reflected light struck upward, robbing the place of mystery. In the Great Hall they had already removed the tree. He watched household staff hanging draperies, carrying in stacks of gilded cane chairs. On the Minstrels' Gallery a pile of odd-shaped boxes proclaimed that the orchestra had arrived.

At fourteen hundred hours he walked back to the TV lounge. A quick glance assured him she wasn't there. The bar was open; Hans, looking as big and suave as ever, had been pressed into service to minister to the guests. He smiled at Mainwaring and said, 'Good afternoon, sir.' Mainwaring asked for a lager beer, took the glass to a corner seat. From here he could watch both the TV screen and the door.

The screen was showing the world-wide link-up that had become hallowed Christmas afternoon fare within the Two Empires. He saw, without particular interest, greetings flashed from the Leningrad and Moscow garrisons, a lightship, an Arctic weather station, a Mission in German East Africa. At fifteen hundred the Fuehrer was due to speak; this year, for the first time, Ziegler was preceding Edward VIII.

The room filled, slowly. She didn't come. Mainwaring finished the lager, walked to the bar, asked for another and a packet of cigarettes. The unease was sharpening now into something very like alarm. He thought for the first time that she might have been taken ill.

The time signal flashed, followed by the drumroll of the German anthem. He rose with the rest, stood stiffly till it had finished. The screen cleared, showed the familiar room in the Chancellery; the dark, high panels, the crimson drapes, the big *Hackenkreuz* emblem over the desk. The Fuehrer, as ever, spoke impeccably; but Mainwaring thought with a fragment of his mind how old he had begun to look.

The speech ended. He realized he hadn't heard a word that was said.

The drums crashed again. The King said, 'Once more, at Christmas, it is my . . . duty and pleasure . . . to speak to you.'

Something seemed to burst inside Mainwaring's head. He rose, walked quickly to the bar. He said, 'Hans, have you seen Miss Hunter?'

The other jerked round. He said, 'Sir, *shh* . . . please . . .'

'*Have you seen her?*'

Hans stared at the screen, and back to Mainwaring. The King was saying, 'There have been . . . troubles, and difficulties. More perhaps lie ahead. But with . . . God's help, they will be overcome.'

The chauffeur licked his mouth. He said, 'I'm sorry, sir. I don't know what you mean.'

'Which was her room?'

The big man looked like something trapped. He said, 'Please, Mr Mainwaring. You'll get me into trouble. . . .'

'*Which was her room?*'

Somebody turned and hissed, angrily. Hans said, 'I don't understand.'

'For God's sake, man, you carried her things upstairs. I saw you!'

Hans said, 'No, sir . . .'

Momentarily, the lounge seemed to spin.

There was a door behind the bar. The chauffeur stepped back. He said, 'Sir. Please . . .'

The place was a storeroom. There were wine bottles racked, a shelf with jars of olives, walnuts, eggs. Mainwaring closed the door behind him, tried to control the shaking. Hans said, 'Sir, you must not ask me these things. I don't know a Miss Hunter. I don't know what you mean.'

Mainwaring said, 'Which was her room? I demand that you answer.'

'I can't!'

'You drove me from London yesterday. Do you deny that?'

'No, sir.'

'You drove me with Miss Hunter.'

'No, sir!'

'Damn your eyes, where is she?'

The chauffeur was sweating. A long wait; then he said, 'Mr Mainwaring, please. You must understand. I can't help you.' He swallowed, and drew himself up. He said, 'I drove you from London. I'm sorry. I drove you . . . *on your own.'*

The lounge door swung shut behind Mainwaring. He half-walked, half-ran to his room. He slammed the door behind him, leaned against it panting. In time the giddiness passed. He opened his eyes, slowly. The fire glowed; the Geissler stood on the bookshelf. Nothing was changed.

He set to work, methodically. He shifted furniture, peered behind it. He rolled the carpet back, tapped every foot of floor. He fetched a flashlight from his case and examined, minutely, the interior of the wardrobe. He ran his fingers lightly across the walls, section by section, tapping again. Finally he got a chair, dismantled the ceiling lighting fitting.

Nothing.

He began again. Halfway through the second search he froze, staring at the floorboards. He walked to his case, took the screwdriver from the pistol holster. A moment's work with the blade and he sat back, staring into his palm. He rubbed his face, placed his find carefully on the side table. A tiny ear-ring, one of the pair she had worn. He sat a while breathing heavily, his head in his hands.

The brief daylight had faded as he worked. He lit the standard lamp, wrenched the shade free, stood the naked bulb in the middle of the room. He worked round the walls again, peering, tapping, pressing. By the fireplace, finally, a foot-square section of plaster rang hollow.

He held the bulb close, examined the hairline crack. He inserted the screwdriver blade delicately, twisted. Then again. A click; and the section hinged open.

He reached inside the little space, shaking, lifted out the recorder. He stood silent a time, holding it; then raised his arms, brought the machine smashing down on the hearth. He stamped and kicked, panting, till the thing was reduced to fragments.

The droning rose to a roar, swept low over the house. The helicopter settled slowly, belly lamps glaring, downdraught raising a storm of snow. He walked to the window, stood staring. The children embarked, clutching scarves and gloves, suitcases, boxes with new toys. The steps were withdrawn, the hatch dogged shut. Snow swirled again; the machine lifted heavily, swung away in the direction of Wilton.

The Party was about to start.

Lights blaze, through the length and breadth of the house. Orange-lit windows throw long bars of brightness across the snow. Everywhere is an anxious coming and going, the pattering of feet, clink of silver and glassware, hurried commands. Waiters scuttle between the kitchens and the Green Room where dinner is laid. Dish after dish is borne in, paraded. Peacocks, roasted and gilded, vaunt their plumes in shadow and candle-glow, spirit-soaked wicks blazing in their beaks. The Minister rises, laughing; toast after toast is drunk. To five thousand tanks, ten thousand fighting aeroplanes, a hundred thousand guns. The Two Empires feast their guests, royally.

The climax approaches. The boar's head, garnished and smoking, is borne shoulder-high. His tusks gleam; clamped in his jaws is the golden sun-symbol, the orange. After him march the waits and mummers, with their lanterns and begging-cups. The carol they chant is older by far than the Two Empires; older than the Reich, older than Great Britain.

'*Alive he spoiled, where poor men toiled, which made kind Ceres sad . . .*'

The din of voices rises. Coins are flung, glittering; wine is poured. And more wine, and more and more. Bowls of fruit are passed, and trays of sweets; spiced cakes, gingerbread, marzipans. Till at a signal the brandy is brought, and boxes of cigars.

The ladies rise to leave. They move flushed and chattering through the corridors of the house, uniformed link-boys grandly lighting their way. In the Great Hall their escorts are waiting. Each young man is tall, each blond, each impeccably uniformed.

On the Minstrels' Gallery a baton is poised; across the lawns, distantly, floats the whirling excitement of a waltz.

In the Green Room, hazed now with smoke, the doors are once more flung wide. Servants scurry again, carrying in boxes, great gay-wrapped parcels topped with scarlet satin bows. The Minister rises, hammering on the table for quiet.

'My friends, good friends, friends of the Two Empires. For you, no expense is spared. For you, the choicest gifts. Tonight, nothing but the best is good enough; and nothing but the best is here. Friends, enjoy yourselves. Enjoy my house. *Frohe Weihnachten* . . . !'

He walks quickly into shadow, and is gone. Behind him, silence falls. A waiting; and slowly, mysteriously, the great heap of gifts begins to stir. Paper splits, crackling. Here a hand emerges, here a foot. A breathless pause; and the first of the girls rises slowly, bare in flamelight, shakes her glinting hair.

The table roars again.

The sound reached Mainwaring dimly. He hesitated at the foot of the main staircase, moved on. He turned right and left, hurried down a flight of steps. He passed kitchens, and the servants' hall. From the hall came the blare of a record player. He walked to the end of the corridor, unlatched a door. Night air blew keen against his face.

He crossed the courtyard, opened a further door. The space beyond was bright-lit; there was the faint, musty stink of animals. He paused, wiped his face. He was shirt-sleeved; but despite the cold he was sweating.

He walked forward again, steadily. To either side of the corridor were the fronts of cages. The dogs hurled themselves at the bars, thunderously. He ignored them.

The corridor opened into a square concrete chamber. To one side of the place was a ramp. At its foot was parked a windowless black van.

In the far wall a door showed a crack of light. He rapped sharply, and again.

'*Hundenmeister* . . .'

The door opened. The man who peered up at him was as

wrinkled and pot-bellied as a Nast Santa Claus. At sight of his visitor's face he tried to duck back; but Mainwaring had him by the arm. He said, '*Herr Hundenmeister*, I must talk to you.'

'Who are you? I don't know you. What do you want? . . .'

Mainwaring showed his teeth. He said, 'The van. You drove the van this morning. What was in it?'

'I don't know what you mean . . .'

The heave sent him stumbling across the floor. He tried to bolt; but Mainwaring grabbed him again.

'What was in it? . . .'

'I won't talk to you! Go away!'

The blow exploded across his cheek. Mainwaring hit him again, backhanded, slammed him against the van.

'Open it . . . !'

The voice rang sharply in the confined space.

'*Wer ist da? Was ist passiert?*'

The little man whimpered, rubbing at his mouth.

Mainwaring straightened, breathing heavily. The GFP captain walked forward, staring, thumbs hooked in his belt.

'*Wer sind Sie?*'

Mainwaring said, 'You know damn well. And speak English, you bastard. You're as English as I am.'

The other glared. He said, 'You have no right to be here. I should arrest you. You have no right to accost *Herr Hundenmeister*.'

'What is in that van?'

'Have you gone mad? The van is not your concern. Leave now. At once.'

'Open it!'

The other hesitated, and shrugged. He stepped back. He said, 'Show him, *mein Herr*.'

The *Hundenmeister* fumbled with a bunch of keys. The van doors grated. Mainwaring walked forward, slowly.

The vehicle was empty.

The captain said, 'You have seen what you wished to see. You are satisfied. Now go.'

Mainwaring stared round. There was a further door, re-

cessed deeply into the wall. Beside it controls like the controls
of a bank vault.

'What is in that room?'

The GFP man said, 'You have gone too far. I order you to
leave.'

'You have no authority over me!'

'Return to your quarters!'

Mainwaring said, 'I refuse.'

The other slapped the holster at his hip. He gut-held the
Walther, wrists locked, feet apart. He said, 'Then you will be
shot.'

Mainwaring walked past him, contemptuously. The baying
of the dogs faded as he slammed the outer door.

*It was among the middle classes that the seeds had first been
sown; and it was among the middle classes that they flourished.
Britain had been called often enough a nation of shopkeepers;
now for a little while the tills were closed, the blinds left drawn.
Overnight it seemed, an effête symbol of social and national
disunity became the* Einsatzgruppenfuehrer; *and the wire for
the first detention camps was strung. . . .*

Mainwaring finished the page, tore it from the spine, crumpled it and dropped it on the fire. He went on reading. Beside
him on the hearth stood a part-full bottle of whisky and a glass.
He picked the glass up mechanically, drank. He lit a cigarette.
A few minutes later a new page followed the last.

The clock ticked steadily. The burning paper made a little
rustling. Reflections danced across the ceiling of the room.
Once Mainwaring raised his head, listened; once put the ruined
book down, rubbed his eyes. The room, and the corridor outside, stayed quiet.

*Against immeasurable force, we must pit cunning; against
immeasurable evil, faith and a high resolve. In the war we
wage, the stakes are high: the dignity of man, the freedom of
the spirit, the survival of humanity. Already in that war, many
of us have died; many more, undoubtedly, will lay down their
lives. But always, beyond them, there will be others; and still*

more. We shall go on, as we must go on, till this thing is wiped from the earth.

Meanwhile, we must take fresh heart. Every blow, now, is a blow for freedom. In France, Belgium, Finland, Poland, Russia, the forces of the Two Empires confront each other uneasily. Greed, jealousy, mutual distrust; these are the enemies, and they work from within. This, the Empires know full well. And, knowing, for the first time in their existence, fear. . . .

The last page crumpled, fell to ash. Mainwaring sat back, staring at nothing. Finally he stirred, looked up. It was zero three hundred; and they hadn't come for him yet.

The bottle was finished. He set it to one side, opened another. He swilled the liquid in the glass, hearing the magnified ticking of the clock.

He crossed the room, took the Lüger from the case. He found a cleaning rod, patches and oil. He sat a while dully, looking at the pistol. Then he slipped the magazine free, pulled back on the breech toggle, thumbed the latch, slid the barrel from the guides.

His mind, wearied, had begun to play aggravating tricks. It ranged and wandered, remembering scenes, episodes, details sometimes from years back; trivial, unconnected. Through and between the wanderings, time after time, ran the ancient, lugubrious words of the carol. He tried to shut them out, but it was impossible.

'*Living he spoiled where poor men toiled, which made kind Ceres sad . . .*'

He pushed the link pin clear, withdrew the breech block, stripped the firing pin. He laid the parts out, washed them with oil and water, dried and re-oiled. He reassembled the pistol, working carefully; inverted the barrel, shook the link down in front of the hooks, closed the latch, checked the recoil spring engagement. He loaded a full clip, pushed it home, chambered a round, thumbed the safety to *Gesichert*. He released the clip, reloaded.

He fetched his briefcase, laid the pistol inside carefully, grip uppermost. He filled a spare clip, added the extension butt and

a fifty box of Parabellum. He closed the flap and locked it, set
the case beside the bed. After that there was nothing more to
do. He sat back in the chair, refilled his glass.

'*Toiling he boiled, where poor men spoiled . . .*'

The firelight faded, finally.

He woke, and the room was dark. He got up, felt the floor sway
a little. He understood that he had a hangover. He groped for
the light switch. The clock hands stood at zero eight hundred.

He felt vaguely guilty at having slept so long.

He walked to the bathroom. He stripped and showered,
running the water as hot as he could bear. The process brought
him round a little. He dried himself, staring down. He thought
for the first time what curious things these bodies were; some
with their yellow cylinders, some their indentations.

He dressed and shaved. He had remembered what he was
going to do; fastening his tie, he tried to remember why. He
couldn't. His brain, it seemed, had gone dead.

There was an inch of whisky in the bottle. He poured it,
grimaced and drank. Inside him was a fast, cold shaking. He
thought, 'Like the first morning at a new school.'

He lit a cigarette. Instantly his throat filled. He walked to
the bathroom and vomited. Then again. Finally there was
nothing left to come.

His chest ached. He rinsed his mouth, washed his face again.
He sat in the bedroom for a while, head back and eyes closed. In
time the shaking went away. He lay unthinking, hearing the
clock tick. Once his lips moved. He said, 'They're no better
than us.'

At nine hundred hours he walked to the breakfast room. His
stomach, he felt, would retain very little. He ate a slice of toast,
carefully, drank some coffee. He asked for a pack of cigarettes,
went back to his room. At ten hundred hours he was due to meet
the Minister.

He checked the briefcase again. A thought made him add a
pair of stringback motoring gloves. He sat again, stared at the
ashes where he had burned the Geissler. A part of him was
willing the clock hands not to move. At five to ten he picked

the briefcase up, stepped into the corridor. He stood a moment staring round him. He thought, 'It hasn't happened yet. I'm still alive.' There was still the flat in Town to go back to, still his office; the tall windows, the telephones, the khaki utility desk.

He walked through sunlit corridors to the Minister's suite.

The room to which he was admitted was wide and long. A fire crackled in the hearth; beside it on a low table stood glasses and a decanter. Over the mantel, conventionally, hung the Fuehrer's portrait. Edward VIII faced him across the room. Tall windows framed a prospect of rolling parkland. In the distance, blue on the horizon, were the woods.

The Minister said, 'Good morning, Richard. Please sit down. I don't think I shall keep you long.'

He sat, placing the briefcase by his knee.

This morning everything seemed strange. He studied the Minister curiously, as if seeing him for the first time. He had that type of face once thought of as peculiarly English: short-nosed and slender, with high, finely shaped cheekbones. The hair, blond and cropped close to the scalp, made him look nearly boyish. The eyes were candid, flat, dark-fringed. He looked, Mainwaring decided, not so much Aryan as like some fierce nursery toy; a Feral Teddy Bear.

The Minister riffled papers. He said, 'Several things have cropped up; among them, I'm afraid, more trouble in Glasgow. The fifty-first Panzer division is standing by; as yet, the news hasn't been released.'

Mainwaring wished his head felt less hollow. It made his own voice boom so unnecessarily. He said, 'Where is Miss Hunter?'

The Minister paused. The pale eyes stared; then he went on speaking.

'I'm afraid I may have to ask you to cut short your stay here. I shall be flying back to London for a meeting; possibly to-morrow, possibly the day after. I shall want you with me, of course.'

'Where is Miss Hunter?'

The Minister placed his hands flat on the desktop, studied the nails. He said, 'Richard, there are aspects of Two Empires culture that are neither mentioned nor discussed. You of all people should know this. I'm being patient with you; but there are limits to what I can overlook.'

'*Seldom he toiled, while Ceres roiled, which made poor kind men glad . . .*'

Mainwaring opened the flap of the case and stood up. He thumbed the safety forward and levelled the pistol.

There was silence for a time. The fire spat softly. Then the Minister smiled. He said, 'That's an interesting gun, Richard. Where did you get it?'

Mainwaring didn't answer.

The Minister moved his hands carefully to the arms of his chair, leaned back. He said, 'It's the Marine model, of course. It's also quite old. Does it by any chance carry the Erfurt stamp? Its value would be considerably increased.'

He smiled again. He said, 'If the barrel is good, I'll buy it. For my private collection.'

Mainwaring's arm began to shake. He steadied his wrist, gripping with his left hand.

The Minister sighed. He said, 'Richard, you can be so stubborn. It's a good quality; but you do carry it to excess.' He shook his head. He said, 'Did you imagine for one moment I didn't know you were coming here to kill me? My dear chap, you've been through a great deal. You're overwrought. Believe me, I know just how you feel.'

Mainwaring said, 'You murdered her.'

The Minister spread his hands. He said, 'What with? A gun? A knife? Do I honestly look such a shady character?'

The words made a cold pain, and a tightness in the chest. But they had to be said.

The Minister's brows rose. Then he started to laugh. Finally he said, 'At last I see. I understood, but I couldn't believe. So you bullied our poor little *Hundenmeister*, which wasn't very worthy; and seriously annoyed the *Herr Hauptmann*, which wasn't very wise. Because of this fantasy, stuck in your head. Do you really believe it, Richard? Perhaps you believe in

Struwwelpeter too.' He sat forward. He said, 'The Hunt ran. And killed . . . a deer. She gave us an excellent chase. As for your little Huntress . . . Richard, she's gone. She never existed. She was a figment of your imagination. Best forgotten.'

Mainwaring said, 'We were in love.'

The Minister said, 'Richard, you really are becoming tiresome.' He shook his head again. He said, 'We're both adult. We both know what that word is worth. It's a straw, in the wind. A candle, on a night of gales. A phrase that is meaningless. *Lächerlich*.' He put his hands together, rubbed a palm. He said, 'When this is over, I want you to go away. For a month, six weeks maybe. With your new car. When you come back . . . well, we'll see. Buy yourself a girl friend, if you need a woman that much. *Einen Schatz*. I never dreamed; you're so remote, you should speak more of yourself. Richard, I understand; it isn't such a very terrible thing.'

Mainwaring stared.

The Minister said, 'We shall make an arrangement. You will have the use of an apartment, rather a nice apartment. So your lady will be close. When you tire of her . . . buy another. They're unsatisfactory for the most part, but reasonable. Now sit down like a good chap, and put your gun away. You look so silly, standing there scowling like that.'

It seemed he felt all life, all experience, as a grey weight pulling. He lowered the pistol, slowly. He thought, 'At the end, they were wrong. They picked the wrong man.' He said, 'I suppose now I use it on myself.'

The Minister said, 'No, no, no. You still don't understand.' He linked his knuckles, grinning. He said, 'Richard, the *Herr Hauptmann* would have arrested you last night. I wouldn't let him. This is between ourselves. Nobody else. I give you my word.'

Mainwaring felt his shoulders sag. The strength seemed drained from him; the pistol, now, weighed too heavy for his arm.

The Minister said, 'Richard, why so glum? It's a great occasion, man. You've found your courage. I'm delighted.'

He lowered his voice. He said, 'Don't you want to know why

I let you come here with your machine? Aren't you even interested?'

Mainwaring stayed silent.

The Minister said, 'Look around you, Richard. See the world. I want men near me, serving me. Now more than ever. Real men, not afraid to die. Give me a dozen . . . but you know the rest. I could rule the world. But first . . . I must rule them. My men. Do you see now? Do you understand?'

Mainwaring thought, 'He's in control again. But he was always in control. He owns me.'

The study spun a little.

The voice went on, smoothly. 'As for this amusing little plot by the so-called Freedom Front; again, you did well. It was difficult for you. I was watching; believe me, with much sympathy. Now, you've burned your book. Of your own free will. That delighted me.'

Mainwaring looked up, sharply.

The Minister shook his head. He said, 'The real recorder is rather better hidden, you were too easily satisfied there. There's also a TV monitor. I'm sorry about it all, I apologize. It was necessary.'

A singing started inside Mainwaring's head.

The Minister sighed again. He said, 'Still unconvinced, Richard? Then I have some things I think you ought to see. Am I permitted to open my desk drawer?'

Mainwaring didn't speak. The other slid the drawer back slowly, reached in. He laid a telegram flimsy on the desk top. He said, 'The addressee is Miss D. J. Hunter. The message consists of one word. "*Activate.*"'

The singing rose in pitch.

'This as well,' said the Minister. He held up a medallion on a thin gold chain. The little disc bore the linked motif of the Freedom Front. He said, 'Mere exhibitionism; or a deathwish. Either way, a most undesirable trait.'

He tossed the thing down. He said, 'She was here under surveillance of course, we'd known about her for years. To them, you were a sleeper. Do you see the absurdity? They really thought you would be jealous enough to assassinate your

Minister. This they mean in their silly little book, when they talk of subtlety. Richard, I could have fifty blonde women if I chose. A hundred. Why should I want yours?' He shut the drawer with a click, and rose. He said, 'Give me the gun now. You don't need it any more.' He extended his arm; then he was flung heavily backward. Glasses smashed on the side table. The decanter split; its contents poured dark across the wood.

Over the desk hung a faint haze of blue. Mainwaring walked forward, stood looking down. There were blood-flecks, and a little flesh. The eyes of the Teddy Bear still showed glints of white. Hydraulic shock had shattered the chest; the breath drew ragged, three times, and stopped. He thought, 'I didn't hear the report.'

The communicating door opened. Mainwaring turned. A secretary stared in, bolted at sight of him. The door slammed.

He pushed the briefcase under his arm, ran through the outer office. Feet clattered in the corridor. He opened the door, carefully. Shouts sounded, somewhere below in the house.

Across the corridor hung a loop of crimson cord. He stepped over it, hurried up a flight of stairs. Then another. Beyond the private apartments the way was closed by a heavy metal grille. He ran to it, rattled. A rumbling sounded from below. He glared round. Somebody had operated the emergency shutters; the house was sealed.

Beside the door an iron ladder was spiked to the wall. He climbed it, panting. The trap in the ceiling was padlocked. He clung one-handed, awkward with the briefcase, held the pistol above his head.

Daylight showed through splintered wood. He put his shoulder to the trap, heaved. It creaked back. He pushed head and shoulders through, scrambled. Wind stung at him, and flakes of snow.

His shirt was wet under the arms. He lay face down, shaking. He thought, 'It wasn't an accident. None of it was an accident.' He had underrated them. They understood despair.

He pushed himself up, stared round. He was on the roof of Wilton. Beside him rose gigantic chimney stacks. There was a lattice radio mast. The wind hummed in its guy wires. To his

right ran the balustrade that crowned the façade of the house.
Behind it was a snow-choked gutter.

He wriggled across a sloping scree of roof, ran crouching.
Shouts sounded from below. He dropped flat, rolled. An
automatic clattered. He edged forward again, dragging the
briefcase. Ahead, one of the corner towers rose dark against
the sky. He crawled to it, crouched sheltered from the wind.
He opened the case, pulled the gloves on. He clipped the stock
to the pistol, laid the spare magazine beside him and the box of
rounds.

The shouts came again. He peered forward, through the
balustrade. Running figures scattered across the lawn. He
sighted on the nearest, squeezed. Commotion below. The
automatic zipped; stone chips flew, whining. A voice called,
'Don't expose yourselves unnecessarily.' Another answered.

'*Die konmen mit den Hubschrauber* . . .'

He stared round him, at the yellow-grey horizon. He had
forgotten the helicopter.

A snow flurry drove against his face. He huddled, flinching.
He thought he heard, carried on the wind, a faint droning.

From where he crouched he could see the nearer trees of the
park, beyond them the wall and gatehouses. Beyond again, the
land rose to the circling woods.

The droning was back, louder than before. He screwed his
eyes, made out the dark spot skimming above the trees. He
shook his head. He said, 'We made a mistake. We all made a
mistake.'

He settled the stock of the Lüger to his shoulder, and waited.

The White Boat

Becky had always lived in the cottage overlooking the bay.

The bay was black, because there a seam of rock that was nearly coal burst open to the water and the sea had nibbled in over the years, breaking up the fossil-ridden shale to a fine dark grit, spreading it over the beach and the humped, tilted headlands. The grass had taken the colour of it and the little houses that stood mean-shouldered glaring at the water; the boats and jetties had taken it, and the brambles and gorse; even the rabbits that thumped across the cliff paths on summer evenings seemed to have something of the same dusky hue. Here the paths tilted, tumbling over to steepen and plunge at the sea; the whole land seemed ready to slide and splash, grumble into the ocean.

It was a summer evening when Becky first saw the White Boat. She had been sent, in the little skiff that was all her father owned, to clear the day's crop from the lobster pots strung out along the shore. She worked methodically, sculling along the bobbing line of buoys; the baskets in the bottom of the boat were full and bustling, the great crustaceans black and slate-grey as the cliffs, snapping and wriggling, waving wobbling, angry claws. Becky regarded them thoughtfully. A good catch; the family would feed well in the week to come.

She pulled up the last pot, feeling the drag and surge of it against the slow-flowing tide. It was empty, save for the grey-white rags of bait. She dropped the tarred basket back over the side, leaned to see the ghost-shape of it vanish in the cloudy green beneath the keel. She sat feeling the little aches spread in shoulders and arms, narrowing her eyes aganst the evening haze of sunlight; and saw the Boat.

Only she didn't know then that White Boat was her name.

She was coming in fast and quiet, bow parting the sea,

raising a bright ridge of foam. Mainsail down and furled, tall jib filling in the slight breeze. The calling of the crew came clear and faint across the water; and instinct made the girl scurry from her, pushing at the oars, scudding the little craft back to the shelter of the land. She grounded on the Ledges, the natural moles of stone that reached out into the sea, skipped ashore all torn frock and thin brown legs, wetted herself to the middle in her haste to drag the boat up and tie off.

Strange boats seldom came into the bay. Fishing boats were common enough, the stubby-bowed, round-bilged craft of the coast; this boat was different. Becky watched back at her cautiously, riding at anchor now in the ruffled pale shield of the sea. She was slim and long, flush-decked, a racer; her tall mast with the spreading outriggers rolled slowly, a pencil against the greying sky. As she watched, a dingy was launched; she saw a man climb down to rig the outboard. She scrambled farther up the cliff, crouched wild as a rabbit in a stand of gorse, staring down with huge brown eyes. She saw lights come on in the cabin of the yacht; they reflected in the water in wobbling yellow spears. The afterglow flared and faded as she lay.

This was a wild, mournful place. An eternal brooding seemed to hang over the bulging cliffs; a brooding, and worse. An enigma, a shadow of old sin. For here once a great mad priest had come, and called the waves and wind and water to witness his craziness. Becky had heard the tale often enough at her mother's knee; how he had taken a boat, and ridden out to his death; and how the village had hummed with soldiers and priests come to exorcize and complain and quiz the locals for their part in armed rebellion. They got little satisfaction; and the place had quietened by degrees, as the gales went and came, as the boats were hauled out and tarred and launched again. The waves were indifferent, and the wind; and the rocks neither knew nor cared who owned them, Christ's Vicar or an English king.

Becky was late home that evening; her father grumbled and swore, threatening her with beating, accusing her of outlandish crimes. She loved to sit out on the Ledges, none knew that better than he; sit and touch the fossils that showed like coiled springs in the rock, feel the breeze and watch the lap and splash of water and lose the sense of time. And that with babies to be fed and meals to stew and a house to clean, and him with an ailing, coughing wife. The girl was useless, idle to her bones. Giving herself airs and graces, lazing her time away; fine for the rich folk in Londinium maybe, but he had a living to earn·

Becky was not beaten. Neither did she speak of the Boat.

She lay awake that night, tired but unable to sleep, hearing her mother cough, watching between the drawn blinds the thin turquoise wedge of night sky; she saw it pale with the dawn, a single planet burn like a spark before being swallowed by the rising sun. From the house could be heard a faint susurration, soft nearly as the sound the blood makes in the ears. A slow, miles-long heave and roll, a breathing; the dim, immemorial noise of the sea.

If the Boat stayed in the bay, no sound came from her; and in the morning she was gone. Becky walked to the sea late in the day, trod barefoot among the tumbled blocks of stone that lined the foreshore; smelling the old harsh smell of salt, hearing the water slap and chuckle while from high above came the endless sinister trickling of the cliffs. Into her consciousness stole, maybe for the first time, the sense of loneliness; an oppression born of the gentle miles of summer water, the tall blackness of the headlands, the fingers of the stone ledges pushing out into the sea. She saw how the Ledges curved, in obedience it seemed to some cosmic plan, became ridges of stone that climbed the dark beach, curled away through the dipping strata of the cliffs. Full of the signs and ghosts of other life, the ammonites she collected as a child till Father Antony had scolded and warned, asked her once and for all time, if God created the rocks in seven days could He not have created those markings too? She was close to heresy, the things were best forgotten. She brooded, scrinching her toes in the water, feeling the sharp grit move and suck. She was fourteen, slight and dark, her breasts beginning to push at her dress.

It was months before she saw the Boat again. A winter had come and gone, noisy and grey; the wind plucked at the cliffs, yanking out the amber teeth of stone, sending them crashing and bumbling to the beach. Becky walked the bay in the short, glaring days, scrounging for driftwood, planks, broken pieces of boats, sea-coal to burn. Now and again she would watch the water, thin brown face and brilliant eyes staring, searching for something she couldn't understand out over the waste of sea. With the spring, White Boat returned.

It was an April evening, nearly May. Something made Becky linger over her work, hauling in the great black pots, scooping the clicking life into the baskets she kept prepared, while White Boat came sidling in from the dusk, driven by a puttering engine, growing from the vastness of the water.

'*Boat ahoy . . .*'

Becky stood in the coracle and stared. Behind her the headland cliffs, heaving slowly with the movement of the sea; in front of her the Boat, tall now and menacing with closeness, white prow cutting the water, raising a thin vee of foam that chuckled away to lose itself in the dark. She was aware, nearly painfully, of the boards beneath her feet, the flapping of the soiled dress round her knees. The Boat edged forward, ragged silhouette of a man in her bows clinging one-handed to the forestay while he waved and called.

'Boat ahoy . . .'

Becky saw the mainsail stowed and neat-wrapped on its boom, the complication of cabin coamings and hatches and rigging; up close she was nearly surprised to see the paint of White Boat could have weathered, the long jib-sheets frayed. As if the Boat had been nothing but a vision or a dream, lacking weight and substance.

The coracle ground, dipping, against the hull; Becky lurched, caught at the high deck. Hands gripped and steadied; the great mast rolled above her, daunting, as White Boat drifted slow, moved in by the tide.

'Easy there . . .' Then, 'What're ye selling, girl?'

From somewhere, a ripple of laughter. Becky swallowed, still staring up. Men crowded the rail, dark shapes against the evening light.

'Lobsters, sir. Fine lobsters . . .'

Her father would be pleased. What, sell fish afore landing

'em, and the price good too? No haggling with Master Smythe up in the village, no waiting for the hauliers to fetch the stuff away. They paid her well, dropping real gold coins into the boat, laughing as she dived and scrabbled for them; swung her clear, laughing again, called to her as she sculled back into the bay. She carried with her a memory of their voices, wild and rough and keen. Never it seemed had the land loomed so fast, the coracle been easier to beach. She scuttled for home, carrying what was left of her catch, money clutched hot in her hand; turned as White Boat turned below her in the dusk, heard the splash and rattle as her anchor dropped down to catch the bottom of the sea. There were lights aboard already, sharp pinpoints that gleamed like a cluster of eyes; above them the rigging of the Boat was dark, a filigree against the silver-grey crawling of the water.

Her father swore at her for selling the catch. She stared back wide-eyed.

'*The Bermudan* . . .' He spat, hulking across the kitchen to slam dirty plates down in the sink, crank at the handle of the tall old pump. 'You keep away from en . . .'

'But f—'

He turned back, dark-faced with rage. 'Keep *away* from en. Doan't want no more tellin' . . .'

Already her face had the ability to freeze, turn into the likeness of a dark, sculpted cat. She veiled her eyes, watching down at her plate. Above in the bedroom she heard her mother's racking cough. There would be spatters of pink on the sheets come morning, that she knew. She tucked one foot behind the other, stroking with her toes the contour of a grimy shin, and thought carefully of nothing at all.

The exchange, inconclusive as it was, served to rivet Becky's attention; over the weeks, the strange yacht began to obsess her. She saw White Boat in dreams; in her fantasies she seemed to fly, riffling through the wind like the great gulls that haunted the beach and headlands. In the mornings the cliffs resounded with their noise; in Becky's ears, still ringing with sleep, the bird-shouts echoed like the creaking of ropes, the ratchet-clatter of sheet winches. Sometimes then the headlands would seem to sway gently and roll like the sea, dizzying. She would squat and rub her arms and shiver, wait for the spells to pass and worry about death; till queer rhythms and passions reached culmination, she stepped on a knife blade, upturned in the boat, and slicing shock and redness turned her instantly into a woman. She cleaned herself, whimpering. Nobody saw; the secret she hugged to herself, to her thin body, as she hugged all secrets; thoughts, and dreams.

There was a wedding once, in the little black village, in the little black church. At that time Becky became aware, obscurely, that the people too had taken the colour of the place; an air-borne, invisible smut had changed them all. The fantasies took new and more sinister shapes; once she dreamed she saw the villagers, her parents, all the people she knew, melt chaotically into the landscape till the cliffs were bodies and bones and old beseeching hands, teeth and eyes and crumbling ancient fore-heads. Sometimes now she was afraid of the bay; but always it drew her with its own magnetism. She could not be said to think, sitting there alone and brooding; she felt, vividly, things not readily understandable.

She cut her black hair, sitting puzzled in front of a cracked and spotted mirror, turning her head, snipping and shortening till she looked nearly like a boy, one of the wild fisherboys of the coast. She stroked and teased the result, while the liquid huge eyes watched back uncertainly from the glass. She seemed to sense round her a trap, its bars thick and black as the bars of the lobster pots she used. Her world was landlocked, encompassed by the headlands of the bay, by the voice of the priest and her father's tread. Only White Boat was free; and free she would come, gliding and shimmering in her head, unsettling. In the critical events of adolescence, after the fear her pride in the shedding of her blood, the Boat seemed to have taken a part. Almost as if from under the bright mysterious horizon she had seen, and could somehow understand.

Becky kept her tryst with the yacht, time and again, watching from the tangles of bramble above the bay.

The sea itself drew her now. Nights or early iron-grey mornings she would slide her frock over her head among the piled slabs of rock; ease into the burning ice of the water, lie and let the waves lift her and move and slap. At such times it seemed the bay came in on her with an agoraphobic crowding, the rolling heights of headlands grey under the vast spaces of air; it was as if her nakedness brought her somehow in power of the place, as if it could then tumble round her quickly, trap and enfold. She would scuttle from the water, thresh into her dress. The awkwardness of her damp body under the cloth was a huge comfort; the cliffs receded, gained their proper aloofness and perspective. Were once more safe.

As a by-product, she was learning to swim.

That in itself was a Mystery; she felt instinctively her father and the Church would not approve. She avoided Father Antony; but the eyes of icons and the great Christos over the altar would still single her out in services to watch and accuse. By swimming she gave her body, obscurely, to assault; entered into a mystic relationship with White Boat, who also swam. She needed fulfilment, the shadowy fulfilment of the sea. She experienced a curious confusion, a sense of sin too formless to be categorized and as such more terrifying and in its turn alluring. The Confessional was closed to her; she walked alone, carefully, in a world of shadows and brittle glass. She avoided now the touches, the pressures, the accidental gratifications of her body that came nearly naturally with walking and moving and working. She wished in an unformed way to proscribe at least a vague area of evil, reduce the menace she herself had sought and that now in its turn sought her.

The idea came it seemed of its own, unlooked for and unwanted. Slowly there grew in her, watching the yacht swing at her mooring out in the darkening mystery of the water, the knowledge that White Boat alone might save her from herself. Only the Boat could fly, out from the twin iron headlands to a broader world. Where did she come from? Why did she vanish so mysteriously, and why return?

The priest spoke words over her mother's grave, God looked down from the sky; but Becky knew the earth had taken her to squeeze and squeeze, make her into more black shale.

The Boat came back.

She was frightened now and unsure. Before, with the less cluttered faith of childhood, she had not questioned. The Boat had gone away, the Boat would return. Now she knew, that all things change, and change is for ever. One day, the Boat would not return.

She had passed from knowledge of evil to indifference; for that, she felt herself already damned.

The thing she had rehearsed and dreamed of blended so with reality that she lived another dream. She rose silently in the black house, hearing the squabbling cough of a child. Her hands shook as she dressed; in her body was a fast, violent quivering, as if some electric force had control of her and drove her without volition. The sensation, and the mad thumping of her heart, seemed partially to cut her off from earthly contact; shapes of familiar things, chairbacks, dressertop, doorlatch, seemed to her fingertips muffled and vague. She slid the catch back carefully, not breathing, listening and staring in the dark. It was as if she moved now from point to point with an even pace that could not falter or check. She knew she would go to the bay, watch the Boat up-anchor and drift away; her mind, complicated, reserved beneath the image others that would be presented in their turn, in sequence to an unimagined end.

The village was black, lightless and dead; the air moved raw on her face and arms, a drifting of wet vapour that was nearly rain. The sky above her seemed to press solidly, dark as pitch except where to the east one depthless iron-grey streak showed where in the upper air there was dawn. Against it the tower of the church stood tall and remote, held out stiffly its ragged gargoyle ears.

In the centre of the bay a shallow ravine conducted to the beach a rill dribbling from the far-off Luckford Ponds. A plank bridge with a single handrail spanned the brook; the steps that led down to it were slimy with the damp. Once Becky slipped on a rounded stone; once felt beneath her pad the quick recoil of a worm. She crossed the bridge, hearing the chuckle of water; a scramble over wet rock and the bay opened out ahead, barely visible, a dull-grey vastness. On it, floating in a half-seen mirror, the darker grey ghost of the Boat. She crossed the beach, toes sinking in grit, feeling with her feet among the planes of tumbled stone. The water rose to calves and knees, half-noticed; before her was a faint calling, the hard *tonk-tonk-tonk* of a winch.

Rain spattered on the dawn wind, wetting her hair. She moved on, still with the same mindless steadiness. The stone ledge, the mole, sloped slowly, water slapping and creaming where it nosed under the sea. She floundered beside it, waist deep, feet in furry tangles of weed. Soon she was swimming, into the broad cold madness of the water. As the land receded she fell into a rhythm of movement, half-hypnotic; it seemed she would follow White Boat tirelessly, to the far end of the world. The aches increasing in shoulders and arms were unnoticed, unimportant. Ahead, between the slapping dark troughs of waves, the shadow of the Boat had altered, foreshortening as she turned to face the sea; above the hull had grown a taller shade that was the raising of the gently flapping jib.

To Becky it seemed an accident that she was here, and that the sea was deep and the cliffs tall and the Boat too far off to reach. She nuzzled at the water, drowsily; but the first bayonet stab in her lungs startled something that was nearly an orgasm. She retched, and kicked; felt coldness close instantly over her head, screamed and fought for air.

And there were voices ahead, a confusion of sounds and orders; the shape of the Boat changing again as she turned back into the wind.

There were hands on her shoulders and arms; something grabbed in her dress, the fabric tore, she went under again gulping at the sea. She wallowed, centred in a confusion of grey and black, white of foam, glaring red. Was hauled out thrashing, landed on a sloping deck, lay feeling beneath her opened mouth the smoothness of wood. The voices surged round her, seeming like the lap and splash of the sea to retreat and advance.

'*That one . . .*'

'Bloody fishergirl . . .'

The words roared quite unnecessarily in her ear, receded in

their turn. She stayed still, panting; water ran from her; she
sensed, six feet beneath, the grey sliding of the sea. She lay
numbly, knowing she had done a terrible thing.

They fetched her blankets, muffled her in them. She sat up
and coughed more water, hearing ropes creak, the slide and
slap of waves. Her mind seemed still dissociated from her body,
a cool grey thing that had watched the other Becky spit and
drown. She was aware vaguely of questions; she clutched the
rough cloth across her throat and shook her head, angry now
with herself and the people round her. The movement started
a spinning sickness; she was aware of being lifted, caught a last
glimpse of the black land-streak miles off as the boat heeled to
the wind. One foot caught the side of the hatch as they lowered
her; the pain jarred to her brain, ebbed. She was aware of a
maze of images, disconnected; white planking above her head,
hands working at the blankets and her dress. She frowned and
mumbled, trying to collect her thoughts; but the impressions
faded, one by one, into silence.

She lay quiet, cocooned in blankets, unwilling to open her eyes.
Soon she would have to move, go down and rake the stove to
life, set the pots of gruel simmering and bubbling for breakfast.
The house rolled faintly and incongruously, shivering like a
live thing; across beneath the eaves ran the chuckling slap of
water. The dream-image persisted, stubbornly refusing to fade.
She moved her head on the pillow, rubbing and grumbling,
fought a hand free to touch hair still sticky with salt. The fingers
moved back down, discovering nakedness. That in itself was a
sin, to tumble into bed unclothed. She grunted and snuggled,
defeating the dream with sleep.

The water made a thousand noises in the cabin. Rippling
and laughing, strumming, smacking against the side of White
Boat. Becky's eyes popped open again, in sudden alarm. With
waking came remembrance, and a clawing panic. She shot
upright; her head thumped against the decking two feet above.
She rubbed dazedly, seeing the sun reflections play across the
low roof, the bursts and tinkles and momentary skeins of light.
The cabin was in subtle motion, leaning; she saw a bright yellow

oilskin sway gently, at an angle from the upright on which it hung. Perspectives seemed wrong; she was pressed against a six-inch wooden board that served to stop her rolling from the bunk.

The boy was watching her, holding easily to a stanchion. The eyes above the tangle of beard were bright and keen, and he was laughing. 'Get your things on,' he said. 'Skipper wants to see you. Come up on deck. You all right now?'

She stared at him wild-eyed.

'You'll be all right,' he said. 'Just get dressed. It'll be all right.'

She knew then the dream or nightmare was true.

Tiny things confused her. The latches that held the bunk-board, she had to grope and push and still they wouldn't come undone. She swung her legs experimentally. Air rushed at her body: she scrabbled at the blankets, came out with a thump, took a fall, lost the blankets again. There were clothes left for her, jeans and an old sweater. She grabbed for them, panting. Her fingers refused to obey her, slipping and trembling; it seemed an age before she could force her legs into the trews.

The companionway twitched aside to land her among pots and pans. She clung to the steps, countering the great lean of the boat, pulled herself up to be dazed by sunlight.

And there was no land. Just a smudge, impossibly far off across the racing green of the sea. She winced, screwing her eyes; the boy who had spoken to her helped her again.

The skipper sat immobile, carved it seemed from buttercup-yellow oilskin, thin face and grey eyes watching past her along the deck of the Boat. Above him was the huge steady curving of the sails; behind the crew, clinging in the stern, watching her bold-eyed. She saw bearded mouths grinning and dropped her eyes, twisted her fingers in her lap.

Before these people she was nearly dumb. She sat still, watching her hands twine and move, conscious of the nearness of the water, the huge speed of the boat. The conversation was unsatisfactory, Skipper watching down at the compass, one arm curled easy along the tiller, listening it seemed with only the smallest part of his mind. The faces grinned, sea-lit and uncaring. She had jammed herself into their lives; they should have hated her for it but they were laughing. She wanted to be dead.

She was crying.

Somebody had an arm round her shoulders. She noticed she was shivering; they fetched her an oilskin, wrestled her into it. She felt the hard collar push her hair, scratch at her ears. She must go with them, they couldn't turn back; that much she understood. That was what she had wanted most, a lifetime ago. Now she wanted her father's kitchen, her own room again. Shipbound, caught in their tightly male and ordered world, she was useless. Their indifference stung; their kindness brought the welling, angry tears. She tried to help, in the little galley, but even the meals they made were strange; there were complications, nuances, relishes she had never seen. White Boat defeated her.

She crawled forward finally, away from the rest, clung to the root of the mast with one arm round the metal hearing the tall halliards slap and bang, seeing the bows fall and rise and punch at the sea. Diamond-hard spray flew back; her feet, bare on the deck, chilled almost at once. The cold reached through the oilskin; soon she was shivering as each cloud shadow eclipsed the boat, darkened the milk green of the sea. The dream was gone, blown away by the wind; White Boat was a hard thing, brutal and huge, smashing at the water. She could work her father's little cockleshell through the tides and currents of the coast; here she was awkward and in the way. A dozen times she moved desperately as the crew ran to handle the complication of ropes. The calls reached her dimly, '*Stand by to go about,*' '*Let the sheets fly;*' then the thundering of the jib, scuffle of feet on planking as White Boat surged on to each new tack, changed the angle of her decking and the flying sun and cloud shadows, the stinging attack of the spray. The horizon became a new hill, slanting away and up; Becky looked into racing water where before she had seen the sky.

They sent her food but she refused it, setting her mouth. She was sulking; and worse, she felt ill. She needed cottage and bay now with a new urgency, an almost ecstatic longing for solidness, for things that didn't roll and move. But these things were lost for all time; there was only the hurtling green of the water, fading now to deeper and deeper grey as the clouds grew up across the sun; the endless slap and tinkle of ropes, the misery at the churning pit of her stomach.

They offered her the helm, in the late afternoon. She refused. White Boat had been a dream; reality was killing it.

There was a little sea toilet, in a place too low to stand. She closed the lid and pumped, saw the contents flash past through the curving glass tube. The sea opened her stomach, brought up first food, then chyme, then glistening transparent sticky stuff that bearded her chin. She wiped and spat and worked the pump and sicked over again till the sides of her chest were a dull pain and her head throbbed in time it seemed with the thumping of the waves. The voices through the bulkhead door she remembered later, in fragments, like the recalled pieces of a dream.

'Then we'll do that, Skipper. Hitch a few pounds of chain to her feet, and gently over the side . . .'

The voice she knew. That was the boy who had helped her. The angry rising inflection she didn't know; that was the voice of Wales.

Something unheard.

'How can she talk, man, what does she bloody know? Just a bloody dumb kid, see . . .'

'Make up the log,' said the skipper bitterly.

'Don't you see, man?'

'Make up the log . . .'

Becky leaned her head on her arms, and groaned.

She couldn't reach the bunk. She arced her body awkwardly, tried again. The blankets were delicious heaven. She huddled into them, too empty to worry about the after-scent of vomit on her clothes. She fell into a sleep shot through with vivid dreams; the face of the Christos, Father Antony like an old dried animal, mouth champing as he scolded and blessed; the church tower in the pre-dawn glow, the gargoyle ears. Then flowers dusty in a cottage garden, her mum bawling and grumbling before she died, icy feel of water round her groin, shape of

White Boat fading into mist. All faint things and worries and griefs, scuttling lobsters, tar and pebbles, feel of the night sea wind, the Great Catechism torn and snatched. She moved finally into a deeper dream where it seemed the Boat herself talked to her. Her voice was rushing and immense yet chuckling and lisping and somehow coloured, blue and roaring green. She spoke about the little people on her back and her duties, her rushing and scurrying and fighting with the wind; she told great truths that were lost as soon as uttered, blown away and buried in the dark. Becky clenched her fists, writhing; woke to hear still the bang and slap of the sea, slept again.

She came round to someone gently shaking her shoulder. Again she was disoriented. The motion of the boat was stopped; lamps burned in the cabin; through the ports other lights gleamed, making rippling reflections that reached to within inches of the glass. From outside came a sound she knew; the fast rap and flutter of halliards against masts, night-noise of a harbour of boats. She swung her legs down blearily; rubbed her face, not knowing where she was. Not daring to ask.

A meal was laid in the cabin, great kedgerees of rice and shellfish pieces, mushrooms and eggs. Surprisingly, she was hungry; she sat shoulder to shoulder with the boy who had spoken for her, had, she realized, argued for her life in the bright afternoon. She ate mechanically and quickly, eyes not leaving her plate; round her the talk flowed unheeding. She crouched small, glad to be forgotten.

They took her with them when they went ashore. In the dinghy she felt more at ease. They sat in a waterfront bar, in France, drank bottle on bottle of wine till her head spun again and voices and noise seemed blended in a warm roaring. She snuggled, on the Welshman's knees, feeling safe again and wanted. She tried to talk then, about the fossils in the rocks and her father and the Church and swimming and nearly being drowned; they scuffed her hair, laughing, not understanding. The wine ran down her neck inside the sweater; she laughed back and watched the lamps spin, head drooping, lids half closed on dark-lashed hazel eyes.

'*Ahoy, White Boat . . .*'

She stood shivering, seeing the lamps drive spindled images into the water, hearing men reel along the quay, hearing the shouts, feeling still the tingling surprise of foreignness. While White Boat answered faint from the mass of vessels, the tender crept splashing out of the night.

She was still barefoot; she felt the water tart against her ankles as she scuttled down to catch the dinghy's bow.

'Here,' said David. 'Not puttin' you to bed twice in a bloody day . . .'

She felt her head hit the rolled blankets that served as a pillow; muttered and grinned, pushed blearily at the waistband of her jeans, gave up, collapsed in sleep.

The miles of water slid past, chuckling in a dream.

She woke quickly to darkness, knowing once more she had been fooled. They had slipped out of harbour, in the night; that heave and roll, chuckling and bowstring sense of tightness, was the feel of the open sea.

White Boat, and these people, never slept.

There were voices again. And lights gleaming, rattle of descending sails, scrape of something rolling against the hull. Scufflings then, and thuds. She lay curled in the bunk, face turned away from the cabin.

'No, she's asleep . . .'

'Easy with that now, man . . .'

She chuckled, silently. The clink of bottles, thump of secret bales, amused her. There was nothing more to fear; these people were smugglers.

She woke heavy and irritable. The source of irritation was for a time mysterious. She attempted, unwillingly, to analyse her feelings; for her, an unusual exercise. The wildest, most romantic notions of White Boat were true; yet she was cheated. This she knew instinctively. She saw the village street then, the little black clustering houses, the church. The priest mouthing silently, condemning; her father, black-faced, unfastening his broad, buckled belt. To this she would return, irrevocably; the dream was finished.

That was it; the point of pain, the taste and very essence of it. That she didn't belong, aboard White Boat. She never would. Abruptly she found herself hating the crew for the knowledge they had given so freely. They should have beaten her, loved her till she bled, tied her feet, slammed her into the deep green sea. They had done nothing, because to them she was worth nothing. Not even death.

She refused food, for the second time. She thought the skipper looked at her with worried eyes. She ignored him; she took up her old position, gripping the friendly thickness of the mast. The day was sunny and bright; the boat moved fast, under the great spread whiteness of a Genoa, dipping lee scuppers under, jouncing through the sea. Almost she wished for the sickness of the day before, the hour when she'd wanted so urgently to die. As White Boat raised, slowly, the coast of England.

Her mind seemed split now into halves, one part wanting the voyage indefinitely prolonged, the other needing to rush on disaster, have it over and done. The day faded slowly to dusk, dusk to deep night. In the dark she saw the cressets of a signal tower, flaring, moving pinpoints; and another answering it, and another far beyond. They would be signalling for her, without a doubt; calling across the moors, through all the long bays. She curled her lip. She had discovered cynicism.

The wind blew chill across the sea.

Forward of the mast, a hatch gave access to the sail locker. She lowered herself into it, curled atop the big sausage shapes of canvas. The bulkhead door, ajar and creaking, showed shifting gleams of yellow from the cabin lamps. Here the water noise was intensified; she listened sullenly to the chuckle and seethe, half-wanting in her bitterness the boat to strike some reef and drown. While the light moved, forward and back across the sloping painted walls. She began picking half-unconsciously at the paint, crumbling little brittle flakes in her palm.

The loose boards interested her.

By the lamplight she saw part of the wooden side move slightly, out of time with the upright that supported it. She

edged across, pulled experimentally. There was a hatch, behind
it a space into which she could reach her arm. She groped
tentatively, drew out a slim oilcloth packet. Then another.
There were many of them, crowded away in the double hull;
little things, not much bigger than the boxes of lucifers she
bought sometimes in the village shop.

On impulse she pushed one of them into the waistband of
her trews. She scurried the rest out of sight again, closed the
trap, sat frowning. She sat rubbing the little packet, feeling it
warm slowly against her flesh, determined for the first time in
her life to steal; wanting some part of White Boat maybe,
something to hold at night and remember. Something precious.

Somebody had been very careless.

There was a voice above her, a moving of feet on the deck.
She scrambled guiltily, climbed back through the hatch. But
they weren't interested in her. Ahead the coastline showed solid,
velvet-black. She saw the loom of twin headlands, faintest
gleam of waves round long stone moles, and realized with a
shock and thrill of coldness that she was home.

She saw other things too, heresies that stopped her breath.
Machines, uncovered now, whirred and ticked in the cabin.
Bands of light flickered pink, moved against a scale of figures;
she heard the chanting as they edged into the bay, seven fathoms,
five, four. As the devil-boat came in, with nobody at the lead ...

The dinghy swung from its place atop the cabin, thumped
into the sea. She scrambled down, clutching her parcelled
dress. Another bundle was lowered, heavier, chinking musically.
For her father, she was told; and to say, 'twas from the Boat. A
bribe of silence that; or a double bluff, confession of a little
crime to hide one monstrously worse. They called to her, low-
voiced; she waved mechanically, seeing as she turned away the
last descending flutter of the jib. The dinghy headed in slow,
the Welsh boy at the tiller. She knelt upright on the bottom
boards till the boat bumped the mole, grated and rolled. She
was out then quickly, scuttling away. He called her as she
reached the bottom of the path. She turned waiting, a frail
shadow in the night.

He seemed unsure how to go on. 'You must understand, see,'

he said unhappily. 'You must never do this again. Do you understand, Becky?'

'Yes,' she said. 'Goodbye.' She turned and ran again up the path to the stream, over the bridge to home.

There was a window they always left open, over the wash-house roof. She left the bundles in the outhouse; the door hinge creaked as she closed it but nothing stirred. She climbed cautiously, padded through the dark to her room. She lay on the bed, feeling the faint rocking that meant mystically she was still in communion with the great boat down there in the bay. A last conscious thought made her pull the package from her waist, tuck it beneath the layers of mattress.

Her father seemed in the dawn light a stranger. There was no explanation she cared to give, nothing to say. She was still drugged with sleep; she felt with indifference the unbuckling of her trews, heard him draw the belt slow through his hands. Dazed, she imagined the beating would have no power to hurt; she was wrong. The pain exploded forward and back through her body, stabbing in red flashes behind her eyes. She squeezed the bedrail, needing to die again, knowing disjointedly there was no help in words. Her body had sprung from rock and shale, the gloomy vastness of the fields; the strap fell not on her but on the headlands, the rocks, the sea. Exorcizing the loneliness of the place, the misery and hopelessness and pain. He finished finally, turned away groping to barge through the door. Downstairs in the little house a child wailed, sensing hatred and fear; she moved her head slightly on the pillow, hearing it seemed from far off the breathing wash of the sea.

Her fingers moved down to coil on the packet in the bed. Slowly, with indifference, she began picking at the fastenings. Scratching the knots, pulling and teasing till the wrapping came away. It was her pleasure to imagine herself blind, condemned to touch and feel. The fingers, oversensitive, strayed and tapped, turning the little thing, feeling variations of texture, shapes of warmth and coldness, exploring bleakly the tiny map of heresy. A tear, her first, rolled an inch from one eye, left a shining track against the brownness of the skin.

She had the heart of White Boat, gripped in her hand.

The priest came, tramping heavy on the stairs. Her father pushed ahead of him, covered her roughly. Her hand stayed by her side unseen as Father Antony talked. She lay quiet, face down, lashes brushing her cheek, knowing immobility and patience were her best defence. The light from the window faded as he sat; when he left, it was nearly night.

In the gloom she lifted the stolen thing, touched it to her face. The heretical smell of it, of wax and bakelite and brass, assaulted her mind faintly. She stroked it again, lovingly; while she held it gripped it seemed she could call White Boat to her bidding, bring her in from her wanderings time and again.

The sun stayed hidden in the days that followed, while she lay on the cliffs and saw the yacht flit in and go. A greater barrier separated her now than the sea she had learned to cross; a barrier built not by others but by her own stupidity.

She killed a great blue lobster, slowly and with pain, driving nails through the membraned cracks of its armour while it threshed and writhed. She cut it apart slowly, hating herself and all the world, dropped the pieces in the sea for a bitter, useless sacrifice. This and other things she did to ease the emptiness in her, fill the progression of iron-grey afternoons. There were vices to be learned, at night and out on the rocks, little gratifications of pleasure and pain. She indulged her body, contemptuously; because White Boat had come cajoling and free, thrown her back laughing, indifferent to hurt. Life stretched before her now like an endless cage: where, she asked herself, was the Change once promised, the great things the priest John had seen? The Golden Age that would bring other White Boats, other days and hope; the wild waves of the very air made to talk and sing . . .

She fondled the tiny heart of the Boat, in the black dark, felt the wires and coils, the little tubes of valves.

The church was still and cold, the priest's breathing faint behind the little carved screen. She waited while he talked and murmured, unhearing; while her hands closed and opened on the thing she carried, the sweat sprang out on the palms.

And it was done, hopelessly and sullen. She pushed the little machine at the grille, waited greyly for the intake of breath, the panic-scrabble of feet from the other side.

The face of Father Antony was beyond description.

The village stirred, whispering and grumbling, people scurrying forward and back between the houses gaping at the soldiers in the street, the shouting horsemen and officers. Sappers, working desperately, rigged sheerlegs along the line of cliffs, swung tackles from the heavy beams. Garrisons stood at alert right back to Durnovaria; this land had rebelled before, the commanders were taking no chances. Signallers, ironic-faced, worked and flapped the arms of half a hundred semaphores; despatch riders galloped, raking their mounts bloody as the questions and instructions flew. A curfew was clapped on the village, the people driven to their homes; but nothing could stop the rumours, the whisperings and unease. Heresy walked like a spectre, blew in on the sea wind; till a man saw the old monk himself, grim-faced and empty-eyed, stalking the clifftops in his tattered gown. Detachments of cavalry quartered the downs, but there was nothing to be found. Through the night, and into the darkest time before the dawn, the one street of the village echoed to the marching tramp of men. Then there was a silent time of waiting. The breeze soughed up from the bay, moving the tangles of gorse, crying across the huddled roofs; while Becky, lying quiet, listened for the first whisper, the shout that would send the soldiers to their posts, train the waiting guns.

She lay on her face, hair tangled on the pillow, hearing the night wind, clenching and slowly unclenching her hands. It seemed the shouting still echoed in her brain, the harangues, thumping of tables, red-faced noise of priests. She saw her father standing glowering and sullen while the cobalt-tuniced major questioned over and again, probing, insisting, till in misery questions became answers and answers made their own fresh confusion. The sea moved in her brain, dulling sense, while the cannon came trundling and peering behind the straining mules, crashing trails and limbers on the rough ground till the noise clapped forward and back between the houses and she put hands to ears and cried to stop, just to stop . . .

They wrung her dry, between them. She told things she had told to nobody, secrets of bay and beach and lapping waves, fears and dreams; everything they heard stony-faced while the clerks scribbled, the semaphores clacked on the hills. They left her finally, in her house, in her room, soldiers guarding the door and her father swearing and drunk downstairs and the neighbours pecking and fluttering over the children, making as they spoke of her and hers the sign of the Cross. She lay an age while understanding came and grew, while her nails marked her palms and the tears squeezed hot and slow. The wind droned, soughing under the eaves; blowing strong and cool and steady, bringing White Boat in to death.

Never before had her union with the Boat seemed stronger. She saw her with the clarity of nightmare, moon washing the tilted deck, sails gleaming darkly against the loom of land. She tried in desperation to force her mind out over the sea; she prayed to turn, go back, fly away. White Boat heard, but made no answer; she came on steadily, angry and inexorable.

Becky sat up quietly, padded to the window. She saw the bright night, the moonglow in the little cluttered yard. In the street footsteps clicked, faded to quiet. A bird called, hunting, while cloud wisps groped for and extinguished the moon.

She shivered, easing at the sash. Once before she had known an alien steadiness, a coldness that made her movements smooth and calm. She placed a foot carefully on the outhouse tiles, ducked through the window, thumped into the deeper shadow of the house wall. She waited, listening to silence.

They were not stupid, these soldiers of the Pope. She sensed rather than saw the sentry at the bottom of the garden, slipped like a wraith through darkness till she was near enough almost to touch his cloak. She waited patient, eyes watching white and blind while the moon eased clear, was obscured again. In front of her the boy yawned, leaned his musket against the wall. He called something sleepily, sauntered a dozen paces up the road.

She was over the wall instantly, feet scuffling. Her skirt snagged, pulled clear. She ran, padding on the road, waiting for the shout, the flash and bang of a gun. The dream was undisturbed.

The bay lay silver and broad. She moved cautiously, parting bracken, wriggling to the edge of the cliff. Beneath her, twenty yards away, men clustered smoking and talking. The pipes they lit carefully, backs to the sea and shielded by their cloaks, unwilling to expose the slightest gleam of light. The tide was making, washing in across the ramps and up among the rocks; the moon stood now above the far headland, showing it stark against a milky haze.

In front of her were the guns.

She watched down at them, eyes wide. Six heavy pieces, humped and sullen, staring out across the sea. She saw the cunning behind the placement; that shot, ball or canister, fired nearly level with the water, would hurtle on spreading and rebounding. The Boat would have no chance. She would come in, on to the guns; and they would fire. There would be no warning, no offers of quarter; just the sudden orange thunder from the land, the shot coming tearing and smashing . . .

She strained her eyes. Far out on the dim verge of sky and sea was a smudge that danced as she watched and returned, insistent, dark grey against the greyness of the void. The tallness of a sail, heading in toward the coast.

She ran again, scrambling and jumping; slid into the stream, followed it where its chuckling could mask sounds of movement, crouched glaring on the edge of the beach. The soldiers had seen too; there was a stirring, a rustling surge of dark figures away from the cliff. Men ran to point and stare, train night glasses at the sea. Their backs were to the guns.

There was no time to think; none to do more than swallow, try and quiet the thunder of her heart. Then she was running desperately, feet spurning the grit, stumbling on boulders and buried stones. Behind her a shout, the rolling crash of a musket, cursing of an officer. The ball glanced from rock, threw splinters at her back and calves. She leaped and swerved, landed on her knees. She saw men running, the bright flash of a sword. Another report, distant and unassociated. She panted, rolled on her back beside the first of the guns.

It was unimportant that her body burned with fire. Her fingers gripped the lanyard, curled lovingly and pulled.

A hugeness of flame, a roar; the flash lit the cliffs, sparkled out across the sea. The gun lurched back, angry and alive; while all down the line the pieces fired, random now and furious, the shot fizzing over the water. The cannonade echoed from the headlands, boomed across the village; woke a girl who mocked and squealed, in her bed, in her room, the noise vaunting up wild and high into the night.

While White Boat, turning, laughed at the guns.

And spurned the land.

The Passing of the Dragons

There's no real reason for an Epsilon Dragon to die. None the less, they do.

By 'real reasons' I don't, of course, include atmosphere, soil and plant pollution, direct and indirect blast effects and ultrasonic fracture of the inner ear. Most of the things that will do for a human being will do for a Dragon. They are, or were, more than humanly affected by high frequencies; the tympani were numerous and large, situated in a row down each side of the body an inch or so above the lateral line. Which you can see for yourself if you can get off your butt long enough to get down to the museum of the Institute of Alien Biology.

The other things that can kill a Dragon are more interesting, as I explained to Pilot (First Class) Scott-Braithwaite a few weeks after our arrival on (or coincidence with) Epsilon Cygnus VI. The specimen under consideration flowed and clattered into the clearing by the lab about thirteen hundred hours, Planetary Time. I was checking the daily meter readings, I didn't pay too much attention till I saw the three sets of whips a Dragon carries on its back flatten out and immobilize. It made the thing look like a little green and gold helicopter squatting there on the grass.

I picked up the stethoscope and the Röntgen viewer and walked outside. A Dragon has eight hearts, situated in two rows of four between the eighth and twelfth body segments. I attached the stethoscope sensors, studied the display. As I'd expected, the first cardiac pair had become inoperative. Pairs two and four seemed to be showing reduced activity; pair three, presumably, were sustaining residual body functions. Since breathing is by spiracles and tracheae, body function isn't all that easy to confirm. I used the viewer and stood up, leaned my hands on the knobbly back-armour. 'Well,' I said, 'our friend here is headed for the Happy Chewing Grounds. Or wherever they go.'

The Pilot (First Class) frowned. He said, 'How can you tell?'

I shrugged and walked round the Dragon. There was a slight injury, in the soft membrane between two body segments; a little fluid had wept across the armour, but it didn't seem critical. If Dragons were arthopods, as their appearance suggests, collapse from a minor abrasion would be understandable; but the body is no fluid sac, they have a blood-vascular system as well defined as that of a mammal. On the other hand the possibility of infection couldn't be ruled out. I fetched a hypodermic from the lab, drew off a fluid sample. Later I'd take tissue cuttings. They'd be clean, of course. They always are.

I'd brought the surgical kit out with me. I rigged a pair of pacemakers, set the collars on the probes to the standard twenty-five-centimetre penetration. I measured a handspan from the median lines, pushed the needles down through the joint membrane, used the stethoscope again. The trace bounced around a bit, and steadied.

He leaned over me. I suppose one might say, 'keen face intent'. He said, 'Working?'

I shrugged, I said, 'Any fool can make a heart pump. It isn't much of a trick.'

He said, 'Then it'll be OK.'

I shook my head. I said, 'It'll die.'

He said, 'When?'

I lifted one of the whips, let it droop back. I said, 'In thirty hours, twenty-eight minutes Terrestrial.'

He raised his eyebrows.

I said kindly, 'Planetary revolution.'

I walked back to the lab. I'd decided to run a cardiograph. Not that it would tell us any more than the thousand or two already on file at IAB. But it's one of the things one does. It's called Making an Effort. Or showing the Flag.

He was still standing where I'd left him. He said, 'I can't understand these damn things.'

Most of his conversation was like that. Incisive. Really kept you on your toes.

I started attaching the sensors of the cardiogram. You should listen to a Dragon's heart sometime. It's like the pulse of a star. Or maybe you're a fan of the Hottentots. They based their style on IAB recordings, so I'm told; so the Dragons, you see, have been of service to mankind.

He said, 'Why planetary revolution?'

I smiled at him. 'Do you know, Pilot, First Class,' I said, 'I have no idea.'

He frowned. He said, 'I thought you scientists had all the answers.'

His repartee certainly was a joy to the ear.

I said, 'I'm not a scientist. Just a Behaviourist.' I smiled again. 'Technician,' I said. 'Second class.'

He didn't answer that one. They don't encourage morbid self-analysis at Space School.

I walked back through the specimen lock. I'd had it rigged some time now. I'd been asked to take a living Dragon back to Earth. Not that it would survive phase-out. They never do. But that's what science is all about for most of us: a lot of little people doing what's been done before, and not succeeding either.

He followed me. He had that trick. He said, 'Can I help?'

I said, 'No, thanks.' I was thinking how difficult it must be for him, lumbered with a type like me. My teeth are less than pearly, my body is less than sylphlike; I don't play peloa, I drink my ale by the pint and what I say sometimes has some relation to what I think. It must have been hell.

He lit a cigarette. At least he had one insanitary habit. Maybe there were more. You can never tell, by appearances.

I switched the recorder on. The traces started zipping along the display. I turned the replay volume up. The sound thudded at us. He winced. He said, 'Do we have to have that?'

I said, 'It soothes me.' I gave the volume another notch. I said, 'You must have heard the Hottentots.'

He said, 'That's different.'

Man, was his conversation uptight. This was being a great tour.

I listened to the heartbeats. The rhythms phased in and out of each other like drums; or bells underground, ringing a change that was endless.

He said, 'And that thing's going to die?'

I didn't answer. I was thinking about the Dragon. Difficult to dissociate the notion of purpose from things that take exactly a day to die. Neither a second more nor less. But it's difficult to dissociate the notion of purpose from anything a Dragon does. Or did. For instance, they built cities. Or we thought they were cities. We were never too sure, one way or the other.

I ejected the sample into a centrifuge, locked the case and switched on. He watched me for a bit. Then he yawned. He said, 'I'm going to have a kip till contact time. Call me if you need me.'

I kept my back turned till the door had shut. With the din I'd set up he was going to be lucky. But some people can sleep through anything. Probably to do with leading a healthy life.

He started on the subject again at suppertime. He'd got a radio running; music was playing, from the room next door. The room we call Earth. My Dragon's jazz was still thumping in the lab. I changed channels, got the Hottentots. It made an interesting counterpoint. He changed back. He said, 'How many of those things do you reckon there are out there?'

'What things? Pop groups?'

He said, 'Dragons.'

I let a can of soup preheat, picked it up, burned my fingers and opened it. I said, 'A hundred, hundred and fifty. That was at the last count. Probably halved by now.'

He frowned. He said, 'What's killing them?'

I did rather take that as a silly question. Epsilon Cygnus VI just happens to have a mineral-rich crust containing about everything Homo Sapiens has ever found a use for, from gold to lithium. My species had blown in ten years back; now the rest of the planet was an automated slagtip.

I started ticking points on my fingers. I said, 'Ecological imbalance triggered by waterborne effluent. Toxic concentration of broad-spectrum herbicides –'

He waved a hand, irritably. He said, 'They've got a whole damn subcontinent to live in. There's no mining here.'

I said, 'So they die from minor abrasions. Maybe they're making a gesture.'

He looked at me narrowly. He said, 'You've got some damn queer ideas.'

I said, 'I'm an observer. I'm not paid to have ideas.'

'But you said –'

'I pointed out psychological factors may exist. Or there again, they may not. Either way, we shall never know. Hence my engrosssment.'

He frowned again. He said, 'I don't follow you.'

'There's not much to follow. I'm fascinated by failure. It runs in the family.'

He shook his head. I think he was grappling with a concept. He said, 'You mean –'

'I didn't mean anything. I was just making light conversation. As per handbook.'

He flushed. He said, 'You don't have to be so bloody rude about it.'

I slung the can at the disposal unit. For once, I hit it. I said, 'I'm sorry, Space Pilot.' I smiled. I said, 'Us civvies, you know. Nerves wear a bit thin. Don't have your cast-iron constitutions.'

I don't have the stoicism of the upper bourgeoisie either. If I cut my finger, I usually whimper.

He flashed me a white grin. That's the most offensive sentence I can think of, so I'll leave it in. It describes what he did so well. He said, 'Forget it, Researcher. I'm a bit on edge myself.'

Oh, those lines! I was starting to wonder whether he had an inexhaustible stockpile of them. There must be an end somewhere, even to aphorisms.

I walked to the blinds, lifted the slats. Night on Epsilon VI is greenish, like the days. Like a thick pea soup, with turquoise overtones. The heartbeat thudded in the next room.

I picked up a handlamp. I said, 'I'm going out to check the patient.' The comic-opera habit was evidently catching.

He said, 'I'll come with you.'

I think his nerves were getting bad. He had an automatic strapped to his hip; on the way through the lab he collected a rocket pistol as well. There are no dangerous fauna on Epsilon VI; in fact at the time of writing I'm predisposed to believe there are no fauna at all. There used to be some pretty big lepidoptera, though. I said, 'You should have brought a scatter-gun. They're difficult to hit with ball.'

He said, 'What?'

I said, 'The moths.'

He didn't deign to answer.

The Dragon squatted where we had left it. I turned the lamp on. The halogen-quartz cut a white cone through the murk. Furry flying things blundered across the light. I swung the beam round. The jungle was empty.

He was standing with his hands on his hips, the holster flap tucked back. He said, 'What are you looking for?'

I said, 'The mourners should be arriving pretty soon.'

'The *what?*'

I said, 'Mourners. But again, I'm theorizing without data.'

'What do they do?'

I said, 'Nothing. Stand around. Generally they eat the corpse.'

He made a disgusted noise.

I said, '*Autre temps, autre mondes . . .*' I switched the light off. I said, 'I like these field jobs, you know. They broaden one.'

He walked back ahead of me to the lab. I closed the door and bolted it, for his peace of mind.

I don't sleep too well these days. Like the poet says, old bones are hard to please. I lay and read a while. Afterwards I drank whisky. The site storeroom had a cellar like nobody's business. It should have had; IAB observer teams had been stocking it surreptitiously for a decade. I poured myself another good slug. No point leaving the stuff to rot; there wouldn't be any more folk coming this way. They'd cleaned up all the easy deposits on Epsilon VI; the archipelago on which we'd landed, a big curve of islands stretching into the southern ocean, was about the only land surface left unraped. It was also the last stronghold of the Dragons.

I put the glass down, sat staring at the dural wall. IAB had

had assurance, of course, from Trade Control; but once assurances start arriving three times a year you know the end isn't far off. The principle of the thing's simple, as simple as all truly great ideas; while a single rumpled little Earthman with spiky yellow shoes can make a single rumpled little spiky yellow dollar, the killing goes on. Any killing. Next season they'd open-caste the islands; the Dragons had had their chance.

The Pilot (First Class) kept his light on well into the night. Maybe he was reading. I wondered vaguely whether he masturbated. I wasn't too concerned, one way or the other; but a Behaviourist gets into the way of collecting odd facts.

I'd turned the playback volume down but left it running. The Dragon's hearts thumped steadily through the thin metal wall. Toward the middle of the night the rhythm altered. I got up, pulled a jacket on and went ouside.

There's no moon on Epsilon; but there is a massive aurora belt. The green sky flashed and flickered; it was like the brewing of a perpetual storm. The Dragon's whips vibrated faintly; the golden eye-clusters watched without interest. I used the stethoscope. The second and fourth heart pairs were dead. I applied a second and third set of pacemakers. Pair two picked up; pair four wouldn't kick over. I decided a stimulant couldn't do any harm. I went back to the lab, checked the chart, filled a syringe. I shot enough strychnine into the heart walls to kill a terrestrial horse. I saw the trace pick up and steady. Interesting. I thought vaguely I should have taken encephalographs as well.

The idea of stimulants was a good one. I went back, drank some more whisky. Then I dozed.

The mourners began to arrive at first light.

I heard the rustling and clattering and got up. I pulled on slacks and a shirt, stared through the lab port. The dawn was as green as the rest of the day; smoky emerald, fading to clear high lemon where Epsilon Cygnus struggled with the mist. A Dragon passed a yard or so away, jerking and lumbering like a thing at the bottom of an ocean. It was a big one, I judged a potential male. Dragons are parthenogenetic most of the time; over the years they sometimes develop sexual characteristics and mate conventionally. The analysis people had an idea it was to do with sunspot activity; but if there's a correlation we didn't give the computers enough hard facts to pinpoint it. The whole thing just made phylum classification a bit more entertaining.

The newcomer stopped a yard or more from the immobilized Dragon, and waved its whips. They were ten or twelve feet long, banded in green, orange and black. Ball and socket joints several inches across joined them to the body armour; round the base of each were tufts of stiff, iridescent hair.

The yellow eyes watched; the whips moved and stroked, touching the body of the dying creature from end to end. The head of the Dragon rotated, the jawparts clicked; then the thing reared its forepart into the air, lapsed into immobility. I'd seen the stance before. So had a lot of folk.

I opened the lab door, stepped outside. The morning air was cool and sweet. I walked up to the new arrival. The eye-clusters stared, like blank jewels. I wondered if it was seeing me.

I heard footsteps behind me. The Pilot (First Class) looked concerned. He said, 'Jupiter, is this the first?'

I nodded. I said, 'Good one, isn't he?'

He rubbed his face. He was wearing a white shirt, open to the waist. On his chest hung a heavy silver cross. Very fashionable.

There was a crackling in the jungle. Number two advanced slowly, through the moving coils of mist. It looked like a brilliant little armoured vehicle. The flowing of the clasper legs was invisible; you could have imagined readily enough that it was running on tracks.

It moved to the bunch of cables I'd stretched from the patient, and checked. The whips shook, stooped; rose again vertically above its back. It didn't seem to object to the cables overmuch; neither did it cross them. It turned, followed their line to the dying Dragon. The same ritual was observed. The whips rustled; then the creature arched itself, lapsed like its fellow into stillness.

The pilot (First Class) had his hand on the butt of the automatic. I shook my head. Dragons are harmless. Their mouthparts could take your arm off; but if you put your fingers between the mandibles they just stop working. I'd told him often enough, but it seemed he wasn't convinced.

He trailed after me back to the lab. He said, 'How many of these things do you expect to arrive?'

I said, 'Ten. Or a dozen.'

'What'll they do?'

I said, 'Like I told you. Stand around.'

He said, 'They're waiting for it to die.'

I set water on to boil. I said, 'Could be.'

He frowned. He said, 'They're obviously waiting.'

I laid out plates and cups. I said, 'It's by no means obvious. "Wait" as a concept depends on human-based time awareness. They may lack that awareness. In which case, they are not waiting.'

He said, 'It's a bit of a quibble though.'

I shook my head. 'Certainly not,' I said. 'Consider a proposition. "The rocks of the valley waited." That's more than a quibble. It's a howling pathetic fallacy.'

He glared at me. He said, 'If they're living, they have time awareness.'

I shrugged. I said, 'Try telling a tree.'

'I didn't mean that.'

'Then trees aren't living. Interesting.'

He said, 'You are the most argumentative bastard I ever met.'

I said, 'Hard words, Captain. In any case it's not true. For argumentative read definitive.'

He swallowed his temper, like a good skipper. My word, these boys have self-control. They're pretty fine male specimens, of course, all the way round.

By midmorning nine of the creatures had arrived. I set up the encephalogram, fixed the probes. A Dragon has a massive brain, situated behind and below the eyes. Capacity betters the human cranium by an average of twenty-five per cent. Nearly the same was once true of terrestrial dolphins. But they never learned to talk.

I watched the pens record. Something like an alpha rhythm was emerging. By thirteen hundred Planetary Time the wave forms were altering, developing greater valleys and peaks. The crisis was approaching; but it was nothing new. I lit a pipe, walked outside. The heartbeats thundered from the open lab door. At thirteen-forty the first pair shut down. Then pairs two and three. I counted the beats on pair four. Then the glade was silent. I said, 'That's it, then.' I logged the time; Earth Standard and Planetary, hours and minutes from sun-up. I pulled the probes out, disconnected them, started coiling the cables.

He stood staring. He said, 'Aren't you going to do anything?'

I said, 'Like what?'

He said, 'Try it with a shot. Something like that.'

I said, 'You can if you like. Speaking from my human-based awareness, I'd say it was a waste of time.'

Dead, the thing looked just as it had when living; but the gold was fading slowly from the eyes.

He sat on the metal step of the lab, and lit a cigarette. He looked shaken up.

The jade-green ring of Dragons made no move. They stood poised through the afternoon, like so many cumbersome statues. Occasionally one or other of the pairs of whips would rise, tremble, sink again; but that was all. I cut tissue specimens for autopsy, stripped the pacemakers, autoclaved the probes. Then I scrubbed up and went through to the living quarters. He was sitting reading a glossy magazine somebody had left about. It had a full-frontal stereograph on the cover. She looked pretty good. I walked back to the lab, ran the tapes and started up. The heartbeat of the dead Dragon filled the air.

I heard him fling the book down. He stood in the doorway, staring. He said, 'Do we have to have that again?'

I said, 'We do. There might be a clue.'

'A *what?*'

I said, 'Think of it as a sort of Cosmic Code. It may help.'

We ate. The Dragons stayed in their circle. Afterwards he walked out. He didn't say where he was going, which is against the rules if you're going strictly by the book. There was a little vertol flier in one of the hangar sheds. I heard it start up, drone away towards the west.

I turned the replay volume up. The heartbeats thudded in the clearing. I got a heavy speaker housing from the lab, set it out on the grass, blasted the noise at the Dragons. It had been tried before, of course. They hadn't reacted then. They didn't react now. I dismantled the rig, put the gear away and shut down. The glade was very still, the veiled sun dropping towards the west.

I got my jacket, and a pair of prismatics. I walked due south, away from the lab. About a mile off, a rocky bluff thrust up through a mustard-green tide of trees. The front of the cliff, golden now in the slanting light, was riddled with holes. I used the glasses. A dozen were occupied; I could see the yellow masks staring down. The rest were empty and blank.

At the foot of the cliff was a roughly circular clearing. In it stood a dozen or more massive structures. The quartz chunks of which they were mainly composed flashed and glittered, throwing back the brilliant light. They formed columns, arcades, porticoes. At intervals openwork platforms pierced the towers; it made them look a little like gigantic rose trellises. Sprays of viridian creeper twined from level to level, enhancing the illusion. It was presumed the Dragons built them; though the proposition had never ben proved. IAB had been interested in them for years, off and on. A docket went round whenever somebody had a bright idea. I'd seen nests, temples and free-form sculpture all put up as propostions. You paid your money, and you took your choice.

The city was the main reason for the siting of the lab. We'd put it a mile away initially in case the Dragons reacted to our presence. The hope had been wild and wilful; nobody had yet seen them react to anything.

I walked back to the lab. There was no sign of the Pilot (First Class). I set the coffee on again, picked up the girlie book, skimmed the pages. I was pleased to see they were letting a few white strippers back in on the act. Emancipation, like everything else, can go too far.

Towards nightfall I checked the port. The ring of Dragons had closed in; one of them was stretching its neck segments, nuzzling forward and back along the corpse like a cat skimming cream from a saucer. After a time the mouthparts settled to a steady motion. I logged the event.

The flier landed. A wait; and I heard the Pilot's footsteps in the clearing. He barged in through the lab door. He said, 'They're eating it. It's bloody horrible.'

I put the mag down. I said, 'The fact has been noted.',

He said, 'It's bloody horrible. And you reckoned those things were intelligent.'

'I can't remember reckoning anything. In any case it doesn't preclude the possibility.'

'You must be joking!'

I said, 'Perhaps it's a religious observance. Which would make it highly sophisticated.'

'A *what?*'

I remembered the cross round his neck. He was a neo-Catholic, of course. He had to be. I said, 'It has all the distinguishing characteristics.'

He sat down heavily, and lit a cigarette. He said, 'You're mad.'

'I wish I was. I'd get more fun out of life. Remember the Dream of the Rood?'

'No.'

I clucked at him. 'Dear me, And part of your course was the Humanities.'

He glowered. I smiled at him. I said, 'Teatime, Skipper. Your turn to undo the cans.'

He said, 'As a matter of fact, I'm not hungry.'

I said, 'Pity. I am. Force of habit, of course. But powerful. Rule One of the Behaviourist.' I got up, started banging pots and pans round in the galley. I said, 'Blood sacrifice. Eat, for this is my flesh. Also see Tennessee Williams. Mid-twentieth century. American.'

He stood. He said, 'I'm going to get cleaned up.'

I said, 'They probably have. It's a very old sofa.'

'*What?*'

'Nothing. Daddy has some timeslip trouble. Bear with an old man.'

He walked out. He'd started slamming doors.

I kicked the girlie stereo under the side table. Not so much from frustration as pique. One dislikes being constantly offered what isn't for sale.

He started singing in the shower. He always sang in the shower. His voice was very good. Light tenor. I expected he used a good aftershave too. I wondered just what the hell a Dragon would make of him anyway. Pink for skin, brown for hair, white for teeth. You could analyse the picture till it fragmented. Then you had a monster of your own.

The bath put him into a better humour. He emerged from his labours at seventeen hundred, Planetary. He was wearing a white uniform jacket, with the braids and brassard of his Order. He capered up to me, spun me round, slapped me on the back. Then he sat in a chair, legs asprawl, grinned and lit a cigarette. He said, 'Judy's coming through. On the Link.'

I said, 'I bet she's your fiancée.'

He looked hurt. He said, 'You know she is. You met her before lift-off. She's a model.'

I said, 'Ah, yes.' It was the Little Girl Look this year, Earthside. Which meant candid blue eyes, golden curls, tits like stoplights. I said, 'Thoughtless of me. I remember her well. A charming person, I thought.'

He looked at the chronometer on the lab bulkhead. He said, 'We're getting married. Straight after this tour.'

I said, 'I expect you are.'

He gave me a dirty look. He said, 'I suppose that fits a behaviour pattern too.'

I said, 'It very well might.'

He said viciously, 'Why don't you run a programme on it? You might come up with some new facts.'

I yawned. I said, 'Fortunately, I don't have to. I read tea leaves. Saves a lot of computer time.'

The buzzer sounded. He started the Richardsons. Earth Control exchanged the time of day; then Judy came on. She was as I remembered her. Love through the Loop; she had the sort of voice that can squeeze sex out of duralumin. He said, 'Hello, darling,' and she said, 'Hello, Drew.' Drew, yet . . . I tried the full effect. Drew Scott-Braithwaite. I got up, went looking for the whisky. I needed something to take the taste away.

She said, 'How are you?'

He said, 'Fine, love, just fine.'

I poured three fingers.

She said, 'How's the project?'

He said, 'Fine.'

I walked out to the lab, started labelling and packing the heart tapes. She said, 'Who's that with you? I can't see, he's not in camera.'

He said, 'Researcher Fredericks. You met him at lift-off.'

She said, 'Are you looking after him?'

He said, 'He's fine.'

The speaker said, 'Give him my love.'

Drew said, 'She sends you her love.'

I said, 'That's fine.'

The Richardson operator said, 'Epsilon, you are in overtime.'

Judy said, 'Gosh, your poor bank balance. Darling, I must go. See you soon.'

He said, ' 'Bye, bunny. Take care now.' I heard the crackle as the link broke. The generators cut, whined down to silence.

He walked to the lab door. He said, 'That was bloody uncivil.'

'What was uncivil?'

He said, 'Walking out like that.'

I said, 'It was your call, not mine.'

'As if that mattered!'

'It mattered to me. Anyway, I had some work to do.'

His face darkened. He said, 'You might as well know, I don't like your attitude.'

I said, 'The fact is noted.'

He took a step into the lab. He said, 'I'm also very well aware you don't like me.'

I said, 'On the contrary. I don't give a damn. Now, if you please. You do your thing. I'll do mine. OK?' I pushed past him, got myself another drink.

He stood and stared for a bit, breathing down his nose. He said, 'What would you do if I belted you between the eyes?'

I said, 'Lose consciousness. Later, in all probability, sue you.' I turned with a whisky in my hand. I said, 'For Christ's sake have a drink, man. And let it go.'

He took the glass, shakily. His moods were starting to switch about a bit. Too much for my taste. Anyway, he cooled down in time. Sat and told me about the place they were buying in the Rockies, his old man having weighed in with a few thousand dollars to help the mortgage; and the Chrysler automat he'd picked up on his last Earth furlough, and all the rest. He didn't quite get round to how many kids they were planning for, but he sailed pretty close. He even gave me a standing invite to view the establishment after they got settled in; which would have been great if I could have afforded the fare. It was all great, life was great. I rejoiced for him. I couldn't help, though, having a momentary picture of the wedding night. You lie this way and I lie that, on sterilized polar sheets; while we devour, ritually, each other's bodies.

I walked out to the Dragons. Chitinous plates lay about; but the corpse had gone. The air was full of a sweet, heavy musk. One of the monsters was still in sight, moving away purposefully to the south.

Purposefully? I was getting as bad as Pilot (First Class) Scott-Braithwaite.

I walked the few yards to the landing vehicle. It stood canted on its fragile-looking legs, heat shields scorched by atmospheric entry. We still use conventional feeders, of course, even with the Richardson Loop; the Loop vehicle was parked somewhere out in orbit. We could probably slice it fine enough these days to make direct planetary landings; fact is, nobody's all that keen to be the guinea-pig. Get the Richardson axes a milli-degree or so out of true and your atoms could just get rammed cheek by jowl, so to speak, with the atoms of a mount-tain top. Nobody's quite too sure whether that would represent a paradox or not. The consensus of opinion is that it would, and there'd be a bloody great bang.

Travelling by Loop isn't too bad; no worse, I suppose, than allowing yourself to be wheeled in for a major operation. But somebody still has to make planetfall the other end, which is a process as primitive as firing a thirty-eight. That's why even middle-aged IAB researchers need pilots; though it's true to say we need them more than they need us. Still, it's nice to have some Clean-Limbed Young Men about the place. Restores your faith in the world.

I woke with a thick head in the morning. I lay in the bunk for a while wondering whether a touch of whisky would scorch the taste out of my throat. I heard the Pilot moving around outside. He called me a couple of times. I swore eventually and answered. I dressed, walked blearily to the lab door. He said, 'We've got a visitor.'

He was squatting on his haunches a yard or two away in the clearing. Beside him was a Dragon. It was one of the smallest I'd seen. The whips, longer in proportion than the whips of an adult, were folded across its back. He was feeding it leaves off one of the palms; it was twisting its golden-eyed head and munching steadily. He looked up, grinning. He said, 'It's friendly.'

I said, 'It's eating.'

He frowned. He said, 'It's the same thing.'

I said, 'One statement is an observation. The other is a surmise.'

He said, 'Maybe it's thirsty. Does it want a drink?'

I said, 'They get all they need from vegetable fibres. You're wasting your time.'

He got a dish from the lab anyway, filled it with water and set it down under the thing's forelegs. He really thought he'd got some sort of green and gold, kingsize puppy dog there. The Dragon, of course, ignored it. He said, 'I've christened him. His name's Oscar. Do you know, I think he answers to it?' He crooned the name in a variety of voices, snapping his fingers and waving his arms. The Dragon twisted its head, keeping his hands in sight. He said, 'There, what about that?'

I said, 'Try throwing it a stick. Also, its ears aren't in its head. You'd be better off shouting at its arse.'

I put the coffee on to boil, and shaved. He played around with the thing half an hour or more longer. Finally he came inside. The Dragon stood where he had left it, motionless in the clearing. He watched it anxiously through the port while he was eating. He said, 'How old is he? I hope he stays around.'

I really think he was starting to get lonely.

We had a trip planned for the day. I strapped myself into

the flier; he climbed in beside me, jetted up a couple of thousand feet and flew south. I sat with the instrument box on my knees and watched the treetops slide underneath. The sea became visible after a few minutes; a greenish shawl, fringed with an edging of paler lace. Farther out, a maroon stain spread across the horizon. A few biggish fish were floating belly-up. There were no other signs of life.

He turned west, following the coastline of the island. I waved to him to take the machine lower. Half a dozen clearings passed beneath, each with the curious towers of wood and stone. From above they looked vaguely oriental, like outlandish pagodas. Nowhere was there movement; the sites lay open, and deserted.

We crossed the sea again, flew over the northerly islands. Half an hour later I touched his arm. I'd seen a clearing bigger than the rest, glimpsed something bronze-green moving in the jungle. I said, 'Set down.'

He said, 'Here? You must be joking.' He took the machine in, all the same, skimmed to a perfect landing between two of the glittering towers. He killed the motors. I sat while the miniature duststorm we had created subsided, then opened the cab door.

The air struck warm. A Dragon surveyed me indifferently from the edge of the jungle. Another, the one I had seen, was lumbering a hundred yards or so away. I walked towards it. It turned, whips waving, headed back into the trees. I let it go.

Clustering on the edge of the clearing were a series of curious six-sided structures, like pale green organ pipes a few sizes too large. The Pilot stood beside them, dusting his immaculate slacks. He said, 'What are these?'

I said, 'Were.'

'Well. What were they?'

I said, 'Nests. Moonstone termites. They were rather a pretty species. But they produced a formic acid variant that upset the chronometers at Transhipment Base. Earth lost a couple of freighters; they're still out somewhere in the Loop. So we cooked up a little systemic. It was pretty good; did the job in a couple of years.'

He fingered one of the mortared columns, and frowned.

I said, 'Never mind, old son. Can't stand in the way of Progress.'

Beyond the clearing a low earth bank was covered by sprays of dense viridian creeper. Regularly spaced holes showed blackly. All but one were deserted; in the nearest showed a familiar green and gold mask.

He said, 'Are these places where they live?'

'What?'

'The Dragons.'

I said carefully, 'These are where they are usually to be found.'

He nodded up at one of the quartz structures. 'They build those?'

I said, 'It seems probable. Nobody's seen them at it yet.'

He said, 'What the hell are they? What are they for?'

I said, 'We have no idea.'

He said, 'There's got to be a reason.'

'That's a comforting philosophy.'

He glared at me. I was starting to get under his skin again. For a Pilot (First Class) he was pretty touchy. He said, 'Everything has a reason.'

I said mildly, 'Most things have explanations. But if we could explain why these things were built it might not strike us as a reason. Since we're hardly likely to explain them anyway, speculation is pointless.'

I walked forward. All the caves were tenanted; and all but a handful of the Dragons were dead. The bodies were flabby with decay, giving off the same sweet odour I'd smelled in the clearing. I counted forty-seven corpses. None of them showed any signs of damage. He frowned finally, pushed his cap back on his head. He said, 'Anyway, these weren't eaten.'

I said, 'Maybe there wasn't time. They all went together.'

'Do you think so?'

I said, 'It's possible.'

I sat on a rock and filled my pipe. He wandered off. A few minutes later I heard him call. I got up and walked in his direction.

There was a tower lower than the rest. On the timber staging were piled a dozen or more Dragons. I didn't care to approach too closely. The bodies were pretty far gone.

He said, 'That settles one thing anyway.'

'What?'

He gestured irritably. He said, 'They're burial platforms. It's obvious.'

I said, 'Or they climbed up there of their own accord. They were shuffling solemnly around, worshipping the sun, when they were struck with the same idea at precisely the same time.'

'What idea?'

I said, 'The idea our friend had in the clearing.'

'Which was?'

I said, 'You work it out.'

He said slowly, 'You think they're suiciding.'

I said, 'One possibility among many.'

He said angrily, 'It doesn't make sense.'

I said, 'Try not looking for the answers. You'll sleep easier.'

It was as if I'd challenged his Faith. He said, 'Everything makes sense.'

'Haciendas in the Rockies make sense. Laying women makes sense. Of a sort. Dragons don't.'

He shook his head. He said, 'I just don't understand you.'

'No,' I said. 'And we're the same species. Awe-inspiring, isn't it?'

He walked back to the flier. I followed him. We searched the rest of the islands, landed a couple of times. We found nothing living. It seemed our local group of Dragons now represented the universal population.

We were back at the laboratory by nightfall. The little Dragon still squatted where we had left it. He seemed overjoyed to see it; started scurrying about pulling down armfuls of leaves. He sat while I brewed coffee, prodding them patiently at its jaws. I though he might sling a blanket roll beside it to make sure it didn't stray.

There wasn't much to do round camp. He fed Oscar and tried to teach him to sit up and beg; I logged the meter readings, processed fluid and tissue samples, collected droppings for analysis. The Dragons sat in their caves and watched us; we watched the Dragons. Each day at seventeen hundred hours Planetary we reported to Earth Control, and they reported to us. We listened to Earth news via the Loop; and twice more the Pilot's fiancée spoke to him. The second time they had a considerable heart-to-heart. I left them to it, risking his wrath; there were a lot of tears flying about Earthside, the thing seemed pretty private. I repeated the experiment with the heartbeat recordings, beaming a ring of loudspeakers on to Oscar. He didn't respond, which was hardly surprising, though the Pilot pronounced himself delighted with his progress. If you tickled his foreleg joints with a stick for long enough, he'd sometimes rear. It didn't strike me as exactly a critical development.

We took the flier across to Continent Three. It wasn't much of a trip. I remembered the place as vivid green, furred with trees. Now drifts of puce and ochre dust stretched to the horizon. Heavy automats were working. They looked like magnified versions of the Dragons. The wind was blowing strongly, racing across the ruined land; you could see the trails of dust smoking along the ground, dragging their long shadows over the dunes.

We didn't land.

He was moody at supper. It transpired he wanted to get back to Earth. Something had gone a bit wrong with his scene, he wasn't too specific about it. 'It's all right for you,' he said bitterly. 'Nobody gives a damn how long you sit staring at bloody great insects, you've got nothing to get back to. If it lay with me, I'd just report the damn things extinct and clear out. Nobody's going to know the difference anyway.'

I sucked at my pipe. It was pulling sour again. 'Can't be done, my son,' I said. 'Impatience of the young, and all that. Can't brush science aside, y'know.'

'Science,' he said. 'Two men stuck here on a bloody dustball, watching a handful of incomprehensible objects die off for no good reason. You might be devoted to research . . .'

I chucked the pipe down, reached for the whisky. 'On the contrary,' I said, 'I couldn't care less.'

He stared at me. 'Then why're you here?'

'Because,' I said, 'I'm paid to be. Also, here's as good a place as the next.'

He shrugged. 'I'd say that was a pretty dismal outlook,' he said. 'It doesn't seem to me you've made much of your life. Anyway, that's your concern. I'm not going the same way, I can tell you.'

I said, 'Then you're a lucky man.' I filled a glass, shoved it across. He stared at me; then to my surprise picked it up and drained it at a gulp.

He called me next morning, early. I walked from the lab and stared. Oscar had immobilized; the whips thrust out at right angles from the body, producing that curious helicopter effect, and the eyes were lustreless. He was waggling greenstuff beneath the mandibles, but there was no response.

I set the meters up. It looked as if this might be one of the last chances we should get to gather data. The hearts failed, in their set pattern; I drove the probes, started the pacemakers, laid the syringes ready with the stimulants. The Pilot (First Class) took it hard. His pet was dying, certainly; there was no doubt of that. But the noise he made, you'd have thought he was losing a woman at the very least. He fumed and fretted, made trips out into the jungle to bring back this or that goody; he tried Oscar with tree leaves, bush branches, the pale green tubers that grew round the hangar sheds and landing pad. None of it, of course, made the slightest difference. The heart-pairs of the little Dragon faltered on through the night; the Planetary chronometers ran up their thirty hours; on cue, Oscar died.

The Pilot seemed broken up by the whole business. He vanished for a couple of hours or more; when I saw him again he was waving a whisky bottle. He took to his room, finally, in the afternoon. I presumed he was sleeping it off.

It was just as well. The funeral party arrived about fourteen hundred Planetary. They were commendably prompt. The ceremony didn't take long, the volume of the deceased being fairly small. They left the sherds of armour stacked neatly in the shadow of the lab; I heard the whips trail and rustle as they headed back south, toward the rock city and the quartzite towers. I labelled the new recordings, logged the time, took the routine call from Earth Control. I'd closed down the generators when I heard the lab door open and shut. I looked round, frowning. I'd no idea he'd managed to leave his room.

He didn't look too good. He had a bottle of rye in one hand and the rocket pistol in the other, which struck me as a bit unnecessary. Still, it was dramatic.

He flung the bottle down. It broke. He said, 'I was going to bury him. Those bloody murderers. With their bloody whips. Shaking their bloody whips . . .' He advanced, unsteadily. I suppose I should have told him to put that thing down before somebody got hurt. I didn't. It was the sort of line that would have come better from him.

He was fairly through his skull. I thought perhaps he didn't have too high a capacity; a lot of these clean-cut young men haven't. Also when they blow they really blow. He waved the pistol around a bit more and told me what was going to happen if I interfered within the next hour or so. I gathered a man had to do what a man had to do. Anyway when he finally staggered out I took him at his word. The girlie mag lay on the table; I got a bottle of whisky, poured myself a stiff one and started leafing through it. After all, there's nothing like curling up with a good book.

In time there was a hefty, rolling bang from the south, and another. Then some higher cracks that I took it were the automatic. I hoped he'd remembered to pack a few spare clips. After a bit the noise started up again, so it seemed he had.

I chucked the book down, lay back. I finished the bottle, sat watching the dawn brighten the green sky. It had been quiet a long time now; I wondered if he'd slipped on the bluff and broken his fool neck.

The lab door opened. He stood framed in the doorway, the gun still in his hand. His uniform was torn, his face haggard and dirty white. He said, 'I don't know what happened. I don't know what happened.'

I said, 'All?'

He said, 'It was their eyes. Staring. Their bloody eyes. They let me do it, they didn't move . . .' He rubbed a hand across his face. He said, 'If you waved at them, they didn't blink . . .'

I put the glass down, carefully. I said, 'One point, Space Pilot. Did you notice any signs of ritual behaviour among the survivors during the . . . er . . . event? If so, it should go on the report. You might have added to our store of Knowledge.'

He brought the gun round slowly. He said, '*You bastard. You bloody bastard . . .*'

I stayed where I was. I don't find life universally sweet, but that particular mode of exit has never appealed. I said as pleas-ántly as I could, 'I don't think that would be a good idea. I'm not worth it; you've still got Judy to think about.' The gun barrel wavered; and I smiled. 'If you've put all those rounds through that thing,' I said, 'it needs a clean. There's some water on next door; nip and sluice it through. I'll get some coffee going; you look as if you could use it.'

He stood a while longer, staring like a ghost; then it seemed it sank in. He turned silently, closed the door behind him.

'Next door' was my specimen lock. Amazing what auto-suggestion can do. I clamped my foot on the floor switch, heard the bolts shoot home. He yelled something, started banging the wall; and I valved gas. A steady hissing, then a thump.

And blessed peace.

I bespoke Earth Control on the emergency frequency, ex-plained the salient facts and got a clearance.

Lugging him to the shuttle wasn't the easiest part. I made it finally, strapped him in the couch, closed the hatches, ran through what countdown checks I could remember and gave myself back to Earth. Wire-flying through the Loop isn't a thing to be thought on too closely; but they made it. I transferred to the Richardson vehicle, tied myself down once more; and Earth pulled the tit, plastering our substance and the substance of the freighter thinly round the parameters of paradox.

When I regained coherence we were in stable Earth orbit, and the relief vessels were coming up to us. The Pilot (First Class) was awake, and saying quite a lot. He would probably have backed up speech with action in some unpleasant form or another, only I'd taken the precaution of tieing him down again. I listened for a while; eventually I got tired. I switched his voice circuit direct to Earth Control, and he had enough sense left to button his lip. I spent the time till docking thinking how interesting we are as a species. One and all, we build round ourselves little protective shells; but inside, when we're bottomed, we're really quite inhuman.

So IAB never got their Dragon. I was out of circulation for a time; when I got back I was told Trade Control had already issued authority for the automats to be programmed into the islands. Epsilon Development were losing money each day they didn't mine; they underwrote the cost of the station without too much complaint and endowed a research grant that will keep me in crusts for the next five years at least. I settled down to catalogue what had been learned of the humanoids on Proxima Centauri IX before Epsilon's power station ran supercritical; and the Dragons were forgotten.

Except that a few days later I had a visitor. I used the door sensors because only the week before there'd been a mugging a dozen floors below. But I hadn't got that sort of trouble this time. I opened the door and poured myself a whisky.

She was as pretty as her stereo. She'd been crying; and she was wearing the season's newest. I gave her a chair, but she wouldn't have a drink. She crossed her legs, tried them the other way. Didn't like that either. Finally she said, 'Remember me?'

I said, 'It's coming. Don't help me.'

She smiled. She said, 'I always expect Researchers to be much older men.'

I put the glass down gently, and sat at the desk.

She said, 'I've come from . . . from Drew. I wondered if you could . . . tell me a little more. He's so . . . reticent. You know.'

I said, 'There's a report going in tomorrow. It's irregular; but I can arrange for you to see a copy. If you so desire.'

She swallowed. She said, 'I . . . will have that drink, if you don't mind.'

I got it for her, sat down again.

She drank it, put the glass aside. She said, 'Researcher, the report . . . You know why I'm here. Don't you?'

I said, 'I'm always willing to be surprised.'

She stood up, without fuss. She laid her gloves down, unbuttoned her blouse and pulled it open. Then she just stood there, looking at me.

I shook my head and opened the desk drawer. I thumbed through the report and started to read.

'Until day fifty-seven, the life forms designated Epsilon VI brackets three stroke two showed no awareness of the presence of the observing party, and no animosity. Their attack was both sudden and unexpected. My companion, Space Pilot First Class Andrew Scott-Braithwaite, behaved with conspicuous gallantry. To him, certainly, I owe my life; and my final employment of GS 93 was at his instigation, though he himself was imperilled by the release of the gas. Our subsequent return was logged by Earth Control . . . etcetera.'

I tossed the papers over to her. I said, 'You read the rest. The style may be wanting here and there; but at least it's concise.'

She stared at the thing a moment, and burst into tears.

After she had gone Miss Braithwaite glided from the inner room. Miss Braithwaite is my secretary at IAB. She is also fat, fortyish and an optimist; but she cooks good suppers. Right now her eyes were misty with emotion; and she laid a hand shakily on my arm. 'Researcher,' she said, 'that's about the biggest thing I ever saw a person do.'

I patted her. 'That's all right,' I said. 'I'm like that.'

That's the sort of thing one has to live with.

They still have Pilot (First Class) Scott-Braithwaite down at the State Home for Bewildered Astronauts. But I did hear he's been seconded for another tour of duty. Apparently that boy was one of the worst cases of Loop nerves they'd ever seen. Had I not plastered the cracks, he would certainly have been an ex-spacer by now; and Judy would have had to cast those honest wide blue eyes around fairly rapidly. Because Drew's disability pension would hardly have maintained her in the Manner to Which. As things stand, I wonder which would have been the better turn to do him.

I wouldn't have thought he'd have blown like that; but you can never tell. After all, I once spent three years with a woman who closely approximated a Greek goddess. Appearances are deceptive; as a Behavourist, it's the first thing you learn.

The Trustie Tree

His impressions on returning to awareness were two-fold: the play of light behind his closed lids, and the chuckle of water under the boat's forefoot. Though the orange flickering could be further analysed into a play of light and heat combined, while 'chuckle' seemed altogether too imprecise a metaphor. Rather the water sounds were like a series of little harps, struck continuously in some musical scheme that seemed always to be on the point of resolution. He toyed with the idea, and with another vaguely grasped; that of a relationship between the two effects. The pattering of heat against his face seemed contrapuntal to the altering, essentially liquid phrases of whatever melody the little bow-wave played. His mind annoyed itself with the unwanted pun, and he opened his eyes.

The trees here, lining the waterway, were of considerable height. To either side the slim trunks stretched away in aisles and arcades of golden-green; above, the small rounded leaves hung still like sprays of newly minted coins. He raised himself slightly, moving his elbows with care, and saw how ahead the canal stretched arrow-straight, infused with that same misty glow. The movement, though small, woke the pain once more. He rested a while, drifting his eyes closed. With concentration the stabbings could be made apparently to shift, from knee to ankle to thigh and groin. Though intellect understood, the animal brain could be confused. Logic suggested that by a similar exertion the agony might be reduced, perhaps to vanishing point; but the experiment, if possible, was beyond his powers.

To his left, slightly below the stretcher on which he lay, stood a cup and decanter of what appeared to be cut crystal. What it was the Kalti had given him he had no idea; but it was effective, though the swallowing of it turned lips and palate for an hour or more to purring velvet. He moved again, screwing his eyes; then stretching his left hand to the decanter base, reached with his right to withdraw the faceted stopper. He laid it down, transferred his grip to the cup, rested the neck of the decanter against its rim. Instinct bade him drink at once; but some perversity made him first reverse the process, replacing the stopper as carefully as it had been removed. Only then did he feel free to steady the cup to his lips. In his all but supine position, drinking posed an additional difficulty. He managed it by degrees, dribbling the precious liquid a spot a time into his throat. After the first sips it was easier; the action of the drug was immediate, and his hands were steadier. He set the cup down, rubbed his mouth and the unaccustomed fringe of beard. The stuff had a faint, antiseptic tang. He felt it must cling to him; and welcomed it. There were other scents, which he was pleased to mask; for he was a fastidious man.

He lay drowsily, feeling the trickling anaesthesia spread, watching the feathery gliding of the treetops. Between them the ribbon of sky was an intense, nearly metallic blue. From time to time birds, the little fishing birds of the swamps, flitted across his angle of vision, darting like sparks from bank to bank.

From where he lay, in the bows of the enormously long boat, the sound of her engine was all but inaudible, its pounding reduced to a murmur scarcely louder than the wash of ripples driven against the stone-lined banks. In places the stones had fallen in, releasing little slides of brownish-yellow mud. Between them, like moss-grown sockets, showed diminutive tunnel mouths. Birds scuttled beneath the trailing bushes; once a small furred animal plopped into the water, dived and was gone. He saw it surface some thirty metres ahead, a black dot trailing a smooth chevron of ripple. Later the canal narrowed between stands of tall orange-flowered bushes. The air was heavy with their musky scent. On Earth, no doubt, there would have been the steady drone of insects; but Xerxes, mercifully, owned almost no flying forms. He brushed his forehead, where a rivulet of sweat had started, turned his wrist to stare at the chronometer. The figures swam momentarily before his eyes; and he let his arm fall slack.

From the cabin at his back came the momentary rattle of some utensil; but none of the Kalti came near. Nor had they come near, since they lifted the brushwood stretcher into the bows; was it the morning before? They placed the decanter beside him and the cup, and said no word; these square, short, seamed-faced folk in black, with their broad-brimmed round-crowned hats and expressionless, slightly slanting eyes. They reminded him of old-fashioned nursery toys; or Chesterton's grim, simple little priest.

A breeze stirred momentarily, swaying the tops of the trees; and he wrinkled his nose. Twice now, of necessity, he had urinated through the stretcher; and there was the other stink, from the dressings on his leg. He wondered if in their way the Kalti were fastidious too.

He moved once more, settling his shoulders against the broad, sloping buttress of the cabin end; and was warned by the searing flash from his knee that the drink was a palliative only. He lay, breath held, while the pain throbbed through its many overtones, faded along the nerves. His leg twitched, and was still.

He returned to his contemplation of the gliding banks and trees; and a former notion, that of microcosm, came back to him, to some extent with greater force. The stately variation of perspectives, the sense of a progression both effortless and inevitable, gave the concept strength. 'Like life,' he thought; but the idea was complex, defying further pursuit. To be expressed perhaps in the emblem-writing of the Kalti; but not in words. He thought idly then more intently of the pictograph blazoned on the name panels of the boat, the blue swirls fountaining above the white bar that is earth, security and God; and that can mean trust. Something growing was surely represented, a bush or tree. He turned the phrases round his tongue, lips moving; and a memory came, bringing with it first the tang of pain, later a pleasure curiously powerful and unalloyed. He spoke the new words aloud, tasting their flavour.

> *'I lean'd my back unto an aik,*
> *'I thocht it was a trustie tree . . .'*

Then like a passage in the shadow-show his life had become,
sense faded; and he slept.

When he woke the notion of the long hull beneath him,
gliding so effortlessly night and day, was ready in his mind to
comfort him. He welcomed it, as he welcomed the remembered
words. A part of him, that in other times would have dominated, protested perhaps that never yet was boat called the
Trustie Tree; but he was satisfied. He raised himself a little;
and saw how beyond the upswept bow the woods drew back
enclosing a broad pool, its surface still and milky green. At its
far edge the canal plunged into a cutting of dark red rock;
across the face of the little bluff, hung with creeper that trailed
like Spanish Moss, hawked a solitary golden bird.

For two days, to his waking knowledge, they had met with
no other boat; and the pool was likewise empty. None the less,
he knew the marshlands, to be full. He saw, vividly, the drifting
of the endless black hulls, like particles drawn by a single
current through the great vascular system of the Northern
Continent's waterways. Midsummer was near, and the Kalti
festivals at Bran Gildo and Hy Antiel. Somewhere beyond the
cutting lay the low hill range that fringes the Salt Lagoon; and
on the lagoon edge lay Bran Gildo itself and Earth Base, the
trading complex and the Terran Hospital. He saw the city with
equal brilliance, white walls clustered beneath green mops of
palm, the watchtowers like squat terrestrial minarets; and
wondered at the clearness of his mind.

As the long boat nosed into the cutting, the Kalti woman
reappeared. She rigged a little canopy over him, of blue and
yellow striped cloth, its edges frothed and scalloped with lace.
He smiled at her as she worked and said, 'Bran Gildo.' She
paused, crinkling her leathery face, and nodded; but made no
other sign. After she had gone, and the diamond-lighted cabin
doors were closed, he wondered why the protection had been
necessary. Then as the sides of the cutting narrowed, shrubs
and bushes arched dim overhead; and great spots of water began

to fall, like an icy and persistent douche. He smiled again at that; for the Kalti were not unaware.

He fell to watching the strands of fern slide by to either side. Some, the longest, brushed the black-painted hull; others, disturbed by the faint air-mass the boat drove before it, swayed gently, discharging from their pointed tips their cargo of pellucid drops. The fronds were greyish, he saw; but the sides of the defile were by no means of uniform hue. Between the bastions of brick-red rock were lozenges of purple and maroon; through the strata ran veins of copper and dull gold. The updraught touched his face, dank-smelling and pleasantly cool. He closed his eyes, recalling just such another bluff, seeing, with the troubled yet very clear vision vouchsafed him, the flyer as it lay side-shattered, crumpled against the rock. De Valera's body, lying smashed amid a tangle of crimson-flowered cane; the burst and gutted first-aid chest; the saplings of the little clearing stripped of bark and foliage by the machine's descent. One spar of the flyer, driven javelin-fashion, had passed cleanly through the trunk of a tree; he remembered lying dazed, his back against a low earth bank, watching the trickling of dark sap or resin from the wound. In places the fluid, balked by a knot or stump, welled into tiny pools; in others it overflowed suddenly, streaking down glutinously a yard or more. Round him the air was motionless and warm; and somewhere a bird was singing. The image, arbitrarily recalled, filled him with a curious sense of desolation and loss; a sensation, he decided, that was primal as the pang of birth, the pain the thinking spirit must feel at the violence of the inanimate, the blindness of chance. He lay a day or more beneath the tree, while the impermeable dressing clamped to his leg turned first pink, then to poppy red. In the days that followed, the colour changed once more; and he covered the thing with bandages, roughly torn.

The violence of the descent, that disembowelled the flyer, had been indirectly his salvation. When the first shock and sickness passed, leaving only the pain, he commenced crawling laboriously between the twisted struts, finding here a treasure in the shape of a water flask or brandy bottle, there a morsel of food; an unsplit vacpak, a slab of emergency chocolate. He found a tube of white pills, that for an hour at a time partly relieved the pain; later he crawled to de Valera, fiddled with the wrist strap on the outflung arm. But the radio was dead as well. For all he knew, the flyer's main set might be unharmed; but it hung ten feet above his head, and was inaccessible. There were limits to what the white pills could achieve.

Later he wondered, as he wondered now, why he had not long since used the pistol at his belt, the standard nine shot semi-automatic space regs compelled him to carry. He could recall no driving will to live; yet the notion of violent self-destruction seemed none the less monstrous. He felt himself at one with the dead of all the ages; obscurely, it was as if his own extinction would make their ends the more complete. Later the thought was driven away by one still more irrational. He fumbled the gun from its holster, sat staring at it and trying to laugh. Held in his hand, the pistol still seemed a toy; that a bullet might be accelerated sufficiently to tear the flesh was a patent absurdity. How the conviction had come to him, he could not say. But come it had; and finally he put the rubber thing away, more useless than a catapult.

He rested in the shade, sipping from a water bottle, eating the little white tablets; and in time it seemed his strength grew rather than decreased. He wondered, disinterestedly, at the stubbornness with which the body clings to life. Finally, to occupy his mind and hands, he made shift to cut himself a pair of crutches from the tough stems of the bamboo. At first his mind, illogically obstinate, refused to admit that the things might have a purpose at all. Later, when their use was conceded, there was still no notion of actual employment. Their manufacture was an exercise, and nothing more; a gesture in the face of futility.

The knife he carried was barely adequate for the task; he discovered a machete in the remains of the Incidents Box that speeded the job a little. He made crosspieces for the tops of the poles, succeeded after several failures in lashing them more to less firmly to the shafts. Later he wrapped the makeshift joints with strip after strip of the flyer's silvery skin. The job finished, he set himself to fabricate slings. From them he suspended the last of the water bottles, and what ration containers remained; and finally he found himself, after a dozen false starts and as many pain-blenching falls, hobbling slowly and with infinite care away from the clearing, down the long slope into the forest.

With the primarily agricultural economy of the Northern Continent must be considered the remarkable subculture of the Kalti, the Boatmen of Xerxes. The origins of this people are obscure. Reinhardt (op. cit) argues a Southern derivation, detailing the many resemblances between the emblematic script of the Boatmen and the stelae of Barene and Defling in the subcontinent of New India. Agreement is by no means general however, and the field is a rich one for historian and ethnologist alike. The views of the Boatmen themselves add to rather than detract from the uncertainty. Some claim descent from a legendary ancestor, Bar-Zenno, sole survivor of a terrific and ubiquitous flood, while others assert that their forebears were once rulers of Antiel and Bran Gildo, till driven like the Tarquins to take refuge in the swamps with which the continent abounds. Their religious beliefs are likewise confusing to the outworlder, centred as they are on the notion of the Silent One, the Being who is at once Godhead, the epitome of the virtues and the tutelary spirit of the waterways, the canal complex on which from birth to death the Boatmen live, move and have their being. The symbol of his many manifestations is the Bar-Ko, the white or blue hyphen round which most Xerxian pictographs are built. . . .

He smiled and said to himself, 'The voice of the guidebook is heard in the land.'

The crutches served after a fashion; though after each few hours' travel he found he must sit and painfully re-tie the padded heads. Despite his efforts, the bamboo chafed him, so that the sides of his shirt beneath the arms became crusted with dried blood. He accepted the extra pain, unquestioning; for he had happened, dimly, on the first of several notions that were to sustain his journey, that of expiation.

The land at first trended steadily downward, aiding his progress. He knew approximately the direction in which he must travel; he made slow but steady time, guiding himself by the sun. Later, when he reached the lower ground, his difficulties multiplied. The soil here was spongy, clad with a carpet of vivid green moss; the tips of the crutches sank deeply, throwing his weight unexpectedly to either side. When this happened the tip of his maimed leg scraped the ground, and flashes like white fire woke inside his head. Once he fell, and lay for most of an afternoon before summoning the strength to continue. His water, now, was all but exhausted. More was to be had readily enough, by pressing his cupped hands into the moss; but it was tart and stinking, he didn't care to drink it. He contented himself with rubbing it on his lips, which still in time grew cracked and sore.

Also he found his mind was wandering. The simplest tasks he set himself, like the re-tying of the crutches, were hard to concentrate on and took far too long. Also it was becoming increasingly difficult to make his hands obey him; they wobbled and shook, possessed seemingly of a life of their own. These signs of impending collapse at first caused him acute distress. In time he came to view his state once more with something like dispassion. He was, he reminded himself, rather like the soldier in the poem, from whom successive pieces are carved and shot away until he is reduced to little more than a head. Later still, when the white pills were gone, he realized why the doggerel had at one time affected him with such horror. The soldier forgets to curse; even his God.

So he was reduced finally to crawling; in which condition earth banks assumed the proportions of low hills, bush clumps reared like the rain forests of an endless continent. Till on the fourth or fifth day his sense of the scale of things was once more altered; then it seemed, to his befuddled brain, that his body in its blunderings spanned light-years. He elbowed his way to Earth between the stars, thrusting aside whole galaxies. In this way he came to the water, on which the long boats passed like dreams.

He rested awhile at the crest of the final slope before scramb-

ling and clawing the hundred metres or so to the bank. He sat
the remainder of the day, nibbling his chocolate squares while
his leg, resting in the cloudy water, was soothed to bearable
numbness. The rushes whispered, rustling, and the black hulls
puttered and thudded past, each like the next. First would come
the rearing prow, with its knotwork and filigree; then the round
portbrasses of the cabin, the endless cargo space tented with
tarpaulin-like cloth; the engine house with its thin, vibrating
chimney, so like the chimneys of the narrow boats that had
once plied on Earth, and like them haloed by a haze of diesel-
blue. Finally the nameplates with their bursting hieroglyphs,
the tiny stern grating, the steersman gripping his bright-
banded oar. Through the day none of the Kalti so much as
glanced at the bank; and he for his part waved and smiled,
understanding with perfect amity. For the Silent One, who gave
the *Bar-Ko* for his sign to men, sends pain and joy both in
their season; all things are decreed to be.

Why they stopped their boat, the *Trustie Tree*, no one can
say. Why they stilled their engine and drove their stakes, came
thumping and squelching back along the overgrown bank, is a
mystery as great as the Boatmen's origins. An hour or more they
must have stared, the dumpy woman and the dumpy men, alike
as pegtop toys in their suits of solemn black. No word passed
between them, certainly; but at the end of that time they wove
the stretcher, and raised him from the water with care. Once
while lifting him aboard they jolted him. He – the central,
thinking part – was indifferent; but the body screamed. They
did speak at that; the clicks and guttural bangs that pass for
syllables among their kind. They lashed the stretcher, and
brought the drink; and then they let him be.

By early evening of the planet's short day the boat had
cleared the cutting. The thudding of her engine, amplified by
the close rock walls, faded once more; the ripples reasserted
themselves. He saw he travelled now on a high embankment,
twenty feet or more above the level of the surrounding land.
To right and left, stretching to the horizon, ran a sea of sun-
baked yellow grass, dotted with clumps of scrub and low,
mounded bushes. Beside the embankment crouched thorny,

bulbous-stemmed trees. From his vantage point he saw an
animal break cover, trotting daintily; hornless, and something
of the size and colouring of a terrestrial goat. He watched the
grass heads wave, marking its passage. Some memory of Jefferies
came to him then, and the sick magnificence of the Sun Life;
uncomprehended before, realized now in a flash of insight. It
seemed he too was one with what his senses recorded; the beast
in the grass, the star hanging in the sky. The thought bred
another, yet more fleeting and elusive. He understood, dimly,
what world-union might mean to the Kalti and their flowing
Tree, the boat that bore him; understood too his part in an
ultimate scheme in which the very certainty of change, growth
and death and birth, was an expression of the immutability of
the Most High. The notion, as grandiose as it was vague,
brought none the less a further upsurge of the pleasure that
had buoyed him, a sensation almost of ebullience, a lightening
of the spirit that seemed as carefree as a bird. He knew himself
to be on the verge of greater revelations, and wished for pencil
and paper with which to record his thoughts. There was nothing of the sort to be had; but no matter. In Bran Gildo, he
would write of this. Later his leg set up a devil's hammering;
and he drank some more of the anaesthetic wine.

When he opened his eyes again the Kalti woman had lit the
great running lamps on either side of the cabin roof. To Planetary West a cauldron of dull light marked the setting of the sun.
Ahead, breaking the dimness of the veld, low hills rose rounded
against the sky.

The lamps were beyond his immediate range of vision. By
twisting his head he caught glimpses of the filigree of brass,
black against the brilliance of the coloured panes; red to the
left, blue to the right. The glow reflected in moving ghostly
patches to either side; beyond, a warmer diffusion more sensed
than seen told him the cabin lamps were burning. The Kalti
family, perhaps, was sitting to a meal; but day and night, the
boat would never stop. He watched the hills grow slowly
against the sky. Beyond lay the Salt Lagoon; beyond again,
Bran Gildo. Rushingly, the *Trustie Tree* was swimming
home.

*For all but a fraction of the working year the Boatmen
lead their solitary lives in the fastnesses of the canal country,
transporting their cargoes of wood, coal and road stone across
the swamps and plains of the Northern Continent. Only at the
midsummer Feast of Bar-Ab does this most taciturn of races
throw off its reserve. Then for a week or more the great fairs
of Antiel and Bran Gildo glow with light. The streets fill;
everywhere, on temple fronts, public buildings, inns, the flower-
wreathed Bar-Ko is seen. The festivities continue unabated
from dusk to dawn; and here too the season's business is trans-
acted. Marriages are arranged, contracts sealed, boats bought
and sold. Though the Feast is evidently the successor of a much
older solstice celebration, it seems fitting that it should be held
now in honour of Bar-Ab, the vigorous and enlightened ruler of
Bran Gildo who four Earth centuries ago first gave to Xerxes
what has remained the planet's major transportation system. . . .*

The canopy had been drawn back. He lay seeing the shapes
of unfamiliar constellations. For some, he knew the Kalti
names: the Anchor, the Fishing Net, Sista's Barge. The
quadrilateral towards which the Barge for ever steered was the
Great Pound; beyond were the Boatmen with his Oar, and the
Hunter Bra'ad. As ever, the night sky of Xerxes held a faint
greenish pallor; to the east, a broad silver streak heralded the
rising of the planet's single moon. The hills loomed now to either
side, black against the glow.

The sleep that claimed him was the deepest he had enjoyed.
Round him, unheeded, were the night-sounds of the boat's
passage; creak and thump of gates, rattle of paddle gear, roar
of unseen sluices. The long hull ground and jolted, unheard;
the shouts, rasp and scrape of footsteps, groan of ropes, seemed
small as the flutterings of moths. The moon of Xerxes declined,
sinking towards the west. Far below, the grass plain showed
now pale as bone. The swamps, and the rising massif beyond,
were a dark rim to the world; and still, by the hour, *Trustie Tree*
climbed and climbed. As scores of her kind had climbed before
her, and scores would climb after. Somewhere, far back in the
hills, the mile-long reservoir that fed the summit was showing

its reedy bed; in two weeks' time, when the last black hull had locked back to the east, it would be empty.

There seemed no sharp transition between the states of sleep and waking. He knew only that his eyes were open; and that he smiled at the boat, and the hills, and the sky. The sky was flushed now, chequered with pinkish light. At the zenith flickered the last star of the Pound; and a wind was on his face. A dawn wind, fresh and cold, overlaid with the great tang of the sea.

He sat up, nearly with a shout. Along the horizon, like a dimly shining sword, stretched the Salt Lagoon. Between hills and sea the land was dark, overlaid with the moving shimmer of mist; and from the dark, climbing towards him in a breathless sweep, rose the locks of the Bran Gildo flight. Beside each lock, the pale patch of its sidepond; above each the *Bar-Ko*, vaunting in its wrought-iron frame; and from pound after pound the gleaming stars, red and blue, red and blue, that were other boats, locking down to the city and the sea.

In the bows, poised impassively, stood the little Kalti boat-woman. He called to her, pointing and laughing; then it seemed the inside of his head took fire, catching brightness from the curious drink, so that he cried to her he was a sick Earthman coming home, and that the penance was done; that he was a Breton, and his forbears had been Bretons, and fishers of the sea. Some nonsense there was too of other boats, and the journeyings of the *Trustie Tree*; all of which she ignored, as was the way of her people. Though once she came to him, catching his chin in her pinching horny fingers, lifting his lids to stare into the pale-coloured eyes. She pulled at the stretcher, tugged the lashings that held it firm; rearranged the patterned quilting over him, turned back to the bow. Her presence warmed him; so he told her of Ben Cruachan, and the road that angles round the mountain's flanks, through the Pass of Brander to Dalmally and Glen Orchy and Rannoch Moor. He talked of finding Crearwy, and taking her there; and what it was like to love her, and how they went, and where they stayed. And the pink rocks of Iona and the Ross of Mull, the night boat raising a diadem of lights in Oban Bay. Many things, secret things, he remembered now; the wooden towns of Wessex, the teashops and castles, fossils and chalk Gods; barrows crowning the grey ridge-sided downs, Portland tower bawling at the mist. He told her of the Star and the Mermaid and the Hare and Hounds; and renting the cottage for Crearwy who was Marie, the cottage with the yellow pine stairs and hearth of new Ham stone where they toasted legs and calves and laughed at the night-sound of the wind. And Kensington and Chelsea, Holland Park and Salisbury and the Great West Road. Once the Kalti nodded, over her shoulder, wielding the long-shafted hook; and once he thought she smiled.

So, encouraged, he told her the things for which he had never as yet found words; how it is when the Silent One has turned the wheel, when the laughter is dead and the loving and the wind blows empty on the downs, with nobody there to see. The warmth is gone, the stars remain; while over the years the object of love grows realler than when she lay all night at your side. Till you taste her lips, and smell her skin, and see her hair at every empty turn. And the whisky is there in the cupboard and the sandals she didn't want and her dress on the hanging rail. While *Trustie Tree* drove forward and down, forward and down, and the woman laughed and didn't understand. But how could they understand he asked himself, laughing in his turn; these folk who dressed in black, and used colours for their words?

Every year, they race the great Bran Gildo flight; a full day's work for a full-crewed boat, from Summit Pound to the Lagoon. From dusk to dawn the paddles crash, the sluices churn their streams of water and brown foam and stalks of weed. The blue haze rises, fed by the many exhausts; the shoremen curse, young and old alike, strain shoulders to the yard-thick beams, swing on the gates over the froth and boil. The cabin brasses dance, lamps sway and tick; feet are broken and hands, but the boats can't stop. Beyond lie the city and the sea, and a fever – the only fever ever to grip a Boatman – is in the blood.

The diesels bellow, the painted stern-oars dip; and through it all the boats sail out, at the end, between the reed clumps of the

Salt Lagoon. The tide whispers and lops; the seabirds wheel; and Bran Gildo is half a night away.

In the noise and flurry, amid the roar of water, he at last understood that through suffering he was saved; so he sang, an old sea song – light on the engine room, no more – and laughed again because no hurt can last for ever, no time is too late, no clock runs that cannot be unwound. He knew the *Bar-Ko* and the Tree that sprang from it, the Tree that is life itself; he knew the words he would say, the healing, blinding words, sprung from wisdom that springs in turn from pain. They formed a pattern that glowed and flashed, Constantine's diadem of stars; a pattern that enclosed all things, Marie and the mountains, the *Bar-Ko*, Salisbury Spire, Earth Base, the Loop where they ravel the atoms of a man like coloured beads against a velvet sky. The tall reeds whispered to either side; the night birds called from the land; and he was grateful, with all his heart, to the Kalti, and their Lord, and the great boats of the North.

> '*I lean'd my back unto an aik,*
> '*I thocht it was a trustie tree . . .*'

The lamps, the engine-rooms, and Bar-Ab great prince, faded in his mind.

The early light lay grey and cold across the lagoon of Bran Gildo. A little swell was running, here so near the open sea; so the river boat, unused to open water, pitched and creaked, rolling to show her weed-stained sides. The light, brightening, gleamed on the complex knotwork at her bow, on her running lamps and burnished port rims. It gleamed on the stern oar, still held by the Kalti steersman; and on the painted name-boards, the *Bar-Ko* and the Tree. Beside the Kalti his woman stood head bent. The words she muttered were harsh and hurried as the gabbing of a bird; he frowned, inclining his own head in reply. She spoke again; then turned away, climbed to the catwalk above the cargo space. Along it she trudged, dumpy and foreshortened, secure as if she walked on land; while to either side the mist, thinning, disclosed the shapes of other boats, and

others, and still more. On each prow, the headropes of the God;
on each side, somewhere, the Sign; on each cabintop the fading
gleam of lamps of beaten brass. At them the Kalti mother
stared; then closed with her hard fingers the eyes of the man
who lay in the brushwood stretcher, slipped the Ferryman's
golden coin under the root of his tongue.

The Lake of Tuonela

The dawn had been overcast, but by midmorning the weather had cleared. The small yellow sun of Xerxes burned in the planet's blue-green sky, waking shimmers and sparks from the little bow-wave the long boat drove ahead of it. The banks of the canal, lower here, were clothed with bushes and some stouter trees. Mathis, leaning his forearms on sun-warmed wood, felt their shadows stroke his cheek, touches of light and heat combined.

Here, in the bows of the vessel, the thud of her big single-cylinder engine was muted. He glanced back along the tented cargo space, turned once more to lean over the craft's side. The water was milky green; and some trick of light lent greater depth and perspective to the reflections than to the vegetation above. The tree leaves, small rounded sprays backlit to gold, passed smooth and silent fifty feet beneath the hull.

He studied the bow-wave, the fluctuating patterns within its stable form. The main crest curved from an inch or two before the vessel's blunt stem. Behind it the concave slope of water was glassy and clear. Some six inches ahead a smaller ripple began; the ends of this wavered, flicking forward and back in some pattern that seemed at the same time random and predetermined. Into it flowed the detailed images of branches; behind it the blue and gold melted into streaks that vanished in the deep green shadow of the hull.

He moved his shoulders, feeling the aches from the day before in back and arms. Thirty locks, in three flights of ten, had taxed his strength to the limit. The gates, unused for years, were grass-grown, nearly too stiff to move; also leaks had started, round the heel plates and worn paddle gear. Chamber after chamber refused to fill; it had taken the weight of the boat, butting at the timbers, to force the gates back. Locking down, the problem would be aggravated; but he had no intention of turning back.

He glanced at the chronometer strapped to his wrist, stared ahead again. For two days the canal had paralleled the course of GEM tracks, raw swaths of earth curving through the scrub and marshland that comprised much of Xerxes' Northern Continent; but the last of these had long since swung away. There were no signs of civilization, either Terrestrial or Kalti, and no sounds save the sporadic piping of birds. The boat moved through a silence that the thudding of the engine only seemed to make the more complete.

He wondered, with something approaching interest, whether his absence had yet been noticed. A week had passed since leaving the lagoon that fringed Bran Gildo on the seaward side, climbing the vast lock flight that leads inland from the city. Mathis shrugged. If an alarm had been raised, it mattered little enough. Hidden for most of the time beneath the lapping tangle of branches, the boat would be invisible from a flyer; while the canals of the Southern Complex forked and meandered endlessly, joined by watercourse after watercourse, some natural, others artificial. The hamlets they had served, the mills and tiny manufactories, lay deserted now, the scrub growing up to and lapping across their walls; once lost in that complex, a spotter craft might search for a week and be no wiser at the end.

The air was humid beneath the trees. He wiped at his face and arms. On Earth, flies and midges would have made life burdensome; but the few flying insects of Xerxes, jewel-like creatures resembling terrestrial dragonflies, had no interest in blood. He watched one now, darting and hovering beneath the miniature moss-grown cliff of the bank. The thing swooped, took something from the surface of the water, vanished with a bright blur of wings. The water, he noted, still flowed steadily. The current came via bypass sluices from the high Summit Level ahead. It was an encouraging sign.

In front of the boat a purple-flowered shrub hung low across the water. Her cabin passed beneath its branches with a scrape and rustle. A dozen times already she had been forced to a halt, while Mathis and his steersman used machetes to hack a way through the half-choked watercourse; but in the main the navigability of the canal after so many years' disuse was a monument to the half-legendary Bar-Ab and his engineers.

Four Earth centuries ago, so ran the stories, Bar-Ab had been Prince of Bran Gildo, the palm-fringed city by the Salt Lagoon. He it was who in war after war had swept away the barbarous tribes of the interior, driving their remnants into reserves or into the sea; he also who had given to Xerxes the vast network of canals that, till Terran Contact, had remained the planet's major transportation system. From his line the Kalti, the Boatmen of Xerxes, claimed descent, when they troubled to claim anything at all. From the first, Mathis had been intrigued by them; the little dumpy men and the little dumpy women with their wide-brimmed, round-crowned hats and suits of Sunday black. Though the Kalti were a fast-vanishing race themselves. In every direction, through the swamps, across the uplands with their mile on mile of spindly forest, ran the broad trackways of the Ground Effect Machines; their windy rushing was the night-sound of Xerxes now, replacing the churring of frogs and hunting birds.

Mathis shrugged, and lit a cigarette. From the hundred or so he had brought with him, he allowed himself just two a day. He smoked carefully and slowly, thinking back to his interview with Jefferson, the Bran Gildo Controller. Just ten days ago, now.

He'd pushed his request as far as a Behaviourist (Grade 2A) reasonably could; and been mildly surprised at the result. A small but important circus had assembled to consider the proposition; Ramsden, head of Biology; an Engineer/Controller from the survey section; and Figgins from Liaison, complete with Earth-style secretary. It had been Figgins who opened the attack; Figgins fat, and Figgins bearded.

'John, I feel I must make one point at the outset. This sort of thing is hardly your Department's concern.'

The Terran Complex, an air-conditioned cube of dural and glass, overlooked the brick-red ruins of the Old Palace; the place where Bar-Ab once sat, planning the network of waterways that would span a continent. A boat was passing, on the broad green moat that fronted the ruins, gliding above its mirror-image like a swan. A gay-striped awning covered it; on the foredeck lay a bare brown girl. Mathis shrugged. Difficult to keep his attention on the matter in hand. He said slowly, 'I never claimed my Department was involved. It's a personal project; and I've got a slab of leave come due.'

Figgins' secretary crossed her legs, looking bored. Ramsden, a neat, bald, compact man, ran his finger across an ornamental carafe – Kalti work – and frowned. The engineer doodled on a scratchpad. A little wait, while the Controller decided not to speak; and Figgins carried on.

'Speaking off the record,' he said, 'what would your object be in making a trip like this? What would you hope to prove?'

Mathis said, 'It's all in the report.'

Another wait. Nobody helped him.

The boat was nearly out of sight. He turned back from the window, unwillingly. The words sounded dry; meaningless with repetition. He said, 'We've been on Xerxes about one Earth generation. When we arrived we found a flourishing native culture. Backward on the sciences maybe but well up in the arts. We found a sub-culture, the Boatmen. They had a picto-graphic writing system like nothing we'd ever seen, and a religion we still haven't properly understood. One generation, and that culture is dying. I don't think we have that sort of privilege.'

Jefferson laid down the stylus he had been fingering. The click of metal on the rainbow-wood desk served to focus attention. Obscurely, Mathis wanted to smile.

The Controller said, 'I think we're rather wandering from the point. There are a lot of side effects to culture-shock that none of us much like. But they're inevitable given the situation in which we find ourselves.'

He glanced at Mathis, eyes bright blue beneath shaggy brows. It was a standard mannerism; a look calculated to convey old-world kindliness combined with shrewdness. 'We might not have learned as much as we ought from three hundred planets,' he said. 'But this much we do know. The day we made contact with Xerxes, existing social patterns were doomed. Mr Mathis, you mentioned privilege just now. Let's all be logical.' He turned briefly to the big coloured map that covered most of one wall. 'The hinterland of the Northern Continent is largely swamp,' he said. 'In time, that swamp will be drained and reclaimed. Better standards of living are going to bring a higher birthrate, more mouths to feed. We shall need that land. As of this moment . . . one Ground Effect Machine will traverse between Bran Gildo and Hy Antiel by any of half a dozen routes in a little under one day Planetary. It'll carry the payload of between five and six Kalti longboats, each of which would take a month on the trip. As I see it, our job isn't to resist a change that's already an accomplished fact. We're here to channel that change, help native cultures through a time of transition as smoothly and quickly as possible. In time, the Boatmen will learn new skills. Readapt. That's the way it has to be.'

Mathis said, 'In time, the Boatmen will cease to exist.'

The Controller nodded gravely. He said, 'That's also a possibility we must allow for.' He leafed through the docket on his desk. He said, 'You're asking for permission to take a Kalti boat through the Southern Complex by way of Hy Antiel Summit. And you still haven't answered Mr Figgins' question. What's your ultimate object?'

Mathis said, 'The word goes that that complex is no longer navigable. That isn't true; and I'm going to prove it. A tenth of what we spent last year on GEM terminals would restore it to full working use – and a hundredth of the labour. I want to see that happen; and I also want the matter of the Kalti culture raised at the next sitting of the Extraterrestrial Council. With your permission, I'm applying for a personal hearing. I want the Boatmen protected, and the entire Northern Continent declared a Planetary Reserve.'

The Controller raised his brows slightly. He said, 'Well, that's your privilege. Ramsden, what do you feel about all this?'

The biologist rubbed his chin. 'There's another factor, of course,' he said in his quiet, precise voice. 'Preservation equals stagnation; stagnation equals deterioration. This sort of thing has been tried enough before. In my experience, it's never worked.'

Figgins grunted. 'It seems to me,' he said, 'that you're starting from unsound premises anyway. These people, the Kalti, I haven't seen many of 'em clamouring for help. Could be they don't want the old way any more than we do. You preservationists are all alike, John. None of you can take the broad view.'

Mathis shook his head, still vaguely amused. How could he explain? If Figgins didn't understand, it was because he didn't want to. Study a Kalti pictograph, the swirls that were tenses, the shadings that were words, and the answer was plain enough. Through every design, like a great hyphen, slashed the *Bar-Ko*, the mark of the One who made water and earth, the green leaves and the sky. At the start of time, He decreed all things to be. If a man was to die, or a culture fail, then these facts were pre-ordained; true a million years ago, and true for ever. This was all you needed; know it, and you knew the Boatmen.

But the Controller was speaking again. This time to the engineer.

'Mr Sito, do you have anything to add?'

Sito shrugged. 'I'd say the whole thing was a pipedream. That cut hasn't been used in thirty years; even the Boatmen don't seem to know much about it any more. I shouldn't think you'd get through to Summit Level; and if you did, do you know the length of that tunnel?'

Mathis said, 'Not precisely, no.'

The other made a face. 'That's my point. Those blighters dug like beavers. There's a tunnel up in the Northern Marshes, Kel Santo, that measures out at twenty kilometres. We've had to put scaffolding through nearly a kilometre to hold the roof; and Kel Santo's never been out of maintenance. Take a boat into Hy Antiel and jam, and you'd not walk back out. It isn't a chance I'd take.'

The Controller nodded. 'Yes, Mr Ramsden?'

The biologist said carefully, 'I have to point out it's not too healthy an area. Most of our cases of Xerxian fever have been brought in from the Antiel range. It's spread by a free-swim-

ming amoeboid, gets into the smallest abrasion. Leave that
untreated, and you're in trouble. I've seen some native cases;
the medics call it the Shambles.'

The Controller said briskly, 'Right, I think that gives us all
we need.' The stylus tapped the tabletop again, with finality.
'I'm not unsympathetic,' he said to Mathis. 'Far from it. As far
as appeals go, I'll forward your case with pleasure; we all
know every frontiersman has that right. But for the rest, I
have to think, first and foremost, of the safety of Base personnel.
Both your own and the party we'd have to send out if you went
missing. So . . . request refused. I'm sorry.' He shuffled the
papers together, handed them across the desk and rose.

Ramsden caught up with Mathis in the outer office. By mutual
consent they took the elevator to the ground-floor bar. Earth
interests on Xerxes were expanding steadily; they were brewing something on the planet now that tasted remarkably like
whisky. The biologist called for doubles, drank, put the glass
down and puffed a pipe alight. He said, 'Hm, sorry about that.
Hardly expected anything else, though. Disappointed?'

Mathis smiled. He said slowly, 'Not particularly.'

The other glanced up sharply; and it occurred to Mathis that
alone of the committee, Nathan Ramsden had understood his
real purpose. Better, perhaps, than he understood it himself.
He'd known the biologist a long time. Once, a thousand years
back on another planet, he'd been in trouble. He rang Ramsden;
and Ramsden had listened till the bursting words were done.
Then he said quietly, 'I see. Now, what's the first thing I can
do to help?'

The older man took another sip of the pseudo-Scotch. He
said, 'As you know, it's not my custom to offer unwanted
advice. But I'm offering some now. Go home.'

Mathis stayed silent. He was seeing the canals; the endless
shadings of green and gold, puttering of the long black hulls,
interlacing of leaf and branch shadows in the brown-green
mirror of the water. By pictograph, an answer might be made.
The white and blue swirls formed themselves unasked, inside
his head.

Ramsden set the glass down. He said, 'This'll be my last tour anyway. I'm looking forward to putting my feet up on an Honorary Chair somewhere. You're still young, John; you've got a year or two left yet.'

Mathis said vaguely, 'I suppose we're as young as we feel.'

The biologist said, 'Hmm . . .' He waited a moment longer; then rose. He said, 'Drink up. I've got an hour before my duty tour; I've got someone I'd like you to meet.'

The steersman called behind him; a high, sharp sound, like a yap. The Kalti waved and grinned, pointing to the bank; and Mathis smiled, nodding in return. Ahead rose a line of hills, outliers of the Hy Antiel massif. An arm of forest swept down to the canal; it enclosed a grassy clearing, quiet and golden with sunlight. The Boatman swung the painted shaft of the stern oar, nosing the big craft in towards the bank.

In the Lagoon, close under the old white city walls, the long vessels lay tied each to each; the sun winked from brass-strapped chimneys and round portglasses, gleamed on the painted coamings of cabins. On each stempost, knotted rope-work was pipeclayed to whiteness; above each roof were the big running lamps with their filigree-work of brass; on each side, somewhere, was the mark of the God, the *Bar-Ko* with its sprays of leaves, gold and white and blue. Ramsden strolled beside the bright herd of boats, wiping his face and neck with a bandanna. He paused finally beside a craft tied up some distance from the rest, and called. 'Can't get my tongue round these Kalti names,' he said. 'I just call him Jack.'

The Boatman who bobbed from the diminutive bow cabin was slimmer than most of his people. His bland face with the dark, slightly tilted eyes looked very young; to Mathis, he seemed little more than a boy. He grinned, ducking his head, showing a half-moon of brilliant teeth. Ramsden said, '*Hoki*, Jack. *Hoki, a-aie?*' The Kalti grinned again and nodded, waving a slender hand. The biologist stepped across to the raised prow, dropped, grunting, to the foredeck. Mathis followed him.

Hoki, the coffee-like beverage brewed by the Boatmen, had not at first been to Mathis' taste; but he had grown accustomed to its sharp, slightly bitter flavour. He squatted in the cramped cabin, the thin-shelled, brightly painted cup in his fingers, waited while Ramsden mopped his face again. 'He speaks a bit of Terran,' he said. 'Not much, but I think you'll get by. His parents are dead. He's twenty-five; usually their marriage-contracts are settled before they're out of their teens but Jack's still working single-handed. Bit of an oddball, in many respects.'

The Boatman grinned again. He said, 'Too right,' in a clipped, slightly sing-song voice. He took Mathis' cup, poured more of the brownish fluid. The pot in which it was brewed, like all Kalti artifacts, was gaily decorated; the little discs of copper hanging round its circumference tinkled as he set it down.

Mathis looked round the cabin. It wasn't usual for Terrans to be invited aboard a Kalti boat. Nests of drawers and cupboards lined the walls. No inch of the tiny living space seemed wasted; there were earthenware bowls, copper measures and a dipper, a barrel for water storage, a minute stove. He wondered vaguely how Ramsden had come to know the Boatman. He seemed well enough at home.

The biologist lit his pipe again, staring through the open doors at the sparkling expanse of the lagoon. 'This man will take you to Hy Antiel,' he said. 'By the old route, through the Antiel Range. He's a bit of a patriot in his own way too, is young Jack.'

Mathis narrowed his eyes. He said, 'Why're you doing this, Nathan?'

The older man shrugged and raised his brows. 'Because,' he said, 'if you intend to go, and I feel you do, I'd rather you have a good man with you. That way you stand a chance of coming back.' He prodded at the pipe bowl with a spent match. 'Just one thing,' he said, 'if they drag you out by the back hair, as they probably will, I shan't know a thing about it. I've got troubles of my own already. . . .'

He had one final memory: of sitting on the cabin roof of the great boat later that day, watching a vessel come in from Plane-tary West. Through the glasses she seemed to make no pro-gression, hanging shadowlike against the glowing shield of water. The figures that crowded her rocked, as she rocked, slowly from side to side. From them drifted a thread of sound – a single note, harsh and unnatural, taken up and sustained by voice after voice.

Mathis touched the young Kalti on the shoulder, pointed. 'Jack,' he said, 'what's that?'

'*Kaput*,' said the Boatman unexpectedly, 'all finish.'

Mathis said musingly, 'All the decks were dense with stately forms . . .' He glanced down sharply. He said, 'You mean it's a funeral.'

'All finish,' said Jack. 'Yes. Bloody bad luck.'

The canal shallowed towards the edges, banked with fine silt. He heard the slither and bump as the flat-bottomed craft grounded, and shrugged. A few minutes' work with the poles would shift her, at first light. For safety's sake he still carried a line ashore. The ground, unexpectedly soft, wouldn't hold a mooring spike. He tethered the boat instead to a sapling at the water's edge. He sat a while watching the shadows lengthen, the gold fade from the little space of grass. From the cabin at his back came shufflings, once a tinkle as the Kalti worked, preparing the mess of beans on which the Boatmen habitually lived. With the dusk a little breeze rose, blowing from the hills, heavy with the scent of some night flower.

The Kalti bobbed from the cabin slide. 'All done,' he said. 'Too quick.'

Mathis turned, stared up at the high line of hills losing themselves in the night. 'Jack,' he said, 'are we going to make it?'

The Boatman nodded vigorously. 'One time,' he said. 'No sweat. Too bloody quick.'

He had conned De Witt at Base into knocking him up a generator and headlamp to supplement the lighting of the Kalti boat. It rested now on the forward cabintop, an untidy arrangement of batteries and wires. He ran a hand across the motor casing as he smoked his final cigarette. The canal was restless; cheepings sounded and close plops, once a heavier crashing of branches followed by the *swack-swack-swack* of a bird taking off from water. The banks, and the shaggy bushes lining them, were mounded velvet; between them the water gleamed, depthless and pale. It seemed the canal itself gave off a scent; chill, and pervasive. The moon of Xerxes was rising as he sought his sleeping bag.

The morning was difficult. The channel, much overgrown here, had silted badly; time and again the boat grounded, sliding to a halt. The pole tip sank in the softness, raising blackish swirls that stained the clear green. The Kalti, patient and expressionless, worked engine and steering oar, using the boat's power now to drive her forward, now to draw back from an impassable shoal. The sun woke shimmers from the thread of water remaining, while Mathis sweated and heaved. By midday, he guessed they had covered little more than a mile. They rested a while, drawn beneath a tangle of bushes; and he heard the echoing whistle of a flyer, somewhere to the north. He waited, frowning. For a time the machine seemed to circle, the sound of its motors eddying on the wind. Then the noise faded. It did not return.

By mid afternoon the condition of the waterway had improved. The boat resumed its steady pace, gliding still between high mounded bushes. Some of the branches bore viciously sharp thorns; Mathis, standing in the bow, swung a machete, lopping a path clear for the steersman. That night he was glad of his rest.

Next morning they reached the foot of a long lock flight that climbed steadily into the hills. The chambers were well spaced, the pounds between them a mile or more in length. Over each pair of gates the *Bar-Ko* rusted in its bright iron frame, a valediction from the long-dead Prince. Viridian creepers had wound themselves into and through the scrollwork of the supports; their long tendrils brushed Mathis' face as the boat glided beneath. On the following day they entered the first of the cuttings.

For some time the ground to either side had been trending steadily upward; now the canal sides, still heightening, closed together, becoming near-vertical cliffs of dark purple rock. The strata of which they were composed were seamed and cracked; between the layers massive trees somehow found lodgement.

The root bosses, gnarled and lichened, glistened with water that oozed its way steadily through the stone. Above, the higher trunks were festooned with the brilliant creeper. Some inclined at precarious angles, meshing their branches with those of their fellows on the opposite bank. From them the tendrils swayed, dropping masses of foliage to the water fifty or sixty feet beneath. Later the cutting, still immensely deep, opened out; here lianas, as thick as or thicker than Mathis' arms, stretched pale and taut from the leaf canopy to the shelving rock. They did not, he saw, descend vertically but inclined on both sides at a slight angle to the water; so that driving between them was like passing through the forest-ribs of an enormous keel.

The cutting had one advantage; the height and density of the trees had thinned out secondary growth. The water still ran clear and green; the rock, though friable, seemed not to discolour it. Mathis sat in the damp warmth, hearing the magnified beat of the engine echo back from the high cliff to either side. In time he grew tired of staring up; then it seemed his sense of scale was altered. The bank beside which the boat slid, the foot or so of rock at the water's edge, became in itself a precipice, sheer and beetling. The sheets of lichen, the tiny mosslike plants clinging to the stone, were meadows and trees, above which the menacing shapes drifted like clouds. The tips of the great falls of creeper, touching the boat, discharged showers of drops that fell like storms of icy rain.

He thought vaguely of Ramsden, back at Base; the delight the biologist would take in the strange plant forms surrounding him. With the thought came another, less surely formed; a sense of loss, an aching regret at the necessity for actions. He knew himself better now; and understood more fully the nature of his journey. The notion, once admitted, remained with him, his mind returning to it with the insistence with which the tongue-tip probes the wound of an extraction. This seemed to be the truth; that because nothing, no homecoming, waited beyond the hill range he was drawn forward, because of desolation and emptiness he had to go on. The trees stretched their ranks over the edge of rock above him; beyond he knew lay others and still more, mile on endless mile of forest haunted by rodents and owls. There were empty hamlets, empty villages, empty towns maybe, lapped by the rising green, wetted by rains, warmed by summer suns. He experienced a curious desire, transient yet powerful, to know that land; but know it in detail, hollow by hollow, as he knew the lines of his palms. He wondered at the state of mind, not wholly new to him; and wondered too at a curious notion Ramsden had once expressed that the Loop, in scrambling a man, never reassembled the same being twice. The oddity was allied to another, better known; that over seven years or so the elements of the body, the pints of water and pennorths of salt, are wholly changed so that physically and intimately one becomes a different being. Yet the thinking part, whichever that might be, goes on for ever; hurting, and giving pain.

A mile into the cutting the engine stalled with a thud.

He was amused, momentarily, at the flash of panic aroused in him. The mind, it seems, insists on clinging to patterns once known; maybe to the point of death. The long hull was swinging and losing way, pushed by the faint current from ahead; he fended with the pole, felt the bottom bump gently against mud. He climbed to the catwalk above the cargo space, walked steadily astern.

Round the rear of the vessel, immediately above the propeller, ran a narrow ledge. The Kalti was squatting on it, gripping one-handed, groping with the other arm beneath the water. For the journey, he had affected Terran garb; a sleeveless woollen jerkin, printed with Fair Isle patterns and plentifully daubed with oil, and a pair of frayed and faded jeans. His harsh, longish hair hung forward; between jeans and pullover showed a half-moon of olive skin. He straightened when Mathis spoke, grinning his inevitable grin; Mathis wondered suddenly if it was no more than a reflex of the nerves. 'All stuck up,' he said. 'Jolly bad luck.'

Mathis climbed down beside him. The tip of a nobbled branch protruded from the water; below, its cloudy shape was visible for a foot or more before vanishing in the greenness. He tugged at it. It felt immovable. His reach was longer than the Kalti's; he felt carefully for the propeller boss, traced his finger back along the battered edge of the blade. The log was jammed firmly between propeller and hull.

The Kalti pulled the sweater over his head, balancing with care. He folded the garment neatly and slid into the water. Mathis followed, feeling the buoyant chill.

From this viewpoint, the black hull seemed immense. The mud of the canal bottom sucked at his feet; he grabbed for breath, ducked, surfaced again. He ran fingers across the curving, crusted planks, carefully, remembering Ramsden's injunction. The Kalti heaved at the branch. It moved anti-clockwise an inch or so, jammed again. Half-rotten, the wood was difficult to grip. Mathis clung to the step, exploring again with his free hand. The edge of the big prop had bitten deeply into the waterlogged fibres. He shook his head, made washout motions with his palm above the water.

He paddled to where he could once more swing himself aboard. The ironwood grating at the stern lifted readily enough. Beneath it the shaft gleamed dully, secured to the primitive gearbox by a flexible jawed coupling. He fingered the heavy hand-forged bolts. The Kalti nodded, and grinned again.

De Witt had made up a toolkit for the boat. None of the set spanners fitted; he used an adjustable, working carefully so as not to burr the edges of the nuts. As he worked a light drizzle began, drifting in greyish veils from the heights above.

The nuts came clear, finally. He tapped the bolts back through the fibrous coupling plate, and gripped the shaft. It wouldn't budge.

He sorted the toolkit for the longest crowbar. A wooden wedge pressed against the gearbox end protected the coupling from damage. He leaned his weight carefully. The shaft stayed firm. He took a breath, jerked. The thing slid backward through the packing gland, with a faint creak. He reached behind him, pulled. The branch rolled clear and sank.

He eased the shaft forward, reconnected. He sat back, wiping his hands on a piece of fibrous husk. He said, 'Hoki, Jack?' The Kalti raised his thumbs. He said, 'Dear me, yes.' He scrambled forward, over the cargo space.

By mid-afternoon they were clear of the cutting. Beyond, the land fell away with startling speed to a steep and ragged valley. Across it strode an aqueduct, massive arches built of the same purplish rock. To one side, sluices discharged water from the canal lip with a sullen roar. The spray from the fall drifted back, obscuring the defile. Mathis, gripping the boat's rail, imagined the black hull, topped with the tilted brightwork of the cabins, sliding so high in the air. He saw the vessel from the viewpoint of an observer in the tangled valley bottom. Beyond the great structure the rock walls once more swooped together; and the Kalti moored for the night.

In the second cutting they were delayed again, this time by mud and weed. The weed, slimy strings of it twenty feet or more in length, wrapped itself persistently round the propeller, building a solid ball between blades and hull. As the obstructions formed the Boatman sliced them away patiently. Mathis poled dully, disinterested in time; later the machetes were once more brought into use. Finally the narrows were passed; the second cutting opened up ahead. The rock rose steeply, a hundred feet or more, clothed still for most of its height with living green. Through much of the day the far lip caught the sun; the feathery trees that lined it seemed to burn, haloed with pale gold. Later, clouds grew across the sky. The drizzle returned; and a thin mist, veiling the highest rock. In time the mist crept lower, rolling slowly, clinging in tongues to the water.

He was standing beside the steersman on the little stern grating. The Kalti grunted, pulling his lips back from his teeth. Mathis shook his head; and the Boatman waved an arm. '*Mutta-a*,' he said to the surrounding heights. '*Mutta-a. Kaput.*'

Mutta-a. Mutti, Maman . . . The first sound any mammal's voice will make. Mathis said, 'You mean it's haunted.' Perhaps this was why the Kalti were disinclined to talk.

'*Mutta-a*,' said Jack, nodding vigorously. 'Rather silly.'

Mathis said, 'I can believe it.'

He walked forward. The mist, or cloud-base, had thickened again; the tree-limbs, some bleached, pushed through it, with curious effect. He was interested to find it was still possible to feel unease. He savoured the sensation with some care.

The huge walls angled to the left. The boat edged round the bend; and a black mouth showed ahead. The sloping hillside in which it was set climbed to unguessed height. Bushes clung to it; above were the trunks of the endless forest. The opening itself was horseshoe-shaped, its throat densely black. From fifty yards he smelled its breath, ancient, and chill. Mathis rubbed his face, then swung to the cabin top to start the generator.

This was the Tunnel of Hy Antiel.

He turned the handlamp. The ribbon of water ahead was tarry, non-reflecting. To either side the close brick walls were festooned with red and green slime; larger masses, leprous-white in the light, hung from the half-seen roof. As the boat brushed at them they broke with soft snaps. From the brickwork of the tunnel fell a steady chill rain.

He listened, turning his head. What he had not been prepared for was the din. The thudding of the boat's diesel echoed massively from the curved walls; but there were other sounds. A sighing rose to something like a roar, fled forward and back along the shaft. Maybe the boat had scraped the side, some sprag touched her hull; God only knew. The brick throat threw echoes back on themselves, lapping and distorting. At first the sounds had troubled him; but they had been travelling two hours or more, he had grown accustomed to the place.

He pitched the light farther ahead. For some time now a deeper roar had been growing in intensity. He saw its source finally; a curtain of clear water, sparkling as it fell from the roof. At its base the surface boiled and rippled, throwing up wavering banks of brownish foam.

This was the fourth airshaft he had seen. He ducked, tortoise-fashion, into the little bow castle, heard the cannonade pass down the long tarpaulins of the cargo space to the stern. The big boat rocked; the sighing came again, mixed with the fading roar.

Here, in the encroaching dark, the swimming sense of motion was intensified. A memory returned to him, odd and unconnected; and he nearly smiled. It was of a journey back from

London to his home, when he was a tiny child. On the trip down the monorail whispered and clattered, flashing through tunnel after tunnel beneath the great complexes of buildings; but now the darkness pressed uniform and baffling against the rounded panes of the carriage. He had asked, finally, when this tunnel would end; and his father, momentarily surprised, had dropped a hand to his shoulder and laughed. 'It isn't a tunnel, John,' he said. 'It's the night. . . .'

He leaned back, head against the bulky survival pack. He felt tired and a little dizzy. Maybe it was the fumes that hung in the shaft. He lit his daily cigarette, and closed his eyes. He saw with remarkable clarity the white walls and green palm-clumps of Bran Gildo, the unused watchtowers pushing their dunce-cap roofs into the turquoise sky. It seemed he could smell the hot, spiced air, the fragrance of spike-leaved shrubs where the Terran girls walked with their pleated kilts and strapped native sandals and long bronzed limbs. From beyond the Palace walls came the sounds of the city's traffic, cartbells mixed with the whine of the electric buggies that were a gift from an ever-benevolent Earth. He opened his lids, seeing the slime-hung walls. The two images, so disparate, were yet interlinked; pieces of an equation that one day must be solved.

Later, he must have slept; certainly he dozed, for when his eyes once more opened the engine of the boat was quiet. The cabin lamps were lit; Jack banged and clattered at the little stove.

He rose, awkward in the confined space. For a moment he was disoriented; and the child's confusion returned so that it seemed the boat must have passed the tunnel. Then he saw how the lamplight glowed in fans across wet brickwork; the air he drew into his lungs was chill and stale. He turned to the Boatman; and the Kalti grinned. 'Too far,' he said. 'Not much good.'

They were moored to what seemed to be the remains of a little wharf. Lines of rusting iron rings were let into the brickwork. He swung to the cabintop, started the generator. The lampbeam showed the black, unrippling water stretching ahead. To the right, joining the main line at a sharp angle, was a second shaft. The stonework of the curving groin where tunnels met looked new and fresh. He pointed to the shaft; but the Kalti shrugged, making wash-out motions with his hands. He said again, 'Not much good.'

With the boat motionless, the silence of the tunnel was complete. He lay a long time hearing the quietness hiss in his ears. Finally, sleep came; and with it dreams. They were untenanted, yet precisely detailed. They concerned ancient buildings, places seen once on Earth. A gatehouse, lost in a wood of tall elms; a street of white-walled cottages; a flight of turf steps before a great stone Minster.

Finally it seemed he sat in an upper room of a very large house. The room, a study, looked out on wings of crumbling stone. Beyond were formal gardens, arbours framing leaden nymphs and gods. In the dream he knew with certainty that he would never leave the room, never rise from the chair; and that the light, the afternoon light, would never change.

The Kalti roused him. He was giddy and light-headed; and his eyes seemed gummy, as though he had not slept. He ate the bean stew the boy set before him with little interest. Afterwards he walked to where the jetty, if jetty it was, narrowed, the stone fairing into the smooth brick of the shaft. His purpose satisfied, he stepped back to untie the ropes from the heavy rings. The Kalti swung up the engine; he poled the bow from the wharf, and the journey was resumed.

Twice in the hours that followed echoing roars from ahead warned of fresh ventshafts. Each discharged its torrent of water into the canal; but staring up as the boat approached, Mathis could detect no gleam of outside light. One shaft seemed partially choked; fibrous roots hung twisting in the downpour, their tips pale and rotted. At eleven hundred the boat passed a line of low flood arches. Water from the canal lip poured beneath them in steady greenish sheets. Mathis turned the lamp. At first it seemed a black void opened beyond; but this was a trick of light. The rock, covered with some dark, non-reflectant growth, was very close.

The workings in the tunnel were complex, like none he had

seen. He wondered at their age. He asked the Kalti, shouting above the engine; but the Boatmen shook his head. '*Mutta-a,*' he said. He spread his fingers, and again. Many generations.

The tunnel was very old.

To his other questions there was no reply. The tunnel was very long.

Later in the day the brickwork ended.

The effect was odd. Beyond the shaft sides, a jet half-circle seemed to form and widen. He watched the spreading band a moment, puzzled; then the tunnel was falling away behind. The engine noise, that for so long had pounded in his ears, faded as the stern of the boat drew clear.

He swung the big lamp left and right, discovering no sign of walls; the gloom ahead was likewise unrelieved. At last the abundance of summit water was explained; they had entered an underground lake, of unknown size. He wondered fleetingly if Bar-Ab and his engineers had known. Had they plotted the extent of the cavern, tunnelled to its brink; or had the miners burst into the void, startled and unsuspecting. . . .

On impulse, he angled the light upward. Above, suspended it seemed from an infinite height, the *Bar-Ko,* dark red and dripping, marked the way. Beyond the great iron sign hung another; and another, dimly seen.

He nodded to himself. They had known.

The tunnel had been loud with noise. Running through the void, the opposite effect seemed to hold true. Silence, like the dark, pressed in on the boat; almost it seemed the cavern deadened sound, so that twice he scrambled to the cabin roof convinced the engine was no longer running. Each time he was reassured by the thumping ninety feet astern. Once he tried sounding, with the longest pole, but could touch no bottom. He turned his wrist in the beam of De Witt's spotlight, holding the chronometer close up to his face. He was surprised to see an hour had elapsed since quitting the shaft.

With time, the absence of sensation affected him strongly. The tunnel sounds returned, the whisperings and long sighs; but they were in his ears. Also it seemed that lights appeared, far across the water. It was as if a fairy army drove to meet him, yet for ever receded. He rubbed his face, knuckling at his eyes; and the lights were gone.

Finally a fresher breeze blew from ahead. Also he saw, above the endless line of markers, a fold of stone that was the dipping of the cavern roof. Ghostings of grey appeared to either side; then, suddenly, the cavern walls began to close back in. The slime-hung brickwork returned; and he stared behind him at the velvet dark. He said, 'The Lake of Tuonela.'

Tuonela, where dead spirits walk.

In the outer world the time was thirteen hundred. The abstraction counted for little here. He wound the chronometer, staring up while the bow of the vessel bumped gently at what looked at first sight to be the gate of a stop lock. The journey was ended.

The tilted beam of light rolled slowly, illuminating a slope of wet, smooth rock. At its summit, the side of the second great caisson showed its panels of rusting iron. More iron, columns and tie rods, rose into the dark. Beyond was an engine house. The round-topped windows stared like dim sockets; above them the buttressed column that was the chimney grew up into the stone, thrusting for the open air. Mathis grinned, showing his teeth. He said softly, 'The crazy bastards.'

He sat on the cabin roof and lit a cigarette. He felt closer to Bar-Ab and his men than he would have thought possible. He rubbed the beard-stubble on his chin and asked himself, how could they have done it? How could they carve through twenty miles of rock, with pickaxes and plumb bobs, and keep their line and level? Those engineers in kilts and plumes? Like the Incas, their priests used the Rope of Thorns. Like the Victorians, they knew black powder and the barrow run. Like both, they vanished. They left . . . this.

They built an Inclined Plane, inside a bloody hill.

A sound at his elbow made him turn. The Kalti's face was a pale mark in the gloom. He waved an arm at the monstrousness; the caissons, the engine house, the rails with their great red bogies. He said, 'Make go.'

Mathis threw the half-smoked butt into the water. Sito would

E

have given his back teeth for this. 'Yes, Jack,' he said. 'We must make it go . . .'

There was coal; great bunkers of it, growing here and there a rich skin of mould. Coal, but no kindling. For that they stripped the powdering frames from windows, boards from the engine-house floor. Fuel oil from the boat's depleted tank would fire the furnace. The boiler they filled painfully, a bucket at a time. The top caisson already held water; the gate of the lower for a time refused to close. Mathis rigged a fourfold purchase from a mooring bollard, strained the thick iron partially shut; the boat herself, thundering in reverse, completed the job. Brown foam boiled; the big door closed, with protesting squeals. They lit the furnace then, sat an hour while pressure built to working head. Round the boiler were heavy riveted straps. In time the rivet heads began to sizzle and steam.

There was a bank of gauges, each set in a plate of foliated brass. The markings on the faces made no sense. It was guess-work, all the way.

Mathis edged the regulator forward. A rumbling; rust flew, in a thin rain. Below, the long chains stretched over the rock clanked to tautness. The boat slopped against the chamber side; the engine slowed as the ancient gearing felt the load. Steam roared from a union; and the boat was climbing, inching sideways up the Plane. The headlight, blazing, drew level with Mathis, began to pass. The Kalti heaved at the caisson side, adding his strength to the strength of the machine. He was happy. He had done what the strange Terri wanted; now others would come, with their engines that tore away rock and plucked down trees. And the long cuttings would once more fill. His head made pictures; he saw the blue and red stars that were the lamps of boats, sailing all night long from Bran Gildo to Hy Antiel.

A chain link parted, with a ringing crash. Mathis, sweating, wrenched at the emergency brake with blistered hands. The caisson, with its hundred-thousand-gallon load, lurched back-ward on the slope; and the Kalti's heels shot from under him.

'Oh dear,' said Jack. The bogies, gathering speed, severed his arm, ploughed crashing across his chest. The caisson took the water it had quitted with a thunderous splash. A tinkling; the headlight on the cabin roof swayed sideways and was extinguished.

The tunnel portal was set into a low, mounded hill. Beyond it the canal was fringed with low shrubs that blazed with smoky orange blossom. Above, saplings hung graceful and still, their sprays of rounded leaves catching the sunset light.

To an observer stationed at the tunnel mouth, the twin lamps of the Kalti vessel would have appeared at first like dim brown stars. For some time, such are the curious optics of tunnels, the stars would have appeared to grow no closer; then, suddenly it seemed, they swam forward. Between them the outlines of the boat became visible; the knotted headropes of the prow, the tilted cabin with its ornamented ports. Behind, sliding into the light, came the long tented cargo space; the engine-house, hazed with blue; the stern deck with its grating, the *Bar-Ko* vaunting white and gold on the rounded black sides. The steersman, in once-white slacks and shirt, leaned wearily on the painted shaft of the oar. His face was fringed with a stubble of beard; from time to time he glanced down, frowning, at a bundle near his feet. In places the canvas of which it was composed was soaked and dark; and a runnel of fluid had escaped, staining the boat's dull side.

To Mathis, the transition from darkness to the light seemed curiously unreal. He smelled the sweetness of the grass, heard the wind rustle in the tops of trees and frowned again, shaking his head as if to clear it. His brain recorded, but sluggishly. Ahead and to the left, twin hills marked the position of Hy Antiel. This was the Summit Pound; five miles ahead the lock flight began that led to the city, stepping in green steps down a green and grassy hill. He'd walked beside it often enough, it seemed in some other life.

He squinted up at the high dusting of gold. To the right showed the pilings of a mooring place. Little bushes surrounded it, throwing their branch-shadows across the water. He turned the oar, unused as yet to the boat's response, glided the long vessel to the bank.

He was uncertain of the forms to be employed. He chose a spot finally; a grassy knoll beneath the branches of a broad, spreading tree. He had brought a spade and mattock from the boat; he wiped his forehead, and began to dig. Later he drove a stake into the grass at the head of the fresh-turned mound. To it he lashed a crosspiece for the *Bar-Ko* sign; then there was nothing more to do.

He searched the Kalti's few possessions. He found a breech-cloth of silk, a scarf, a broad-brimmed, round-crowned hat; and a bolero crusted with pearly buttons, the sort of garment a Boatman would wear on a feast-day in Bran Gildo. In a bag closed by a drawstring were two brooches set with semi-precious stones, a nugget of what looked to be iron pyrites and a lock-key charm in gold. There were also a prayer-roll sealed with the *Bar-Ko* mark, and a much-thumbed packet of postcards showing bare-breasted Terran girls. These last he returned to the bag before tucking it carefully away.

He didn't wish to eat. Instead he brewed up the Kalti coffee, drinking several cups. Slightly alcoholic, the drink had a heady effect. He smoked a cigarette, saw to his mooring stakes and spread his sleeping-bag on the cabin roof. The spinning in his head was worse; he closed his eyes, and was quickly asleep.

He woke some time before the Xerxian dawn. To Planetary East, the first faint flush of green heralded the sun. The canal was a silver mirror, set between velvet trees; and Barbara watched him from the bank, her chin in her hand. The light gleamed palely from her hair.

He pushed himself up on one elbow, and smiled. 'Hello,' he said. 'Are you coming on board?'

She considered, smiling in her turn, before she slowly shook her head. 'No, thanks,' she said. 'I think once was enough. I don't think I could go through it all again.'

He said, 'I can't say I blame you. You're better off where you are.'

She chuckled. 'My word,' she said, 'you've certainly changed.'

He said, 'I suppose we all do.' He rubbed his face. 'I wasn't

expecting you,' he said. 'Not here. I thought I'd travelled much
too far away.'

'Oh,' she said, 'you know me, John. I'm the little crab who
always hangs on. Remember?'

'Yes,' he said. 'I do.'

She was quiet a moment, watching along the canal. She said,
'This is a lovely place.'

'It needed you,' he said. 'It was rather pointless before.'

'Where were you going?'

He said, 'Hy Antiel.' He gestured at the bank. 'There were
two of us. But . . .'

She said, 'I know.' She shook her head. She said, 'You haven't
altered all that much, after all.'

'What do you mean?'

'Poor John,' she said. 'You never could understand, could
you? About other people.'

He said, 'I didn't want it to happen. I didn't want him to
be hurt.'

She said, 'You never wanted anybody to be hurt. But you
always forgot.'

He said, 'I'm sorry.'

She said, 'I know. It doesn't matter.'

A little silence. Then he said, 'Please come aboard.'

She laughed. She said, 'No, not now. But I will stay with
you.'

He said, 'Thank you.'

She said softly, 'It's more than you deserve.'

He said, 'You were always more than I deserved.'

He let himself sink back. Later she too dozed, her head
resting on her arm. For that he couldn't blame her. It had been
a long way, from Tuonela.

Sunlight lay in hazy patches on the water when he opened his
eyes. He sat up slowly, pushing back the fabric of the bag, and
saw how clever she had been. The light patch of her skirt was
bright grass seen through a triangle of lapping boughs. The
smooth rootstock of a shrub had made her ankle; and she had
used a glistening branch for the sheen of hair. He moved, and
she was gone. But there were many shadowed places on the

canals, many quiet banks of grass; he found himself not without hope.

The shaking in his legs and arms was bad, but his head felt fractionally clearer. He started the engine, poled the boat from the bank. The canal was wider here and deep, curving gracefully beneath the overhanging bushes. The diesel chugged steadily; the wash ran slapping against earth banks studded with moss-grown holes. The *chikti* made them, the little burrowing mammals of the tropics.

Three miles before the flight a broad green arm of water opened to the left; the Coldstream branch, that once had served the villages to the south of Hy Antiel. He pushed the oar, leaning his weight steadily, watching as the bow began to swing. He had understood a final thing; that pain is life, and death is when the pain has gone away.

Ahead, the lapping of blue and gold repeated itself into distance. Beyond, dimly glimpsed, were the low hills of the watershed through which the canal, broadening and meandering, lost itself once more in the marshlands of the south.

The Grain Kings

The pamphlet was glossy and well thumbed. Harrison leafed the pages indifferently, glancing up from time to time at the bulkhead clock.

> *The principle of the combine harvester,* he read, *dates back to the early years of our century. The first machines were crude and small, and were usually controlled and operated by one man (see illustration opposite).*
>
> *A UN combine has been likened to a small township on caterpillar tracks. Aboard each great machine a crew of up to a hundred must eat, sleep and work for weeks at a time. The superstructure houses construction and repair shops, generator and boiler rooms, a sick bay, laboratories, a gallery; and for off-duty relaxation a restaurant, television lounge, bars and a cinema. A modern combine is big. It has to be; it has a big job to do. In Alaska alone, upward of a hundred thousand square miles of wheat must be harvested in not much more than a month. Wheat that is needed, desperately, to feed the teeming millions of our overcrowded planet.*

The wallclock pinged. Harrison yawned, tossed the booklet down and rose. A belted topcoat hung behind the door. He shrugged himself into it and left the cabin.

The corridor beyond, dim and quiet when he had come aboard, vibrated faintly. The lamps in their wellglasses glowed brightly; the combine had raised running voltage. He turned left and right, climbed a flight of spindly metal stairs. The companionway gave on to B deck and the observation lounge.

On deck he was assailed by an echoing clamour. He stood blinking vaguely, saw without surprise that the combine was in motion. Above and close, the big metal girders of the hangar bay

slid past one behind the next; he stared up, seeing the yellow
bowls of service lights glide by, watching the shifting, repeating
perspectives. Ahead, the exit doors had already rumbled back.
Daylight gleamed outside, faint as yet and grey. The opening
looked like the slit of a pillbox. In a building so vast, perspectives
tended to confuse the brain.

The tannoys in the roof were working again, gobbing out their
words in big, bouncing chunks of sound. The lights gleamed
on the combine's broad forward casings. On her stubby mast,
red and turquoise identification lamps sequenced steadily, like
the landing lights of an aircraft. Harrison found notebook and
stilus, leaned against the deckrail. He wrote: *It doesn't fly, so it
isn't a plane. It doesn't float, so it can't be a ship. It's something
else, something different. Outside experience.* He sneered at the
phrase, scored it through. Beneath it he scribbled; *Clearing
hangar sheds, 07.30 hours. Loudspeakers working; difficult for the
uninitiated to make out the words. They wouldn't mean much if
they did. Big combining already has a language of its own.*

The observation deck was filling now. On the port wing
O'Hara was angling his camera for a shot of the control-room
windows. Alison Beckett had made her appearance, well
muffled. Harrison flicked his fingers at her, walked over to the
photographer. The combine was nearing the exit ramp. Red
lamps sprang into brilliance round the edges of the great doors.
He heard the main diesels catch and thunder. She'd been
running on her auxiliaries then. The engine beats steadied to a
pounding throb. He thought, 'We shall be living with that noise.
For days.' He said to O'Hara, 'Don't forget the old man's hangar shots.'

O'Hara grinned. He said, 'The great sheds sink slowly in the
west.'

Harrison said, 'You take the pictures. I'll write the copy.'

O'Hara rolled film, turned the Bronica, made an adjustment.
He said, 'It's the pictures that matter, boyo.'

'Every one,' said Harrison, 'is worth a thousand words.' He
turned away, hands dug into the pockets of his coat.

A combine is too big to be solid. Rather it humps its way
across the land, like a jointed, gigantic steel carpet. Harrison

watched the forward casings rise steadily, taking the slight slope of the exit ramp. As they nosed into daylight they changed colour from brown to orange-red. The pitch of the engines altered as the main bulk felt the incline.

Beside him stood a stubby, grey-haired man, an off-duty engineer. Harrison said, 'Why were the main diesels only started just now? I thought they'd need longer to warm up.'

The engineer glanced at him, took a pipe from his pocket, tamped the tobacco and struck a match. He seemed in no hurry to answer. Finally he said between his teeth, 'She doesn't run on her mains. They're running 'em up for start of cut. She goes anywhere on her crawlers.'

Harrison said, 'Thank you. I wasn't sure.'

The bulk of the machine was clear of the sheds now. The noise of the loudhailers faded abruptly. In the open air the thunder of the engines was less oppressive. Harrison stared round him. The sky was an indeterminate grey-blue. He saw, or thought he saw, the last spark of a star. The eastern horizon, flat, was slashed with searing yellow.

On the wing, O'Hara was lining up the hangar shots. He'd got Alison to pose against the rail. She was wearing a headscarf. One long strand of hair had come free, was moving in the wind. She put her glove up, tucked it aside. The bridge speakers clicked and said, 'Good morning.'

The voice said, 'I am Controller Cheskin. I welcome you on behalf of the United Nations Organization and the World Food Council. The machine on which you are travelling is an American-built Rolls-Toyota of the Dakota class. She develops a total horsepower of just over a hundred thousand, and harvests on a two-hundred-and-fifty-metre swath. Her codename to base is Combine Patsy. We are travelling east, fifteen degrees north at a speed of ten kilometres an hour. At zero nine hundred hours we shall be turning on to cut.'

The speakers crackled slightly. They said, 'Breakfast is now being served in the C deck restaurant. May I wish you all a pleasant and interesting trip. Thank you.'

Alison came over. She said, 'God, I'm frozen. Aren't you cold?'

Harrison said, 'Not too bad.'

'Coming to breakfast?'

He said, 'I've got some notes to get down. I'll take second tables.'

She said, 'You're too devoted.'

He said, 'I work better first thing.'

He walked back to his cabin, closed the door and hung the coat up. He lay on the bunk, hands clasped behind his head. Now, with the main engines running, the dural walls thrummed faintly. He closed his eyes, feeling the pulse of the combine. He remembered, arbitrarily, how someone once told him he made love to her at dawn, though the fleshly Harrison was two hundred miles away. He shrugged. The borderline between fantasy and fact is vivid and hard. Whoever holds it to be otherwise is either a liar or a fool. Probably the former. He lay now alone, a hardish pillow under his head. The counterpane was striped in sage green and orange, the cabin furnishings looked vaguely Swedish. The air conditioner whistled slightly, the clock hands stood at 08.05. Nothing and nobody would alter these facts.

He had a bottle of whisky in the bedside locker. He sat up, poured himself two fingers, grimaced and added the third. He thought, 'I should kick this early-morning drinking.' He drank, lit a cigarette, laid it in the tray. He was thinking about the flight up. He'd travelled, among others, in the company of a well-known divorcee. Her legs had been superb and she raised hell about the lunch. She left the plane at Kennedy. He thought, 'I should be over the other thing by now. Nine months is a good gestation.'

He opened his eyes again at ten hundred hours. The Scotch still stood on the locker; the cigarette had burned itself out half through. He thought, 'I missed start of cut.' But he could make that bit up. He reached for the notebook, considered for a time and wrote.

The main power system of a combine is diesel-electric. Motors situated above each set of cutter blades. Access from motor gallery forward; maintenance staff permanently on duty. He thought for a moment. Could they withdraw blade sets, service while in motion? He presumed so; still, it was a point worth checking.

The light through the cabin port was bright now. He buzzed the steward, asked for some coffee. While he was waiting he shaved. The coffee when it came was very good. He smoked a cigarette, stubbed it and walked back to the observation deck.

Climate control made these exercises possible. As he emerged into sunlight the combine was flowing past a radiator. The tower stood on tall black struts. Clamped to one of the stilt legs was a board with the legend *Danger. IOKV*. Below it was stencilled another warning: *Do not activate relays without blue and green authorities.* He wondered how service engineers reached isolated towers. Not by helicopter; the downdraught would flatten the wheat.

He stared above him. The sky had a hard, steely brilliance. The decks of the combine stretched out like a scarlet plain; ahead and to either side, the wheat was an immense level sea. He thought, 'Indian summer of technology,' and dismissed the phrase.

The radiator was well astern now. Ahead was a reef signal. The red disc bore a black triangle, point uppermost. He waited for the combine to change course. She didn't appear to; but the signal passed well to port. Beyond it, the smoothness of the grain was unmarred. He wrote: *'Dural girders. Aluminium panels. Ground clearance zero. Patsy is a fragile giant.'*

He thought, 'Aren't we all?'

He watched the horizon, hazed with blue. Nothing to see; no way of marking progression. The combine was on cut; but from up here there was no way of telling. He listened, carefully. Maybe the engine rumble was a fraction deeper, there was a shade more vibration. The endless roaring he'd expected wasn't there. The machine moved majestically, a ship against a yellow ocean. He wondered again about the sea metaphor. As yet he had nothing on which to peg his story. No theme. He watched the cutter coamings a hundred yards away. They rose and fell steadily, rolling with the contours of the land. He imagined he could hear, above the diesels, the sibilance of the blades slicing wheat.

Two dolly-bird reporters came up from below. The taller looked Scandinavian. They glanced at him as they passed, leaned backs turned to him against the rail. They seemed to have a lot to chat about. He walked to the starboard wing, propped the notebook on his knee.

A combine works to a predetermined grid, he wrote. *Strictly, it's flying by wire. Control units, buried by the score, kick out a parcel of signal frequencies; underbelly sensors keep each machine on a true heading. Course and pattern of cut are predetermined at base; onboard computers see to the rest. The system's accurate; you can do a lot with a two hundred and fifty metre datum line.*

He touched the tip of the stylus to his teeth. He wrote; *'Patsy's cutting on a two hundred kilometre grid. Two hundred up, two hundred down. When she gets back to start of cut she won't be running more than a yard from true.*

She could cut on a five hundred kilometer grid, or a thousand, or ten. Distance is no object; all we need is a big enough planet.'

He thought, 'I'm not getting anywhere.' He walked back down the companionway to C deck bar.

The room was wide and long, panelled in satin-finish dural. He'd read some of the Russian combines used mahogany and brass. Windows looked out through the underpinnings of B deck, across the main coamings to the wheat. There were chairs and tables set round, Audubon prints in thin black frames. A coffee machine sang and glugged on the countertop.

O'Hara was playing the Bandit. As Harrison walked in it paid fifty. O'Hara grinned a pale, square grin and said, 'What do I do with these?'

Swissy said, 'Use 'em for washers. Good for de car.'

Harrison said, 'Pint of beer. No, the English.'

Swissy said, 'D'American is very good.'

'I'll stick with this.'

Swissy rubbed his hands. He said, 'A dollar. T'ank you.' He pushed the glass across.

Harrison leaned on the bar and lit a cigarette. Swissy said, 'Where's de li'l girl?'

O'Hara turned back from the machine. He said, 'She's developing.' He winked at Harrison. He said, 'No point keeping these. The crafty bastard won't change 'em.'

Swissy said, 'Give you two dollar for 'em. Haven't counted.'

O'Hara said, 'I'd rather put them back.'

Swissy said, 'Anyway, she's tuned. Pay for t'ree dollar.'

Harrison said, 'You put more than that in it last night.'

Swissy smirked. 'Was wit' syndicate,' he explained. 'Get t'irty per cent anyway. Can't lose if I play wit' four.'

O'Hara said, 'He doesn't understand his systems any more than anybody else.'

Harrison drank beer. He said, 'Got your pictures for today then, Mike?'

O'Hara considered. He said, 'I didn't see you when we turned on to cut, boyo.'

'Quite so. How was it?'

O'Hara said, 'Spectacular.'

Harrison drank another pint, which tasted good. The missed-breakfast feeling was starting to leave him. By the third he was feeling nearly human, which wasn't in all respects a good idea. He walked to C deck restaurant, ate *entrecôte* steak with a scampi starter. You could say this for combiners' food – it was reliable. He signed the bill for the company and walked back to the bar. He had a tour fixed for the afternoon; he'd arranged to meet an engineer called Bertie Pritchard.

Bertie was short, boyish, greying and relatively tired. He looked like an ex-Navy man. He spoke with an explosive punctuation that could turn readily to a stammer. They propped the bar up till three. Swissy was back on duty. He was talking about the last execution in Berne. 'Dey climb up de trees,' he said. 'All de boys, you know? So dey see into de prison yard. Christ, an' down dey come den. Like de blowty apples.'

Somebody laughed.

Bertie said, 'You never *saw* a bloody *execution*.'

Swissy grinned. 'My fader tell me,' he said. 'You know, a man get his head cutted off, he don't stop wit' de blinking?' He mimed, rapidly. He did in fact succeed in looking like a severed corpse. 'Blinkin' de eyes,' he said. 'An' de mout' go, so; and out de trees dey come. Christ, like apples.'

Bertie said, 'Who are you *with?*'

'World Geographic.'

'Good outfit?'

Harrison said, 'Fair. Like the rest.'

Bertie said, 'Christ, listen to the basstard.'

Swissy was saying indignantly, 'Is true. In Zürich, used to know dis chap was apprentice to a butcher. Dey used to drink a lot of blood, when dey killing de calf. Dey go *ksss* on de li'l calf, an' catch an' drink in de glass. Do 'em good.'

Bertie said, 'You are a *repulsive* basstard.'

'No, is true,' said Swissy. 'Can't help what he tol' me, only tell de trut'. All de time.' He smirked. 'You listen, Bertie, you find out a lot. Tell you lot o' t'ings you never hear of.'

Bertie said, 'If you've finished, we'll get out of here.'

Swissy said, 'Chow, bot'. See you next time.'

In the corridor Bertie said, 'Where do you want to go first?'

Harrison said, 'It's your tour.'

They walked forrard. Over a bulkhead door was a stencilled sign, *Crew Members Only*. Bertie ducked through. He said, 'Mind your head.'

Down here, the quality of sound was changed. There was a heavy roaring; Harrison guessed they were close to the main diesels. Bertie turned right and right again. There was a short companionway. He took it at the trot. He said, 'Links. Don't get your *feet* tangled up.'

The corridor, articulated, flexed slightly, moving with the movements of the combine. From somewhere came a faint, persistent squealing. Already, Harrison felt lost. He said, 'How long does it take to find your way about?'

Bertie snorted. He said, 'They're crazy f-fucking objects. Pointless complexity. All the same.'

Harrison said, 'What do they cost?'

'Twenty million. *Give* or take. Everybody gets a nice slice of the pie. Watch your *feet*.'

There was a final hatchway. Harrison stepped through, and stared. They had emerged in the forward casings, directly above the cutter service gantry.

The noise hit him first. It seemed compounded of all frequencies; hum of motors, whirl and clank of chains, *whick-hiss*, *whick-hiss* of the blades, echoing rumble from the combine's tracks. To right and left, long glints of daylight reached under the coamings. The air was yellow, fog-thick; through it the cutters glittered dully, spinning silver drums. Beneath his feet flowed a jostling brown river; the conveyors, edging the grain tons a minute to the threshers in the great belly of the machine.

He watched the men on the gantry. They wore one-piece suits of something that looked like asbestos. Visors covered their faces; on his back, each carried a bulky pack. Tubes from the packs dived beneath the wearers' armpits. Harrison mouthed a question. Bertie shook his head. He said, 'Self-contained systems. Ocy-nitrogen. You can't filter that muck. It gets in everything.'

Harrison said, 'What do these boys earn?'

Bertie said, 'A hell of a lot.' He leaned back, hands in his trouser pockets. He said, 'It's all right while it lasts.'

Harrison said, 'Silicosis?'

'There's quicker than that. Heard of combiner's balls?'

Harrison said, 'No.'

Bertie said, 'It means you don't have any. No skin on the tops of the thighs. It gets up inside the suits. Can't bloody stop it.'

Harrison said, 'They're welcome.'

Bertie said, 'They're the toughest basstards in the world.'

Near at hand, a crew was swinging a blade unit down into operation. One man was beating at the motor housing with a gauntleted fist. Harrison saw him raise his arms, make wash-out motions. He stared down. The movement of the grain beneath his feet was giddying.

Bertie said, 'Seen enough? I can't stand this bloody stuff for long.'

Harrison nodded, stepped back through the hatch. The engineer dogged it shut. The noise diminished. Harrison said, 'Christ.'

Bertie clattered ahead of him, down a flight of steps. At their foot, the decking surged unexpectedly. Harrison grabbed for the rail. Bertie said, 'This is E deck catwalk. We're alongside the threshers. Nothing much to see. The process is totally *enclosed*.'

The catwalk was long, and dim. They glided, it seemed, at eye-level with the wheat. Down here you could really hear the whisper, the sibilance. Glass panels were rigged at head height along the gallery. Harrison leaned close, stared into the endless brown-grey aisles between the stalks. Bertie said, 'That's *virgin*, of course. Julie's coming up from the west. We're cutting east, towards the *Russkie* patch.'

Harrison said, 'It's a new viewpoint.'

Bertie banged the screen with his fist. He said, 'We had to fit these last trip. Had some stupid little *bitch* of a journalist. She put her hand out in it. Said it reminded her of *punting*.' He tittered, soundlessly. 'You should have seen it,' he said. 'A little *blood* goes a long way.'

Harrison turned away. He thought, 'It's graceful, and soft. Touch it, and it opens to the bone.'

Bertie walked ahead. He said, 'This *might* interest you.'

Harrison watched the complex assemblage of levers. The whole device seemed to stride. A rod was poised, plunged into a gap beside the main housings. A pause; and the forward travel of the combine brought the links upright. The rod lifted, gleaming; a dark earth sample was ejected, whirled away, before the corer dipped again. Harrison said, 'What's it taking?' He was still thinking about the wheat.

Bertie said, 'They're checking soil organisms. Bacteria count. It's called a Tom Thumb sampler.'

He opened a bulkhead door. Beyond, a link corridor led to a big darkened space. Heat gusted back, heavily. Harrison saw steel drums rotating behind protective panels of mesh. Lamps gleamed here and there, red-mauve. Bertie said, 'The intake is damped south of the conveyors. Here it's irradiated, and *dried*.' He gestured at the lamps. He said, 'Pig-rearing lights.'

They walked on. In the combine's belly, sound levels varied continually. Sometimes the clatter of an auxiliary room drowned speech, sometimes the roar of the tracks. They walked down a serviceway, its floor panels composed of thick steel mesh. There was a rich, earthy smell; inspection lamps showed stubble flowing a yard beneath. Bertie ducked through a hatch. He said, 'Main tracks.'

The combine jolted and heaved. He reached back, steadied Harrison's arm. He said, 'OK?'

Harrison said, 'Yes.'

Bertie said, 'Don't want to have to scrape you off a bloody *bobbin*. Not while I've signed for you.'

The tracks were also lit. Harrison watched the steel rollers on which they ran bounce and jump. The links, each plate the size of a dinner table, rose up smoothly, passed out of sight overhead. He said, 'How many tracks does she run on?' Bertie said, 'They're rigged on twenty-metre centres. You can do the *sum* yourself.'

In the main diesel room an engineer wearing padded earmuffs waved to Bertie from his gantry. Bertie waved back. Harrison looked at his watch. Already they'd been an hour on the trip. Bertie closed the door behind him. He said, 'We're now going *afft*. Crew's quarters on the left, and sick bay. Laboratories to the right. Can't go there; not my patch.'

There was a door marked *Latrine, male. Field use only.* A part of Harrison's mind recorded the words.

Bertie said, 'When are you seeing the old man?'

Harrison said, 'Tomorrow morning.'

Bertie said, 'He's a queer basstard. Why they let him get hold of this thing I shall never know.'

They passed another door. Bertie said, 'Galleys. Bakehouse.'

Harrison said, 'I shouldn't think there's any shortage of flour.'

Bertie said, 'Under UN regulations, we can't touch our output. They fly the f-flour up from base. Amazing, the workings of the Oriental *mind*.'

There was light ahead. Daylight. He pushed a door open. He said, 'The ass-*end* of the process.'

Harrison walked to the rail. They were on the stern of the combine. Behind and above, unfamiliar from this viewpoint, the control bridge jutted at the sky. Astern stretched the great swath of stubble; again like a wake he thought, the wake of some ponderous geometric ship. Below him, slipways disgorged the produce of the machine like vast parcelled eggs, each pallet the size of a truck. Flying cranes were busy in the middle distance, droning like heavy dragonflies. He saw one settle its hooks into a bale, rise with it and lumber off to the south. The sun, already levelling, lit the great dustcloud, turning the grains to gold. As they entered the brilliance, the service vehicles became shadows. It was blue, and red of coamings, and gold; everywhere, the blue and gold.

Bertie said, 'As far as I'm concerned, you've seen the lot. Anything you want to ask?'

Harrison said, 'Later on maybe. I'm still taking it in.'

Bertie looked at his wrist. He said, 'Can you find your own way back? Got to meet another party. We ran a bit late.'

Harrison said, 'Don't you have a duty watch?'

Bertie said, 'I'm just the bloody liaison man. Tell 'em why the *wheels* go round.'

Harrison said, 'Thanks for the trip. I shall be OK.'

Bertie said, 'See you in the Swiss *Embassy*.' He ducked through the doorway, and was gone.

There was a seat, to one side of the observation deck. Harrison slumped on it, pulled his notebook from his pocket, stared at it for a time and put it away. He closed his eyes; and for a moment he was on a ship. She had just this same easy motion; the thunder of her diesels was muted, as it was muted here; and she was coming into Oban, from Mull. The sea was millpond calm, big vees of ripples starting and starting and spreading for miles. He thought, 'How often you hear that phrase, how seldom you see what it means.' He shut his eyes again. It had been bad all day. He thought, 'We were going there together, only you couldn't quite make it. You weren't on that ship, you bitch, and you are not here.'

Aloud he said, 'That'll do you a lot of bloody good.'

He leaned back, lit a cigarette. He was remembering Cheltenham, and the caryatid figures in the Colonnade, and buying the big buckled lovely handbag for her and the flat she'd taken in the town. He inhaled, blew smoke. He remembered the first months after the break-up. Time had telescoped; he'd lost nearly a year of his life. He hadn't believed such a thing was possible. He thought about the place he'd found in London, and the absurdity of it all, the sheer absurdity. Once, years back, he'd had a really bad pain. He remembered laughing jerkily, in the middle of it; it seemed a ridiculous state of affairs that any one thing could hurt that much. He thought, 'You sleep, not wanting to wake. But you wake. You get up, you get to the office, you trail back to your pad. You eat and speak and shave and wash and write words. Sometimes you can remember what you've done through the day. Sometimes you can't.' He remembered drinking sessions, sessions that started because the office had shut and just went on anyway; and empty Sundays and empty weekends and trailing out West for drag, the go-go dollies. He thought, 'Is there anybody anywhere, for whom pleasure is real, existence meaningful? What happens, inside Bertie? Inside Swissy? Is it any different for them?'

He glanced at the last thing he'd written that morning. *Distance is no object,* he read. *All we need is a big enough planet.*

He thought, 'I'm riding Combine Patsy. And Patsy is cutting a two-hundred-and-fifty-metre swath; and Patsy is a Wonder of the Age.'

Aloud he said, 'I couldn't bloody well care less.'

He looked at his watch. He'd caught himself wondering when the bars would open.

The sun was dropping toward the horizon. The air was keener now; astern, the dust-pall gleamed with a reddish light. He got up, walked back the way he had come. Finding his way through the combine's guts was a harder task then he'd realized. He passed along gantries he hadn't seen. Once he was challenged, made to show his press card. He got to his cabin finally. The thrumming of the walls felt familiar. He thought, 'Nearly like home.'

He took the Olivetti from its case, transcribed what notes he'd made. He added, *'It's the dust you become aware of. It's in the air, a grittiness on the lips. It creaks underfoot as you walk. Nothing's really clean. Put a saucer down for an hour and lift it and you see the yellow bloom, the mark of where it lay. And this is only start of cut.'*

He looked at his watch again. This past few months he'd got into the habit of marking the progression of hours and days. It was as if some bright point, some node of light and warmth, receded steadily; there was a compulsion to mark the regression. There were little anniversaries to be noted, transient things, affairs of hours, months. One day he supposed they would total years.

Loudspeakers were clattering somewhere in the combine. The sound reached him faintly, mixed with the humming of the cabin walls. He wrote, *'In twenty minutes, if my mathematics serve me, we shall end our first pass.'* He rose, took his coat down, put it on. He walked down the corridor, turned left and right, climbed the companionway to B deck.

The sun was low, the western hemisphere a bowl of dusty pink light. He thought, 'Red sky at night, climatologist's delight.' The upper works and rigging of the combine were sharp-cut against the glow. Forward and below, the light seemed to permeate the coamings; the figures on the cutter housings were haloed with brilliance. The combine roared steadily, still forging to the north.

Alison was leaning on the rail. He joined her. She put her hair back, glanced up and half-smiled. She said, 'It's queer somehow. Oppressive.'

He said, 'Did you get your prints done?' She nodded, not answering. He leaned on the rail. He thought, 'O'Hara gets an assistant. Maybe he needs one. I shouldn't take it out on her.'

The masthead lights began sequencing. He wondered vaguely why. The reflections hit her cheek and hair, scarlet, turquoise, scarlet, turquoise. He said, 'Was the stuff OK?'

She had a knack of not looking at him when she answered. She said, 'There's one advantage to big negs.'

'How do you mean?'

She said, 'You can always cut the middle out. It doesn't really matter where you point the camera.'

He thought, 'Maybe she doesn't like O'Hara. But everybody likes O'Hara.'

The bridge speakers clicked and began to breathe. This time there was no formal announcement; it seemed they'd merely circuited on to Control. A voice said, 'Two minutes from end of cut.' He heard Cheskin acknowledge.

A helicopter moved up overhead. The downdraught battered from the metal deck. He thought, 'They have to fly grid patterns too. Always this business about flattening the crop.'

The speakers clicked again and roared. The chopper pilot was talking through a hamburger. He said, 'End of cut, Roger.' The machine surged back, fell away into the gloom astern. A klaxon began sounding somewhere. Alison said, 'All this fuss, just for turning round.'

Harrison said, 'It's a big machine.'

She said, "They're just afraid they'll get on to somebody else's patch.'

Cheskin said, "Time me, please.'

Another voice answered. It said, 'Forty five seconds, and counting.'

The klaxon cut out. Cheskin said, 'Stand by all stations. Ready on mains.'

The speakers said, 'Cut end . . .'

'Cease cut.'

The trembling of the deck eased. The speakers said, 'Half-speed on starboard auxiliaries. Phase differentials.'

Harrison heard the engine stations acknowledge. He turned away, becoming bored. Cheskin said, 'Reverse starboard auxiliaries. All ahead port.'

A couple of stars were visible. Harrison watched their sideways drift. The big cauldron to the west was moving too, swinging round behind the bridge. The combine was vibrating, straining. From below came a confused roar. The speakers said, 'Ninety degrees. One hundred degrees. One hundred ten.'

'Quarter speed on starboard auxiliaries.'

The sunset light was beginning to creep in from the right of the bridge. The combine nosed, questing.

The speakers said, 'I have forty degrees. I have thirty degrees. I have twenty degrees. Line-up good.'

Harrison said, 'Have dinner with me tonight.'

She looked up at him. She said after a pause, 'Yes. All right.'

Something bumped in his chest. He thought, 'That's very odd.'

She said, 'Which restaurant?'

'C deck. They've got lobster thermidor. I don't know how old the lobsters are.'

She said, 'I'm a martyr to my stomach. I think I'm a compulsive eater.'

The speakers said, 'I have line-up.'

Cheskin said, 'All stations stand by. Confirm your line-up.'

The speakers said, 'Green board. I have line-up.'

Cheskin said, 'Outphase differentials. All ahead. Begin cut. Controller to log. Commenced second pass. I have eighteen, repeat eighteen, oh nine hours.'

She made a face. She said, 'Imagine that. Nine minutes late.'

O'Hara was weaving toward them across the observation deck. Harrison said, 'Where shall we meet?'

'Where do you want?'

He said, 'Swissy's bar. Twenty hundred.'

She said, 'You have a date.'

He went back to his cabin. He lay on the bunk and thought, 'One in the eye for you, Michael.' He lit a cigarette, smoked for a while. Then he shook his head, sat up. He rang the steward for a sandwich, said *'Gracias, Manuelo'* when it arrived and plugged in his shaver. He bathed and changed; by that time the wallclock read nineteen hundred hours. He picked up lighter and cigarettes, clicked the ceiling light off and walked round to Swissy's bar.

It was empty. Swissy was leaning on the counter reading a paper. He looked up and smirked. He said, ' 'Evening, Mr Harrison.'

Harrison said, 'Pint please, Swissy. English, not American.'

Swissy said, 'D'American is very good.' He drew the pint, set it on the bartop. He said, 'Looks good. Like in de picture house. Advertisement.'

Harrison lit a cigarette. Swissy said, 'Seen de paper?'

'What's new?'

Swissy said, 'Not'ing. Same blowty ol' t'ing. It don't go for my head.'

'What's that?'

Swissy said, 'Dey make big t'ing. Big fuss. 'Bout de combine. Dey say, Russia, America; blowty big row.'

'Where?'

Swissy showed him. The leader read:

Difficulties were prophesied today concerning the Russian-American grain link-up. Russia has lodged protests concerning what she describes as British-American infringements and infiltration. President Sukharevsky, in a strong note to the West, threatened Russian withdrawal from the World Food Council's biggest experiment to date, the Alaskan Grain Development Area. Harold Jenkinson, British Premier, expressed in the Commons his total disagreement with the Soviet attitude. 'The Alaskan Development,' he said, 'represents the biggest step so far in the cause of world unity and peace. The government of this country views these latest developments with disappointment, and grave concern.' Commentators feel the underlying cause of friction is the refusal of the United Nations select committee to accept Russia's demands for a controlling interest in the project.

Harrison put the paper down. He said, 'Like you said, Swissy. Nothing new.'

Swissy said, 'It be stupid. Blowty stupid.'

Harrison said, 'It doesn't go for my head.'

The dolly birds came in. They bought lager-and-lime and a Bloody Mary. Swissy said, 'I like to have dat one.'

'Which one? The blonde?'

Swissy snorted. He said, 'Ach, she be no good. Norwegian. Say, do dis, do dat . . . same like blowty German.'

Harrison said, 'Are you married, Swissy?'

Swissy shrugged. He said, 'Divowce. Only mistake I made.'

'How so?'

Swissy shook his head impatiently. 'She be no good,' he said. 'French . . .' He leaned on the bar and wagged a finger. 'I tell you dis,' he said. 'I never should have done it. Use to be on de boats. Go round de world, have a good time. Come back, to dis.'

Harrison said, 'Are you drinking?'

Swissy said, 'T'ank you. Have a half.'

Harrison paid. He said, 'Any children?'

'Ya, two,' said Swissy. 'Nice kids.' He produced a bulging, worn-looking wallet. He said, 'Nice kids, no?'

The pictures showed two rather chunky-looking little girls, the smaller gap-toothed. Both were dark. Harrison said, 'Why were you divorced?'

'Ach,' said Swissy, 'I don' know. Some t'ings go wrong, little t'ing, den get bigger all de time. Like I said, I never should leave de boat. Den she say, never should marry eider. I say bit late, bit blowty late for dat. Got de kids den, see? Working in hotel. Den a pub. Never was no good.'

Harrison said, 'Was this in France?'

'No, England. Cheltenham. You know it?'

Harrison said, 'I was there for a time.'

Swissy said, 'Have de children at school in England.' He waved his hand at the bar. He said, 'I do dis for dem. Make more money. Kids come first, all de time. Eh? Not so?'

Harrison said, 'I wouldn't know.'

Bertie came in. He said, 'Got it all written *down*?'

Harrison said, 'I'm working on it.'

Swissy said, 'Had a good day?'

Bertie said, 'Christ, no. Been trying to service an auxiliary since seventeen hundred. Wanted to pull it out of line, but that stupid basstard' – he gestured upstairs – 'won't have it. Says he's dropping behind schedule. As if it *mattered* . . .' He picked the paper up. He said, 'What's new?'

Harrison said, 'Why're you educating the children in England?'

Swissy said, 'Cause it's best. She start dat. De ex-wife. Maybe later I send 'em to Switzerland. I don't know.' He grinned. 'Christ,' he said. 'Have trouble wit' de family.'

'Why so?'

'Ach,' said Swissy, 'dey be pheasants. No, how you say dat?'

'Peasants.'

'Ah. Peasants. Be blowty peasants.'

'How do you mean?'

'Ah,' said Swissy, 'is difficult. Dey not understand. Dey t'ink I give de kids away.'

'You what?'

'Ah, well,' said Swissy. 'In my country, is no boarding school. State school only. All go dere, whatever parent. If you go odder school, eider parents dead, or prostitute . . . dat sort of t'ing.'

Harrison said, 'Can't you explain?'

Swissy said, 'My brodder understand. De rest . . . Christ, got two sister won't speak wit' me. I tell 'em, I no get de kids in de first place, den dere be trouble.'

'Because of being Catholic?'

Swissy brooded. 'Ach, yes, de Cat'olic,' he said. 'Be blowty rubbish.'

Harrison ordered another beer. He sat and wondered about his notes. The combine throbbed; but already it seemed he was accustomed to the noise. Only when he brought his mind back to it could he hear it. He thought, 'I should go on deck. Get the feel of the thing at night.' He remembered the reef markers. He'd been meaning to ask. He said, 'Bertie, those reef warnings. Are they necessary?'

Bertie looked at him blearily. He said, 'If you hit a b-bugger, you'd find out.'

'Can't the radar pick them up?'

Bertie said, 'Not under ten or twelve *feet*. These things only run a yard off the deck, and they're built of silver paper.'

'Couldn't they be levelled?'

Bertie said, 'If you'd tried picking all the rocks out of ten thousand fucking *miles*, you wouldn't ask.'

The Norwegian girl came to the bar with a glass. She said, 'Fill it, please.'

Swissy grinned. He said, 'For you, anyt'ing.'

Harrison drained his beer, lined up another. The bar was very quiet. The clock hands stood at 20.15. A couple of Americans drifted in. It seemed they knew Bertie. They sprawled across the bar, started an engineers' convention. He heard Bertie say, 'Well, what did you expect? The bloody *com* ring was shot.'

He wondered how long she'd be. He finished the beer, started on whisky. She walked in at 20.25.

She was wearing a little black dress. Her legs were delicious. Her hair gleamed; the bar lights made it look very blonde. Swissy grinned and said, 'Christ. Be all right wit' dat one.'

She said, 'I heard that, Swissy. 'Lo, John.'

He said, 'You're looking very nice, love.'

She said, 'I've got a great big ugly face. Compliments don't work.'

He asked her what she was drinking. She said, 'Scotch.'

He asked for a double. He said, 'How were the pictures?'

She perched on the bar stool. She said, 'I thought I wasn't going to make it. Big Brother wanted another batch put through.'

He laughed. He said, 'I thought you two got on.'

She said, 'He's the answer to the maiden's prayer. Didn't you hear?'

He stubbed his cigarette. She said, 'Have one of these.'

He lit up for her. He found himself starting to like her a little. He said, 'Where's the great man now?'

'Got a date. Or so he told me. I wished him luck.'

Harrison said, 'Swissy, do we have to book for the restaurant?'

Swissy said, 'Better, if you want table. No good eat at de bar. Not romantic.' He leered. He said, 'I fix it for you. Ten per cent.'

Harrison said, 'I'll buy your next beer.' It seemed a trite remark, and was. He thought, 'Maybe I'm talking too much. Which is absurd. I'm dead; so I can't be nervous.'

Swissy used the phone. He said, 'Ya, two. Chow, Man'el.' He turned back. He said, 'Got you corner table. Gipsy orchestra.'

Harrison said, 'Have another drink.' While Swissy was pouring he said, 'I wish you'd accept compliments. It's very unnerving.'

She said, 'I'm funny. Somehow I can never believe in them.'

He said, 'You don't like yourself all that much.'

She said, 'Not much. Not often.'

The clock had moved round to twenty-one hundred. Harrison said, 'Let's go on.'

She stood up. She said, 'I'll see you round there.'

He said, faintly surprised, 'I'll wait.'

Bertie looked up and smirked.

Outside, Harrison said, 'That little man did nothing but stare at your legs.'

'Which little man?'

'Bertie. In the corner.'

She said vaguely, 'Oh, he's not too bad.'

Harrison said, 'It was a comment, not a condemnation.'

Walking beside her, he was conscious for the first time how tiny she was. It had never appealed to him before. He caught a waft of her scent. He thought, 'It suits her.'

The restaurant wasn't too busy; half a dozen couples were eating, a few more sitting at the bar. The lighting was soft; they had no orchestra but piped music was playing. The tune was 'Blue Moon'. He wondered how old it was.

Manuelo showed them a corner table, held her chair. Harrison ordered Liebfraumilch. Manuelo offered him the glass. He sipped, knowing there would be nothing wrong. He said, 'OK, I'll pour.'

Manuelo said, 'Thank you,' and left them alone.

She said, 'Swissy said this means Maiden's Milk.'

Harrison said, 'I suppose it does.' He thought, 'You're not like her. But you could be her. Face not your fortune, but the same big eyes.'

Over the main course she said, 'I'm glad you asked me out.'

Harrison said, 'You can't really be "out" in a combine harvester.'

She shook her head. She said, 'O'Hara can be a pig. I was getting really tired of him.'

He said, 'There's an easy answer.'

She said, 'It's not easy for me.'

He said, 'It will sort itself out. How's the lobster?'

'Mmm. John . . .'

'What?'

She said, 'I am enjoying myself.'

He thought, 'This is one of those Rare Moments.' Later he said, 'We could dance. Only there's no floor. Only I don't dance.'

She smiled, and opened her cigarettes. He lit up for her. She said, 'Was Swissy telling you about his family?'

'Yes.'

She said, 'He's divorced, isn't he?'

'I think so. I can't work it out. He's Catholic.'

She said, 'If he married outside the Church he'd have been lapsed anyway. Technically, he was living in sin.'

He said, 'You know a lot about it.'

She smiled, and pushed her hair back. She said, 'I'm a Catholic. Or was. I lapsed about a year ago.'

Harrison said, 'Why?'

She lifted her chin. She said finally, 'I don't know. I just couldn't see it any more. It's no good just doing it.'

He said, 'How did the family take it?'

'They're still trying to get me back. It's quite difficult.'

He said, 'How old are you, Alison?'

She looked at him. She said, 'Twenty-five.'

He said, 'I'm sorry. That was rather personal.'

She blew smoke. She said, 'I'm queer. I was always the rebel. My brother's much more conventional. He went into the family business. I moved out. Came up to Town.'

He examined his cigarette. He said, 'I was trying to work this afternoon. It wouldn't come. I think the photographic section's doing better.' He watched the fall of her hair and thought, *'Get back behind me, you shadow, you bitch.'*

She said, 'It'll come. I wish I could do that sort of thing.'

He offered the last of the Liebfraumilch. She shook her head. She said, 'Thanks. Reached my limit.'

He drank, slowly. In the restaurant the roar of the combine was very loud. Beside him, the long windows were blue with night. He said, 'Shall we have coffee in the cabin? The steward will send it up.'

She watched him a moment. She said, 'If you like. Yes, nice.'

He said, 'This place thrums too much. It gets into one's head.'

She said, 'It is noisy, isn't it? I suppose you get used to it.'

She walked ahead of him. They turned right, and right again. At the door he reached past her to click the light switch. She said, 'Oo, this is nice. Good heavens.'

'What?'

She said, 'What's this?'

He took it from her, carefully. He said, 'Rule one. Or so I'm told. Never wave a gun about till you know it's safe to.'

She said, 'Is it safe?'

He broke the cylinder. He said, 'It is now.'

She said, 'What is it?'

He said, 'Smith and Wesson. Point four five five.'

'It's a revolver.'

He said, 'Yes.'

She said, 'I've never handled a gun before. It's a beauty. Can I close it?'

He buttoned the intercom. He said, 'Just push it shut.'

The steward answered. Harrison said, 'Gaelic, Irish or plain?'

She said, 'Just plain.'

He walked to her. He said, 'Can I show you?' He broke the revolver again. He said, 'It's a very old one. It's what's called a fixed frame. With a hinged frame, the chambers open upwards.'

She said, 'It's not much fun waving an empty gun about.'

He opened the locker drawer. He said, 'Here.'

She said, 'Gosh. Can I do it?'

He thought, 'I don't know quite what's happening.' He said, 'Go carefully, it's rather dangerous. Do it by numbers.'

She frowned, pushing the big cartridges home. Her hair fell forward, cascading. She shook it back. She said, 'Would it shoot now?'

He said, 'When it's cocked. So.'

She said, 'Oh, I see. The cylinder turns round.' She smiled. She said, 'I've found out about revolvers.'

He said, 'Hold it very carefully. Keep it pointing at the floor, else it's bad manners.'

She said, 'If I pulled the trigger now, it would go off.'

He said, 'Yes. But that wouldn't be a good idea so we'll . . . eject. So. Out come the cartridge cases.'

She said, 'I don't understand. Wouldn't they have been fired?'

He said, 'This part is the bullet. The shiny nose. This is the case. There's a cap at the bottom. When the pin hits it, it explodes.'

She collected the rounds carefully, gave them back. She said, 'It's safe now. Can I play with it?'

Harrison said, 'Most girls aren't interested in guns.'

She said, 'I'm not most girls.'

The steward buzzed with the coffee. She rolled back on the bed. She said, 'I'd like a gun. I'd like this one.'

'Whatever for?'

She said, 'To keep the ghosts away.'

He poured coffee. He thought, 'You are a funny little rat.'

She said, 'You know a lot about guns.'

'Not really. I think they're interesting.'

'Where did you get this one?'

He said, 'One of the German riggers at base. I think he was broke.'

She said, 'It would kill a person, wouldn't it?'

He said, 'I rather think it would kill anything.' He smiled. He said, 'Including ghosts.'

'Why did you buy it?'

He handed her the coffee. He said, 'It interested me.' He thought, 'What was it Hans said? "Your English law is stupid. Every man need a gun. For the one time." ' He said, 'For the one time . . .'

'What?'

He said, 'Nothing. Just a thought.'

She drew her knees up, sighted the revolver. He said, 'You look like Pussy Galore.'

She said, 'I feel like Pussy Galore.'

He thought, 'And the dynamo's running, you little bitch. But that's not possible.'

She said, 'You like nice things, don't you?'

'How do you mean?'

She said, 'Like the gun.'

He thought, 'This is out of the question, absurd.' He said, 'Alison, would you mind if I seduced you?'

She looked at him carefully. Then she put the Smith and Wesson down. She said, 'Not in the slightest.'

Harrison said, 'All right then. Better finish your coffee.'

She drank. He gave her a cigarette. They smoked for a while. Then he said, 'Were you serious?'

She said, 'Perfectly. Weren't you?'

He said, 'It was rather a silly question. I'm not sure how one goes about it.'

'Haven't you done it before?'

He said, 'I've been seduced. That's rather different.'

She put the cigarette down. She said, 'I don't want this.' She rose, walked over to him, sat on his knee. She said gently, 'This will do for a start.'

He lay back. She moved with him, softly. She was lithe, and light. She said, 'I'm sorry. I'm all hair.'

He said, 'Don't I know it.' He kissed her. She didn't mind his tongue. He found the cabin lights, dimmed to sleep level. In the half-dark, the thunder of the combine sounded louder.

She nestled, and kissed again. He found her dress clasp. She whispered 'No,' and didn't stop him.

The wine spun in his head. He said, 'Now I can say all the silly things. Like lovely, desirable, sweet. Nice little girl.'

She said, muffled, 'Nice big man . . .'

He stroked her, ran his fingers along her bra strap. He said, 'I'm not much good at this. Fumbly old job.'

The strap parted. She said, 'That wasn't bad for a novice.'

He worked her dress down, feeling satin skin. He thought, 'I'm going to go crazy with this, because it's too good. These things don't happen.' Aloud he said, 'Move your arms.'

'Why?'

'They're in the way.'

She whispered, 'Please. No, please John . . .'

'What's the matter?'

She said, 'It's silly. I'm shy.'

He said, 'You can stop if you want. I don't want to spoil any friendships.'

She said, 'It won't. Honestly. This is nice. Please, John . . .'

She kissed him, wound her arms round his neck. He pulled at the dress, carefully. She sat up then, shivering. She said, 'Well, this is me. For what it's worth.' And he saw it was possible for a blush to spread, across the neck, down the shoulders and back.

He said, 'You're very lovely.' He bowed his head. She squeaked; and he knew he had to be gentle. Incredibly gentle. Her body was like a tight-strung wire; he could feel the responses start, little jumps deep inside her. She said, 'No, please. Not down there.'

He said, 'Yes . . .'

She caught his fingers. She said, 'I've got you now. You can't get away.'

He used a trick. She said, 'I shall fight you . . .'

He said, 'Alison, fight all night. That's what it's all about.'

He held her again, carefully. She lay back, head against the chair. She said, 'You are nice.'

He said, 'Alison, come to bed.'

'No!'

'I shall say please then.'

'John, *no!* It's no good, I just get stubborn. It's too early . . .'

'Then we'll go to bed later.'

She said, 'I'm not ready. Don't try to make me. I shan't do it.'

He said, 'Love, no one shall make you.' He stroked her back, gentling; and she relaxed again. He thought, 'It could be her. She doesn't look like her, she doesn't act like her. But it could be her. I made it happen again.'

Her skirt had ridden up. She said, 'Don't look at me. I shall be decorous.'

He said, 'I'm enjoying you. Don't you like it?'

She said, 'No. Yes. I don't know . . .'

He said, 'What spectacular panties.'

She said, 'I'm a pantie fetishist. They always match my shoes. That's something you know about me now.'

He said, 'I shall blackmail you. Alison, come to bed.'

'*No!*'

'It's all right.'

She said, 'John, no. Don't do that.'

He said, 'You want it and you shall have it.'

'I don't. I don't.'

He said, 'Don't fib.' He thought, 'Three years. She told me it had done me good. That's why I left her. But she was right. I know it now, I know how to make it good.'

She started to struggle. He said, 'Aren't I doing it right?'

She said, 'You're doing it too damned well . . . John, don't make me . . .'

He said, 'Girlie, you're made . . .' and she was moving against him, arcing her body. She pushed her head back, soundlessly;

he thought, 'Contact contact, flaring bloody contact . . .' And it was over; she relaxed against him with the longest, deepest sigh he had ever heard.

Later he said, 'Did I hurt you?'

She nuzzled and whispered, not opening her eyes. She said 'Only in the nicest possible way.'

He laughed, in the near-dark. He said, 'Your bottom's cold.'

She said, 'It's the only part of me that is.'

He watched the clock hands move, feeling her weight against him, hearing the great thunder of the combine. Once she stirred. She said, 'It's been a long time. I was only eighteen . . .' He stroked her till she was quiet. Much later, she pushed away. She said, 'I'm going to be a nuisance. I want to go back to my cabin now.'

He said, 'Stay in this one.'

'I can't.'

'You'll be all right.'

She said, 'You don't know O'Hara.'

'This isn't to do with O'Hara.'

She said, 'He keeps asking me, everybody asks me. The boss asked me. If he found out . . .'

Harrison said, 'Even O'Hara couldn't be that big a bastard.'

She said, 'Care to bet? Please, John . . .'

He said, 'Nobody shall make you do anything, lovie. You know that. Here . . .'

She sat upright, tousled. She said, 'I'm all undressed.'

He said, 'I like you that way.'

Her eyes looked huge. She said, 'I didn't know there were men like you.' She kissed him again.

Afterwards, he eased her to her feet. She tidied herself. He said, 'Lights on?'

She said, 'Yes. Trying to . . . find my comb.'

He swirled brightness back into the little cabin. The walls were the same, the bulkhead clock and the bunk; yet it was all different. Alive.

She stumbled, trying for her shoes. He caught her. He'd known she would be giddy. He thought, 'I did it right. I did something right.' He said, 'You had a trip.'

Her eyes were very sleepy. She said, 'It was lovely. John, I must go.'

He walked her to her cabin. The corridor lights were dimming now, a part of Combine Patsy preparing for sleep. She opened her door, pulled him half inside, kissed him quickly with all her body. He said, 'My head will be rather full of you, of course. I shall want to see you. Is that proper?'

She smiled. She said, 'It's human. I never knew you were. Good night, John.'

He said, 'Good night.' He stayed till the door closed, softly; then he walked away.

In his cabin the bed was rumpled. He walked to the shower cubicle, rinsed his face and hands, lit a cigarette. He stood staring a while. The revolver lay where she had put it. He set it on the locker, twitched the covers straight.

Sleep was far from him. He walked back to C deck restaurant. The lights were out now, the place deserted. A bulb gleamed dully over the bar. Manuelo was drying a glass. He said, 'Coffee, Manuelo?'

The little man grinned and shook his head, jerked his thumb at the wallclock.

Harrison laid a dollar on the counter. He said, '*Por favor.*'

Manuelo grinned again, and walked to the dispenser.

He took the tall mug back to his room, sat and sipped. After a while he frowned, sniffed his sleeve. Her scent clung, faint and delightful. He thought, 'I was trying to make her. To fill a hole in my life. But I didn't know what she was like. I didn't know what she was going to be like.'

He drank again. After a while he thought, 'She trusted me. And she was shy.' The shyness had hooked him through the lip. He thought, 'The other thing was never like that. It couldn't be.' A ghost had faded, seeming past return. He thought, 'It was time. I went looking, and I made it happen again. A new thing.'

He finished the coffee, set the mug down, stood up. At the door he thought, 'That wasn't her voice. Those weren't her eyes. It was all new. Like a flower, opening in the hand.' He wondered, 'Are they all like that? When they're loved?'

He climbed to B deck. The air was rushing, intensely cold.

Above, the bridge superstructure slid against an incrustation of stars. Darkness seemed to enhance the sense of speed. He saw the combine now as a great entity; he knew her blades spun and roared, her dynamoes hummed, her sensors probed with their electric fingers. He felt the exultation grow, and let it well. He thought, 'I paid for tonight. It's mine.' He saw, with heightened vision, Combine Patsy and her sisters; Julie, Susannah, all the rest, strung like beads of light and warmth against the moving dark. He thought, 'I'd forgotten. I'd sunk into the pit, and didn't know my need; and her hands raised me, unbeknown.' He thought, 'It flies at sense and logic; it flies in the face of reason. But we love; and we rejoice, because it sets us apart from the beasts.'

In the east, already, a new dawn was making. The night air was reaching him; he stubbed his cigarette, and turned away. He thought, 'We reap, and we thresh; grain for half the world. We are the Grain Kings, raised of old; and I a new God. A giant God, who was dead.'

2

He lay for a while in a floating half-awareness before opening his eyes. Sunlight slanted into the cabin from the one square port. The patch vibrated slightly, moving with the movements of the dural wall. He turned his head. The Olivetti stood on the side table; on the locker was the Smith and Wesson. These things pleased him. He studied them a while, unmoving. His awareness, his sense of colour and form, seemed unnaturally sharp.

The wallclock read 09.15. The intercom buzzed; he reached for the cord, lazily, thumbed the switch. The speaker said, 'Good morning, Mr. Harrison. Asked me to call you.'

He said, 'Joe. *Gracias.*'

He rose, padded to the shower cubicle. The stinging needle-points enlivened him. In the cubicle the hum of the combine sounded loud. A can of shaving foam clattered softly against a glass shelf. He towelled, shaved, got out clean shirt and shorts, dressed. He found himself humming, vaguely, the theme from Thomas Tallis. He thought, 'That's good music. English west country music.' He picked up his jacket, stooped to wriggle heels into shoes. He'd thought he would never go into the west again. Maybe now he would.

He let his thoughts drift round to her, by slow degrees. Before he'd kept her out of his head, deliciously. He looked round the cabin. He thought, 'She was here, and she was naked. Funny little rat.'

He walked to C deck restaurant, ordered coffee, cereals and toast. He ate slowly, smoked a cigarette. At eleven hundred hours he was due to meet Controller Cheskin. He walked to the observation deck. The combine had turned once more on to a northern pass. He thought, 'Three since start of cut.' The sky was bright steely-blue, the red bridge coamings sharp-cut in sunlight. He watched rigging shadows move, thin dark stripes against scarlet paintwork. The wind buzzed faintly in the mast struts. The morning was very fair.

He thought, 'Maybe she's sleeping it off.'

He walked back to C deck bar. The place smelled of polish and dust. Except for one of the American engineers, it was empty. Swissy grinned at him. He said, 'Here he come. De great lover.'

He was faintly startled. He said, 'What?'

Swissy said, 'How you get on wit' her? De li'l girl?'

Harrison said, 'We had a nice evening.' He settled himself on the bar stool. He said, 'Not beer, Swissy. Fruit juice.'

Swissy stopped, hand over the pump. He muttered, 'Got to keep up de strengt'. . .'

Harrison nodded vaguely. He was remembering the smoothness of her skin, dimly seen, the firm fullness under her scanties, later the bursting of soft dark down between her thighs. He thought, 'These are my memories. It happened. Nobody can take them away.' He sipped orange juice. He thought, 'I feel for her, rushingly. I didn't know how much I wanted her.' The images would revolve now quietly, hour on hour, till he saw her again; as she had lain quiet in his arms. He thought, 'The smell of her was like a drawer of linen. Clean, lavender-fresh.'

Swissy said, 'Been up top?'

He said, 'It's a great morning.'

Swissy leaned on the bar. He said morosely, 'All right for some. I gotta work.'

Harrison said, 'I'm working all the time, Swissy.'

Swissy said, 'Yeah. T'ink about de li'l girl.'

Harrison said, 'You've got a one-track mind.'

The American glanced at his watch, nodded and strolled out. Swissy said, 'I t'ink after all I go back to de boats. Had good time den, real good time. Used to stop 'Frisco, Honolulu. Christ, was a place, dat. I t'ink I go Tasmania, or New Zealand. Lovely country.'

Harrison said, 'Why'd you leave home anyway, Swissy?'

Swissy said, 'Oh, some t'ings go wrong.'

'Family?'

'Ach, no. But some odder t'ing. Dey be pheasant anyway. I t'ink, fowk 'em. You know? See a bit of de world. Five years I was on de boats. Den I come ashore. After dat, go to England. Christ, was bad t'ing, dat.'

The wallclock pinged. Harrison said, 'Got to go. Seeing the old man. Keep my seat warm.'

Swissy said, 'Chow.'

At the bridge steps a guard with UN tabs on his shoulders scanned his press card. He said, 'Wait, please,' and walked away. Harrison stood idly, heard an intercom buzz. The guard came back. He said, 'Follow me, please.'

Here, higher in the combine, the endless sway and roll were more evident. Harrison glanced round him. Officers' country seemed no less spartan than the rest of the machine. He was high above the wheat; a port gave him a view of it, like a sparkling, brilliant-yellow plain.

The guard tapped a door, opened it. He said, 'Mr Harrison, sir.' Harrison stepped through.

The cabin was wide, and carpeted. To one side a wallfire glowed cheerfully; above it was an oil painting in a heavy, ornate frame. There were cupboards of china and glassware; shelves held a further display. Cheskin sat at a polished desk fronting the great range of windows. He rose as Harrison walked toward him, and held out his hand. He said, 'Mr Harrison, how pleasant. World Geographic, I believe.'

Harrison said, 'I'm delighted to meet you, sir.' His mind was far away; down maybe with the racing, rolling wheat.

Cheskin said, 'Be seated, please. A drink?'

Harrison said, 'Thank you. Thanks very much.'

Cheskin said, 'Whisky perhaps.' He tinkled liquid from a decanter. He said, 'Your British whisky is the finest in the world.' He handed the glass. He said, 'Through peat, and over granite. I believe these are the requirements.'

Harrison smiled. He said, 'I've been told so, sir.'

Cheskin nodded briskly. He said, 'You will excuse me for not joining you. For me, it is a little early.' He pushed a box of cigarettes across the desk. He said, 'I have visited Scotland. A most lovely country. Sometime I hope to return, for the salmon fishing. Do you fish, Mr Harrison?'

Harrison said, 'Last time I tried, I managed a pike.'

Cheskin said, 'Ah. Yes.' He leaned back. He said, 'Have you been well looked after?'

Harrison said, 'Excellently. Mr Pritchard has been most helpful.'

Cheskin said, 'Good.' He steepled his fingers. He said, 'First, a few facts about myself. I am, as you undoubtedly know, Russian by birth. America has been for many years my country of adoption. I am a biologist and agriculturalist; during the Moscow crisis I served in the Russian army. My rank was colonel.' He smiled. He said, 'And you?'

Harrison said, 'Rather an ordinary sort of background, sir. Agricultural degree, then jobbing journalism here and there. I'm afraid I haven't led too adventurous a life.'

Cheskin said, 'I see. It is better that we know just a little of each other.'

Harrison's eyes had wandered. Cheskin caught the direction of his glance and turned. He said, 'Ah, the painting. Are you knowledgeable about paintings, Mr Harrison?'

Harrison said, 'Not really. But I think that's very unusual.' He was in a mood to be pleased by anything. He said, 'It's rather lovely.'

Cheskin smiled again. He said, 'It is not lovely. Rather, it is ugly. This is why I keep it.' He rose, walked to the picture. Its colours were sombre: flat reds, and browns. A table was set with a candlelit meal; a shirt-sleeved man sprawled across a bed, holding a stick over which a fluffy white poodle leaped. Cheskin said, 'It is, of course, a facsimile. The original was painted shortly before his death by a great Russian artist, Pavel Fedotov. You have perhaps heard of him?'

Harrison said, 'I'm afraid not.'

Cheskin said, 'He is not known much outside Russia.' He turned back to the canvas. He said, 'At twenty-five, Fedotov was a brilliant young officer of the Finlandsky Regiment of the Royal Guard. At thirty-seven he was dead, a pauper. This he produced in the last year of his life.'

He reached to touch the carved gilt frame. He said, 'The officer is drunk. The surroundings are squalid, suburban. As the dog jumps the stick, so his master is driven by boredom. By ennui. He too is a victim of his circumstances.'

Harrison said, 'I don't think I quite follow you, sir.'

Cheskin said, 'Though Fedotov was great, his life was wasted. The canvas serves to remind me of this. Effort misdirected is wasted. We must see clearly, rejecting dreams and the fantastic, holding at all times to the realities we perceive. We must not become such a man; jumping sticks, though we think we hold them for others.'

Harrison said, 'You seem very . . . aware of your homeland, sir. Have you never wished to return?'

On the desk was a silver-mounted photograph. It showed a blonde, plumpish woman with a dog. Cheskin frowned across at it. He said, 'While my wife lived, perhaps. Now it would be pointless.'

Harrison said, 'I'm sorry, sir. That was extremely personal.'

Cheskin shook his head. He said, 'This is a part of your profession.' He turned to the shelves. He said, 'Here is something that may interest you. It is very rare.'

Harrison rose, walked to him. The Controller lifted a glass drinking vessel, turned it in his thin fingers. He said, 'It is a joke, really, on the part of the glassblower. It was made sometime in the early eighteenth century. Above the goblet, you see, is a fabulous beast; you would call it a chimaera. To taste the wine, you must press your mouth to his. His body fills, as if with blood.'

Harrison took the piece, carefully.

Cheskin said, 'These are modern works, by Tatyana Navrina. The city in which she was born is now called Gorky. Its folk-art is well known in Russia. Here you see a circular composition. Tatyana shows us the fox, the hare and the cockerel. Famous beasts in our folklore. They chase each other round and round, merrily. It is pointless and gay; yet also perhaps a little sad. Like a fairground entertainment.'

Harrison said, 'Do you have a large collection, sir?'

Cheskin said, 'I have a house in America. In New Jersey. Most of my pieces are there. These few, my favourites, travel with me.'

He walked back to the desk. He said, 'A little more whisky. Now, to your article. Have you collected all the information you will need?'

Harrison said slowly, 'I've collected a lot of information. I think the problem now is putting it together, making a shape. I was looking for something to peg the facts on, to get all this across. Maybe a theme.' He took the plunge, feeling good. He said, 'Yesterday I thought I'd got it.'

Cheskin said, 'Ah, this business of a theme. I find it most interesting. You had thought perhaps of a ship? Or an aeroplane?'

Harrison said, 'I suppose everybody does.'

'Yes,' said Cheskin. 'This is most important. Remember the painting. There are no themes; merely realities. This is a large combine harvester. With a model number, known characteristics. I can give you rates of cut and thresh, length of cut, passage time on cut, estimated return to Grid Base. Are these things not enough?'

Harrison said, 'I'm not sure.'

Cheskin said, 'You thought in higher terms? In terms of significance, of poetry?'

Harrison said, 'Don't you approve of poetry, sir?'

Cheskin smiled fleetingly. He said, 'There is perhaps a poetry. Unheard, unsung.' He brooded. He said, 'No. I have no objection to poetry. But it is necessary to apply the proper labels. We should know at all times with what we are dealing.'

Harrison said, 'I'm not quite with you, sir.'

Cheskin said, 'There is your English author, Kipling. You have surely studied his work. He might perhaps render such a theme. He understood much of machines.'

Harrison said, 'I'm afraid I'm no Kipling, sir.'

Cheskin said, 'Perhaps that is as well.' He turned the cigarette box thoughtfully in his fingers. He said, 'In Kipling's work the machines are made to speak. They cannot; but the poet is skilful, and so we believe. Soon too England speaks, as an old grey Mother. The sea speaks to the Danish women, declaring itself a rival for the affections of their men. The little banjo speaks; and what a harmless instrument! So the world, which is as it is, becomes re-peopled; with mirages, and Gods. Soon, for us, stones speak and trees; we feel the touch of phantom hands. Here is a paradox, Mr Harrison. We do not worship stones and trees; yet we listen to our poets.'

He rose, stood back turned, staring down across the miles on miles of wheat. A buzzer sounded on the bridge; Harrison heard the vague pealing of an intercom. Cheskin said, 'For me, the Grain Development Areas represent new hope. Here for the first time our many peoples work together, truly together, for the universal good. Here perhaps, if you search, you may find your poetry. This too is why none of us must be blinded. We must see, very clearly, what we do. We must see it as a good thing, perhaps a great one; but we must find no mystery. Moon and sun do not tug our brains, as they tugged the brains of earlier men. We reap, and we thresh. We are neither Gods nor ants. Our machines are our machines. As in this, so in our lives. Our hands work, our will directs the hands. The rest, our conceits, our grand words, are luxuries. We cannot permit ourselves such luxuries, Mr Harrison, if we are to survive.

Dreaming, we are unaware; from unawareness spring grief, disaster, despair. For our own sakes, we must not dream.'

Harrison said slowly, 'I'm sorry if my ideas annoyed you, sir.'

Cheskin turned, and smiled. He said, 'I am not here to approve or disapprove of your ideas, Mr Harrison. I am not a censor. I merely warn.'

He walked back to the desk. He said, 'And now, if you have finished your drink, I will show you Control.'

At lunch, Harrison ran into O'Hara. He was sitting at a corner table in C restaurant, forging his way through a steak. He waved a fork, a chip impaled tastefully on the prongs. Harrison joined him, not particularly wanting to. He said, 'Hello, Mike. Where's Alison?'

O'Hara watched him palely. He said, 'I'm keeping her busy. It's good for her waistline.'

Harrison ordered Dover sole and a glass of wine. He steered the conversation on to safer grounds. There had been times when he'd felt a compulsion to belt O'Hara on the nose. Today, he might just do it.

He made his escape as soon as he decently could, walked round to C deck bar. Bertie was in evidence. He said, 'The *wanderer* returns. Have a beer.'

Swissy pulled a pint. He said, 'Is paid for.'

Bertie said, 'How'd you get on with the old man?'

Harrison said, 'This is good Russian beer. From the banks of our own Volga river.'

Bertie tittered. He said, 'I know the feeling.'

Harrison said thoughtfully, 'He's a strange bird though. I can't make out whether he loves Russia or hates it.'

Swissy said, 'All Russians funny bastard. Why he is hating it?'

Harrison said, 'I don't know. I had the feeling they maybe got rid of his wife.'

Swissy said promptly, 'Better off be single anyway. Dat way, get no trouble. Tell you sometimes, all de blowty trouble I have. Better off stay in Switzerland.'

Bertie said, 'If you will *do* these things . . .'

Harrison said, 'Are you married, Bertie?'

Bertie said, 'Yes, worse bloody luck.'

Swissy said, 'It don't stop him none.'

Bertie drank beer. He said, 'We've got a *treat* coming up this afternoon. We're meeting the Russians. Did he tell you?'

Harrison said, 'Yes. When will it be?'

Bertie said, 'Fifteen hundred hours. Or should be. We're getting near the end of the *patch*. We swing round north tomorrow. Start cut two.'

Harrison said, 'Are the Russian combines any different from ours?'

Bertie said, 'They cover the *ground* a bit quicker. Got a modified pickup system. They're bloody cagey about it too.' He drained his pint, and pushed it across for a refill. He said, 'You'll get a good enough view anyway. They should pass two swaths out.'

Swissy said, 'Funny bastard, dese Russian. Get on better wit' de German.'

Bertie said, 'You *are* a fucking German.'

Swissy said, 'I be Swiss German. You know dat.'

Bertie said, 'Oh Christ, don't *start*.'

Swissy said, 'I don't start not'ing. Is big difference. You go to Switzerland, you find out.'

Bertie said, 'You go to Switzerland. You're so bloody *fond* of it.'

Harrison looked at the clock. It read 14.30 hours. He wondered about Alison. He said, 'I'd better get on deck.'

Bertie said, 'That's what everybody will do. You'll get just as good a *view* from here.' He set his beer down, lit a cigarette. He said, 'What *did* the old man talk about?'

Harrison said, 'Mainly a painter called Fedotov.'

Bertie tittered again. He said, 'I expect you saw his glassware.'

'Yes,' said Harrison. 'I did.'

Folk began drifting into the bar in twos and threes. Harrison walked over to the windows. Bertie followed him. He said, 'Bring us a couple of beers, Swissy.'

Swissy said, 'You come fetch 'em. Odderwise, plenty more bars.'

Bertie said, 'Oh, do the *other* thing then,' and muttered something less detectable.

The wheat flowed past beyond the main coamings, silently. At 14.55 the intercom speakers crackled. They said briefly, 'Combine Valeri is in sight from Control, and will pass on schedule.'

Harrison wondered again about going up to B deck. He thought, 'Maybe she's there.' Then he remembered, if she was O'Hara would be with her. He decided to stay put.

Just before fifteen hundred somebody said, 'There she is.'

The combine was still well ahead, but coming up fast. Behind her, her dustcloud was a dark yellow funnel trailing on the land. She was big; God, she was big. She made Patsy, ungainly as she was, look elegant and low. On her side she wore the hammer and sickle of the Soviets, above it a big red star. The rest of her was grey; workmanlike, and blank.

Somebody said, 'Here comes bloody St Basil's.'

Bertie said, 'They were putting *onion* domes on 'em last year.'

Harrison said, 'Why did they stop?'

Bertie said, '*Track* weight became *excessive.*'

She passed abeam, trailing the long dustcloud. Somebody said, 'That's it then.' On Patsy's bridge a loudhailer was working faintly.

Bertie turned and shouldered his way out of the crowd. He said, 'That's damn funny.'

Harrison said, 'What's funny?'

Bertie said, 'She was cutting a swath too close.'

Swissy said, 'De blowty Russians never could steer. Not even de aeroplanes.'

Bertie said, 'I'm going to look *into* that. See you blighters later.'

Harrison walked to B deck, stood on the starboard wing. The combine had certainly passed a single cut away. He stared astern. The Russian was still visible, small with distance. The dustcloud smoked away across the stubble. Beyond, the land lay brown and bare to the horizon. He walked to the forward rail. The double swath remaining stretched like a golden road. Nothing to be seen; just the endless perspectives of the land, shimmering a little with heat haze. Patsy thundered steadily.

The bridge intercom had been left live. The speakers clicked and said, 'Mr Puustjärvi to Control, please. Mr Puustjärvi.'

He didn't feel like work. He walked down to D deck. They had a little gift shop there. It sold corn dollies, paperbacks, wooden Russian toys. He thought, 'Flowers were out, anyway. Right last time. Not this.'

A showcase held bracelets and some jewellery. He glanced across the display shelves and said, 'Good Lord.'

The stewardess smiled professionally. She said, 'Can I help you?'

He said, 'Does this shoot?'

She lifted the tiny revolver out. She said, 'They're bracelet charms. They fire blanks.'

He said, 'I shouldn't think they need a firearms certificate.'

She said, 'They didn't say anything when we bought them.'

He said, 'How much?'

'I think there's a ticket. Nine dollars fifty.'

He said, 'You've sold it.'

He walked back to his cabin, lay on the bunk, took the little pistol from its box. It had a hinge-frame action. He broke it and loaded carefully. The tiny thing made a very respectable crack. He thought, 'Good for the littlest ghosts anyway.'

He put the charm in the side locker, picked up his notebook. He made a rough draft of the conversation with Cheskin. At the end he wrote, *Strange to see the china cabinets. Impress of a personality that still isn't Western. After all these years.*

He pushed the papers aside, thought for a time. Then he reached for the intercom lead, pressed the button. He said, 'Joe, do something for me.'

'Certainly, sair.'

'Page E deck. Miss Alison Beckett.'

Joe said, 'It shall be done.'

The wallspeaker was covered by a plain grey grille. It clicked twice and buzzed. Then it said, 'Hello, John.' The voice had an unexpected huskiness.

He said, ' 'Lo, Alison. How's things?'

A pause. The speaker said, 'Fine.'

'Busy?'

She said, 'O'Hara took a lot of shots of the Russians. We're just starting on them.'

He said, 'Shall I see you this evening?'

'Mmm. Yes. Where?'

He said, 'Swissy's bar. About twenty hundred. We can go on a pub crawl.'

She said, 'Done. Sounds lovely. John, I have to go now.'

He said, ' 'Bye, Alison.'

The speaker said, 'See you later. 'Bye.' It clicked, and went dead.

He walked to C deck restaurant, ordered a coffee. He sat over it a while before going back. He spread the notes out, lit a cigarette and daydreamed. He wasn't seeing Cheskin's cabin. He thought, 'The hell with it. It's there to be enjoyed. Like the aftertaste of brandy.' He thought, 'I still can't believe it. But it happened.' Aloud he said, 'You never know what another person's like. Maybe a lot of chances get dropped that way.'

He started on a first draft of the article. It ran well. He read it back, made his corrections, started again. At eighteen hundred hours he bathed and shaved. He walked round to Swissy's bar. In the corridors, evening light lay flaring. Where sunlight hit the satin-finish panels they glowed with minute grains of gold. The noise of the combine was a steady muted rumble.

Bertie was there. He seemed a bit the worse for wear. Swissy had a copy of the *Swiss Observer*. He said, 'Dere. Tell you all about it dere.'

Bertie said, 'The one thing that's always struck me as *curious* is why nobody ever really understood the William *Tell* legend.'

Harrison said, 'What do you mean?'

'Well,' said Bertie, 'look at it this way. For the sake of a few bob a *week*, the basstard was prepared to risk nailing his son between the eyes with a bloody iron bolt. That's the Swiss for you. They haven't altered.'

Swissy said indignantly, 'He be blowty good bloke. I tell you.'

Bertie said, 'Why, you ass . . . oh, what's the use?' He drank his wine, grimaced, and pushed the glass across. He said, ' 'Nother glass of your exorbitant *plonk*. This time, try filling it.'

Swissy shook his head. He said, 'Drinking too much, Bertie. Too much not good for you.' He recorked the bottle, looking pained. He said, 'Anyway, what about ol' Winkelried?'

Harrison said, 'Never heard of him.'

'Ach,' said Swissy. 'All de schoolchildren, dey learned him. Was a battle sometimes, can't remember when. Against de Austrians. Austrians had de long spear, what you call it?'

Harrison said, 'Pikes.'

'Ach. Pikes. Anyway, was no good. Swiss only have de ball wit' spikes. So dey have to make a gap. An' Winkelried say, "Look after de wife an' kids." Den he take all de spear to himself, to de chest. An' de odders run over him.'

Bertie said, 'I can see *you* doing that. Why don't you try?'

Swissy said, 'Christ, no. But was a good chap. He say just like dat, "Look after de wife an' kids . . ." '

Bertie said, 'You *told* it once.'

O'Hara walked in. He slapped Harrison on the shoulder. He said, 'Here's the man who chats up my assistants.'

Harrison thought, 'One day I'll kill you and slice you, you bastard, and eat the strips. And I shall enjoy them.' He said, 'Have a beer, Mike.'

O'Hara sat and swung his legs. He was looking well manicured. The love life must be prospering. He said, 'You'll not get anywhere with her, boyo.'

Harrison said, 'Maybe I'm not trying to.'

O'Hara said casually, 'She's damn near married anyway. Reckon they'll get spliced next trip. Bloke out in Gloucestershire somewhere, breeds horses. Old man's got a packet. Didn't she tell you?'

Harrison looked at his shoes. He said, 'I don't really know much about her.'

A klaxon sounded overhead. Feet pattered on the decking. The bridge tannoys said, 'Duty officer to Control, please. Emergency stations.'

Bertie said, 'Christ.' He put his glass down and ran for the door.

Harrison swung off the stool. O'Hara got ahead of him. He turned right and left, following the Irishman. They collided on the companion steps. O'Hara said, 'No fucking camera.' He ran back the way he had come.

B deck was filling. Somebody pointed. They said, 'Right up. Up ahead.'

Bertie was back, with a pair of heavy prismatics. He trained them and swore. He said, 'The *basstards* shouldn't be there at all.' He handed the glasses across.

She was big, as big as the last. To Harrison she looked like a great lurching biscuit tin on tracks, grinding across the land. He lowered the glasses. She was easily visible now to the naked eye. He stared behind him, up at the bridge windows. There was a pale blur that could have been Cheskin's face. The light was fading fast, dying in long swaths and banners. The dust-cloud ahead caught the last of the sunset, glowed orange against dull red. To right and left the stubble shone darkly, like a land-scape seen on Mars.

The bridge klaxons blasted, driving sound at Harrison's shoulders and back. The intercom speakers said, 'All stations stand by. Maintain revolutions.'

The loudhailer seemed to solidify the air of B deck. The words rolled into distance, a barrage of thunder. Harrison said, 'What's he saying?'

Bertie tittered. He said, 'He's telling 'em to *f-fuck* off.'

Harrison said, 'She's on the next swath. She'll pass us.'

Bertie said, 'She's too close in. She's not even on the *grid*.'

The loudhailer bawled again, fell silent. The Russian machine was closing fast now. The light gleamed on her bridge wings and coamings. In the sudden quiet, the roar of her engines sounded clear.

Bertie turned, stared up at the bridge. He said, 'The crazy *basstard*.'

Harrison said, 'Why doesn't he swing?'

Bertie said, 'Because he can't, he's too bloody *late*.'

The Russian was nearly alongside. A final flurry from the loudhailer; and Cheskin spoke suddenly and urgently in English. He said, '*Emergency. Collision drill. Clear all starboard catwalks. Clear starboard casings. Hurry, hurry.*'

Harrison saw figures run crouching along the cutter housings.

The grey superstructure reared beyond the bridge wing. Identification letters slid by; vast, curling, Cyrillic.

Patsy jarred, and shook. There was a report like a cannon shot, and another. The crowd on B deck surged back. Harrison saw steel handrail rise into the air, loop jerkily. The catwalk sheered, thunderously, back towards the stern. Something hit the deck wing. A glass screen starred and shattered.

Alison was there, holding his arm. He pulled her back instinctively, swung her away. Wire thrummed overhead. Bertie yelled, 'She's clear. She's clear . . .' The superstructure was diminishing, sliding out of sight behind the bridge.

The deck wing was a mess of wire and glass insulators. Somebody said, 'We got her aerial array.' Bertie spoke feelingly, glaring up at the bridge. He said, 'I hope he broke *all* his fucking pots,'

The speakers said, 'Damage reports to Control, please. Reports to Control.'

A crewman was wrestling with the coils of thick wire. Another swore and turned, showed a wrist dribbling scarlet. Alison said, 'Oh, God . . .'

Swissy was there in his white jacket, stogie clamped between his teeth. He said, 'Blowty Russians.' He turned to Harrison, grinning. He said, 'Like blowty Brand 'Atch. . . .'

The speakers said, 'Controller Cheskin. There is no major damage. There is no emergency. I repeat, there is no emergency. Please return to your quarters. We are continuing on cut.'

Bertie said, 'There'll be bloody *hell* to pay for this.'

Harrison swallowed. He said, 'Are you all right?'

She said, 'Yes. Yes, I'm OK.'

He said, 'Better come and have your drink. I think we need it.'

She shook her head, pushed her hair back. She said, 'In a minute. Got to go somewhere.'

He said, 'Are you sure you're all right?'

She said, 'Honestly. Go on down. I'll come.'

The bar was packed already. The American engineers were making most of the noise. A red-necked man with cropped hair was saying, 'Sons of bitches Russians.'

Swissy alone seemed unruffled. He was saying, 'Blowty Brand
'Atch' again. The phrase seemed to have taken his fancy.

Bertie was scribbling on the back of an envelope. His shoulders
were shaking. Harrison jostled his way to the counter, called for
a beer. He said, 'Why didn't he turn?'

Bertie said, 'Because he's bloody *mad*.'

Harrison said, 'What's so damn funny?'

Bertie seemed to be having difficulty controlling himself. He
said, 'The Russians cut to a complicated *pattern*. Two ahead,
close, and a follower. Always groups of three.'

'And?'

Bertie said, 'Well, we've encountered and *dealt* with two . . .'

It dawned. Harrison said slowly, 'Then there's –'

Bertie nodded. He said, 'Another basstard somewhere dead
ahead.'

Harrison said quietly, 'How long?'

Bertie said, 'You can't be sure, of course. O seyen hundred
tomorrow. Give or *take* . . .'

Alison was back. She said, 'O'Hara's gone temporarily
insane.'

'What for?'

'He wanted to wire his pictures out. There's a clampdown.
Official news agencies only.'

Harrison said, 'We're not a news team anyway.'

She said, 'That's what I told him.'

He said, 'So the pictures . . .'

She said firmly, 'Can wait till morning. I've had enough of
friend O'Hara.'

Swissy leered at her. He said, 'Here dey are. De love
bird.'

Harrison bought a whisky. He said, 'I tried to book a call to
the old man. The booths were too crowded.'

She said, 'O'Hara did it for you. They'll page you when it
comes.'

He said, 'That was extraordinarily good of him.'

The bar was getting fuller than ever. He was jostled, beer
spilled on his sleeve. The red-necked man was saying, 'Shoot
the bastards then. All the bastards.'

Somebody said, 'Anyway, why the hell'd they let Cheskin get Controller?'

The red-necked man said, 'Sucking the bastard British.'

Harrison said, 'Let's try D deck. We can still have our crawl.'

She said, 'It won't be much better.'

Harrison said, 'We can try. Chow, Swissy.'

Swissy said, 'Chow.'

D deck bar was quieter, to his surprise. She perched on a bar stool, looking fairly at home. He hadn't had a chance to see her properly before. She was wearing a fawn sweater, a tiny kilt with a big cress pin. She looked about eighteen. He watched how her hair moved against the woolly. The texture contrast pleased him. He said, 'You were terrific last night.'

She frowned. He said, 'Don't you want to talk about it?'

She said, 'It isn't that. You took me by surprise.'

He said, 'What?'

She turned her glass round on the counter. She said, 'I didn't know you thought of me like that. It never showed.'

'Like what?'

She said, 'Well, as a woman.'

He thought, 'I can't have come back, after all these years, to this same arid place.' But his mind had spun already, added and made a total. He thought, 'I can't believe. I won't believe. It's a joke that's gone bad, through too much laughing. Just a joke gone bad.'

He smiled and said the first thing that came to him.

'Manuelo wants to buy the gun.'

She grasped the subject-change eagerly. She said, 'It fascinated me. I've never handled one before. I'd love to fire it, just once.'

He said, 'You were very good with it. But I don't think you'd like it when it went off.'

She said, 'I wouldn't mind. Not if I was ready.'

'You'd flinch anyway.'

She said, 'Is that wrong?'

Harrison said, 'It makes you miss the target.'

He opened his cigarettes. She said, 'No. Have one of these.'

He lit up for her. She blew smoke. She said, 'We could have

done it just now, if we'd known the collision was coming. Nobody would have heard.'

He thought, 'Stop being desperate; for your sake, if not for mine.' He said, 'It's already an international incident. It would really have loused things up if the Russkies found a forty-five slug stuck in the works.'

The intercom speaker said, 'Mr John Harrison, World Geographic. International call.'

He said, 'Excuse me.' There were booths outside in the corridor. He walked to the nearest, closed the door. They took a time establishing the connection. Finally London came through. He listened and said 'Yes' several times. Then he put the handset down, stood staring at it. He thought, 'The mouth moves, and the facial muscles. The words form, while the odds increase to the power of n. Then you walk away. They call it maturity.'

He went back to the lounge. He said, 'That's about it then.'

She said, 'What's happened?'

He said, 'I'm being recalled. They're sending a bigger gun.'

'Who?'

He said, 'Bill Goldie.'

She made a face. She said, 'When do you have to leave?'

He said, 'Day after tomorrow. They're flying him from Tokyo. I take the helicopter back.'

She said, 'I think we're stopping on.'

He said, 'I think so. From what they said.'

She looked at him blandly. She said, 'You're not getting all up tight about it, are you?'

He stared back. He thought, 'Just twenty-four hours, and I've learned you all over again. My ducky little ball of solid brass.' He said, 'No, I'm not getting all up tight.'

She said, 'I'm sorry about on deck. I was scared.'

He said, 'You had every right to be.'

'I didn't think Swissy would ever stop laughing.'

Harrison stubbed his cigarette. He said, 'Would you like to eat?'

She said, 'Not tonight, honestly. I couldn't.'

His skull felt blocked; too much personal stuff going through.

He remembered Bertie and his envelope. He wondered if he should tell her. He said, 'What do you want to do?'

'I don't know. I don't mind, really.'

'Shall we go back to Swissy's?'

She brightened. She said, 'I like him. Yes, all right.'

Outside he said, 'I'm afraid it wasn't much of a crawl.'

She said, 'I'm enjoying myself. I just don't show things much.'

The Americans had gone. Bertie still sat at the bar. He looked in a bad way; his eyes were starting to run. Swissy said, 'Ah, here she come. De untouchable one.'

Alison said, 'Supposition, Swissy. Mere supposition.'

Bertie brightened momentarily, and greyed back over.

Swissy said, 'I was just telling Bertie here, 'bout dis duel. Last duel dey ever have, in Switzerland.'

Bertie said cloudily, 'Another of his horrible *bloody* stories.'

'No, is true,' said Swissy. 'Interestin'.' He turned back to Harrison. 'Dey have de doctor dere,' he said, 'an' one man, he get de end of his nose cutted off.' He started to giggle. 'An' before dey can sticked it back on,' he said, 'is eaten by de Alsatian dog.'

Alison said, 'I still don't understand about bullets. About part stopping in the gun.'

Harrison started drawing on a beermat.

Later she said, 'I know the lot. Matchlock, wheellock, flintlock, percussion cap. Then bullets. The percussion cap's still a bit dodgy.'

Harrison said, 'They only get more complicated. Just remember all guns are really clockwork.'

She said, 'I like finding out about totally new things.'

Swissy said, ' 'Bout time you give me de bar back.'

The time had passed, as any time passes. Harrison stood up. He said, 'G'night, Swissy. Bertie.'

Swissy said, 'Chow.' Bertie hiccuped faintly.

Outside she said, 'Bertie always looks so unhappy. Like a singularly mournful puppy.'

Harrison said, 'Maybe he is unhappy.'

They'd reached his cabin without the question being raised. Which he supposed was another hurdle crossed. He thought,

'I'm not going to leap on you now every time I get the chance. But you're not to know that, of course.' He opened the door, thumbed the lights to full. He said, 'Coffee?'

She sat on the bed. She said, 'Please. I mustn't be long, though. I feel whacked.'

He murmured something like, 'I wouldn't wonder.' It didn't much matter what he said; he'd lost interest in the words.

She drank her coffee, when it came. Afterwards he held his hand out. She looked uncertain. He said, 'Nobody shall take your clothes off. I won't let them.'

She walked to him, sat across his knees, relaxed. The pressure was back, and the warmth. She looped her arms round his neck and said, ' 'Lo.'

He kissed her. Her mouth was very soft. He thought, 'Here we are again then.' He said, 'Were you very mad?'

She said, 'I'm never mad. I just don't react when I should. I think there must be something wrong with me.'

He thought, 'If I stayed surprised for two hours and twenty minutes, I should see a doctor.' He touched her knee.

She said, 'No, John, please. Not tonight.'

He said, 'Very decorous.'

She said, 'I just wanted body contact. It's comforting.'

They lay silent. He watched the wallclock and rubbed her behind. Finally she stirred. She said, 'I was so worried.'

'What about?'

'You. And us. Being friends.'

He said, 'As far as I know, nothing's altered that.'

She said, 'I just don't know about . . . being lovers. I've had so many.'

He said, 'Lovers?'

'No, boys. Well, men. I didn't want you hurt.'

He thought, 'You lying, two-timing bitch and mother of bitches to be, that is the bloody last straw.' Aloud he said, 'I wouldn't worry too much about me.'

She pushed against his shoulder. She said, 'I'm better at . . . well, talking. I'm a great free thinker. That's why it wouldn't be fair.'

'What wouldn't be fair?'

She frowned. She said, 'The physical attraction thing. It always goes. It's only once. Then . . .'

He said, 'It must be very frustrating for you.'

She said, 'I've lost a lot of friends that way.'

He thought, 'How much do you want? Just how much?'

She drew her finger across his lips. Then she put her mouth up. He evaded her. She punched his chest, chuckling. She said, 'Oh, you . . . man . . .'

The wallclock pinged. He thought she'd move but she didn't. After a while she said, 'I don't think I shall ever marry. I don't know. I'm too independent or something. It just isn't me.'

He said very gently, 'My dear, all I have done so far is remove your knickers. There are rather a lot of steps between that and publishing the banns.'

She stiffened, and relaxed. He thought, 'You put your hand out to the flower; because it's perfumed, and lovely, and you're human. And you feel the cold, bristling worm. At last, I know the Enemy.' He felt tireder than he had thought possible; he wanted her weight, that was just a weight, shucked off.

He massaged, gently, the firm swelling of her woolly. She half put his hand away. She said, 'Don't, please.'

He said, 'This isn't sex. This is friends.'

She said, 'It's in between.'

He thought, 'And you're starting to tighten behind the nipple.' He said, 'Come on. I'm taking you home.'

She sat up carefully, smoothed her skirt. She said, 'I shall have to find my comb.'

They walked up to B deck. The diesels roared, in the night. Overside, lamps were slung. Riggers were working, swinging in belts over the moving stubble. Most of the rubbish had been stripped clear. The combine's side gaped for thirty yards or more, iron brackets showing like bones.

The sky was crusted with stars. Not the same stars. She looked up. She said, 'What a lovely night.'

He walked her to her cabin. She stepped forward, kissed him quickly. She said, 'Good night. And thank you.'

He thought, 'And that, God preserve us, was the Regretful Parting Peck.'

He said, 'Good night.'

He walked back to his pad, sat on the edge of the bunk. Then it hit him. He thought, 'Last fling of lonely middle aged man.' He picked the revolver up, broke the cylinder, loaded five. He closed the piece and cocked, hearing the creak of oiled steel. He laid the gun to his face, felt coldness touch temple and cheek. He thought, 'I should have barrelled her across the ear and got stuck in while she was giddy. It would have come to the same thing.' He broke the gun, worked the ejector. The cartridges fell to the bedcover, lay fatly shining. He got up, opened the locker door. The whisky was two-thirds gone. He slid the big gun into his pocket, walked to C deck restaurant. Manuelo was closing up. He said, 'Manuelo. Bottle of whisky. On my bill.'

Manuelo grinned, made a note on a pad. Harrison took the bottle. He said, '*Gracias*. And Manuelo . . .'

'Mr. Harrison?'

He held the revolver out, butt foremost. He said, 'Here'

The little man's face lit up. He said, 'Mr. Harrison. *Gracias, gracias.*'

Harrison said, 'Good night, Manuelo.'

He walked back. On the way he thought, 'To her, it's dirty. She couldn't step right out. They never do.' He opened his cabin door, sat on the bunk. He raised the bottle, squinted through it at the ceiling light. He thought, 'When she hooks her Mister Right, it'll still be dirty. Only there'll be children, for excuses.'

He finished the whisky, cracked the new bottle. He thought, 'There's two cold spaces now. Hers, and the gun's. Odd to become attached to a material object. Any object.'

The wallspeaker clicked, hummed a moment and faded. He thought, 'Odd, too, what a jump that should give the heart.' Later he decided he had imagined the sound. He thought, 'We could have worked. For a little while. Now all the rest comes back. Like rubble, cascading in the mind.' He said aloud, 'I wonder if he did break his bloody pots?' He remembered the Fedotov painting. He'd thought he'd been doing the taking. But he'd been giving again. So much more than he could afford. He said, 'Now, I jump the stick. It isn't even original.'

His lids felt warm and heavy. He lay on the bunk knowing he

wouldn't sleep. The combine was a monstrous weight, useless tracks grinding, useless blades spinning, useless bolts and nuts and chains and levers and wheels. He thought, 'Cheskin knows. As well as I.'

He palmed the ceiling light to dim. He didn't want any more whisky; and he wasn't drunk. He lit a cigarette. The first drag brought phlegm up into his throat. He finished the thing anyway, lay back. The cabin walls trembled and thrummed. He closed his eyes and remembered how her bare hip felt under her skirt. He said, 'Get out, please God. Get out, get out, get out of my skull.'

He fell asleep.

The cabin was grey, when he opened his eyes. He felt chilled to the bone. Maybe the air conditioning had failed. He swayed upright, glared at the clock. He thought, 'Another day, another dollar.'

The hands stood at 06.35. He said, 'In time for the show.' He walked to the shower cubicle. He looked as rough as he felt. He shaved, washed his face, changed his shirt. He thought, 'Last night little Alison bestrode the grain, and was a Queen. Her eyes were stars, her flesh the good brown earth, her hair the golden crop.' He slapped his pockets, located matches and cigarettes. He thought, 'I saw a goddess, from old time. She enjoyed the touch-up.'

The corridor vibrated faintly. He closed the cabin door, turned left and right. He thought, 'One thing, only, is dirty. And that she didn't do. She'll give herself clean, the bells will ring her clean. They call it morality.'

He said, 'And I let her get away with it.'

B deck was crowded. The figures stood muffled, not speaking, watching to the north. The light was growing, across the waste of stubble. He thought, 'Bertie wasn't the only one with an envelope and pencil.'

He stared ahead. There was nothing. The dawn-streaks in the sky were high, clear green. He thought, 'Maybe she isn't on track. Big anticlimax kick.'

Beside him stood the grizzled engineer he'd spoken to on the first day. He said, 'There's nothing there then.'

The man sucked his empty pipe. He turned, looking faintly

surprised. He said, 'They've had radar contact for half an hour. She's there. Reciprocal course.'

High in the combine's rigging a red light started to blink. It lit the backs of the people on the deck. The engine beats stayed steady. He wondered about Alison. He thought, 'If she needs a pair of comforting arms, there's always O'Hara.'

The wind stung his eyes. He rubbed, peering. There was something, after all. A smudge, on the wide, smudged horizon. On Patsy's mast, the identification lights started to sequence. The smudge made no response.

He could see her clearer now. High and square, like her sisters. Bone-pale. Somebody said in a conversational voice, 'Vostok class. Combine Ilya.'

Harrison looked back at the bridge windows. There were faces, staring ahead. He heard the loudhailer circuit start to breathe. The engineer said, 'We're privileged. We're seeing the start of World War Three.'

The path, the swath of uncut wheat, stretched ahead. The gap was closing now with increasing speed. Harrison clenched his fingers on the deck rail. He thought, 'He understands; and I know him. They took his wife, they took his birthright. Now they take his grain.'

He could make out the long rectangles of the bridge windows. Below, the Russian's forward coamings looked higher than the deck on which he stood. He thought, 'Combine Ilya.' The words made no particular sense.

The bridge speakers said, 'Eight hundred metres, sir. Closing speed constant.'

The loudhailers rumbled briefly, and were quiet. The engineer said wonderingly, 'Right on our bloody track.'

The combine was towering now against the horizon. Seen head-on, her silhouette was oddly complex. The speakers said, 'Five hundred metres, sir. Closing speed constant.' The voice was starting to edge up in pitch.

Cheskin said, 'Main beams, please.'

Brilliance burst, above Patsy's cutter coamings. The Russian's bridge windows reflected back a dazzled glare. The speakers said, 'Three hundred metres, sir . . .'

Abruptly, the combine bucked. A rumbling; then a tearing, crashing shock. The deck rail hit Harrison in the chest. He clung, stupidly. Somebody yelled, '*Reef*...' Round him people were tumbling stiffly, legs and arms thrust out. He saw the forward casings fly apart, plates hang in the air like petals of a red steel flower. Something black came ploughing and shrieking. The air was full of din. On C deck promenade the windows bowed and banged.

He saw the body fly out below him, plunge to the main coamings. It seemed they opened to receive it, snapped like a mouth. The victim poised a moment, impossibly. The eyes blinked rapidly; it was as if Swissy once more gave his impersonation of a severed head. Then he was gone, into the tracks.

The emergency beacons were glaring, orange-pink bowls of fire. The klaxon sounded, huge and harsh. The Russian was slowing, slowing. Her prow reared over the coamings like a grey-white cliff. Then she was halted; and the noise of her many motors was a roaring, confused and dim.

The bridge speakers said, 'Emergency procedure, all departments. Give me full dampdown, please.'

There was a deepening whine as Patsy's diesels died.

Harrison laid the suitcase on the bed. He sorted used shirts, shorts and socks, slipped them into a polythene wrapper. He folded handkerchiefs and ties, packed a box of quarto and half a dozen books. He closed the case, slid it to one side. He sat at the table, sorted the transcript sheets into order and pinned their corners with a staple. Somebody tapped the door. He said, 'Come in.'

It was Bertie. He sat on the bunk for a time and puffed. He said, 'Christ almighty, what a bloody day.'

Harrison said, 'There's some whisky in the locker.'

Bertie poured two fingers. He said, 'I don't know where the other *glasses* are, you'll have to get your own.'

Harrison helped himself. He said, 'Cigarette?'

Bertie said, 'Not at the m-minute.' He drank Scotch, grimaced. He said, 'D-did you see old Swissy take a dive?'

Harrison said, 'Yes.' He looked at the papers, frowned and

laid them aside. He said, 'Were there many other casualties?'

Bertie said, 'Six in the cutter casings. They're still picking the *bits* out.' He stared at the Scotch. He said, 'Christ, I needed that.'

Harrison thought, 'I wish there was something I could think of to say. But it doesn't get to me. Any of it.'

Bertie said, 'Swissy's a lucky basstard.'

Harrison turned. He said, 'That's one way to look at it.'

Bertie said, 'Quite seriously. The basstard got away with it. They got him out. I think he lost a foot.'

Harrison said, 'Good God.'

Bertie finished the whisky at a gulp and stood up. He said, 'I've got to get on. Just thought you'd like the news.'

Harrison said, 'How badly are we damaged?'

Bertie said, 'It just about took her *guts* out. H-hell to pay.' He shook his head, clucked sorrowfully and closed the door.

Harrison called sick bay. The speaker said impersonally, 'The patient is sleeping. His condition is satisfactory.'

Harrison said, 'Thank you,' and broke the link.

The wallclock pinged. He frowned at it. In thirty minutes Cheskin was due to make a statement. He wondered if there was anywhere he could get a beer.

C deck was a shambles of girders and wire. To his surprise, the bar door was ajar. Manuelo was behind the counter, shovelling glass into a bucket. He said forlornly, 'Not much on, Mr. Harrison. All bottles go smash.'

Harrison said, 'Christ, what a mess. Any beer?'

Manuelo said, 'American.'

Harrison said, 'That's fine.'

He walked to the windows. The glass had gone. Below, they had a heavy tackle rigged. Crewmen were lifting aside a buckled hatch cover. Ahead, the forward coamings were split as clean as by an axe-cut.

He finished the beer, got another. A tired-looking party of men came in. They were blackened with oil, one had an arm bandaged. Manuelo said, 'Sorry, sirs. American beer only.'

Harrison lit a cigarette. Sun patterns were moving on the

dural walls; the polished panels glistened. He took the glass back to the counter, walked up to the bridge.

A flying crane was hovering alongside the combine. The downdraught beat at his clothes. He showed his pass to the security man, stepped into the cabin. The crane moved away.

The place was hazed with cigarette smoke. He found a seat. The dolly birds were there; one flashed him a frozen sort of smile.

Cheskin was sitting behind the desk. He said, 'Mr Harrison. Now, I think we are all here.' He looked at a paper. He said, 'At o seven fourteen hours this morning, the combine ran foul of a hitherto-unmarked reef. We have sustained heavy damage to engines and plant, and can no longer function as a field unit. I regret to inform you that nine lives were lost. Under the circumstances, other injuries were remarkably slight.'

Somebody said, 'Have the Russ – the Russians been helpful, sir?'

Cheskin said, 'A medical team from Combine Ilya is at present working with our own sickbay staff. The seriously injured are being flown to base hospital. We are in contact with combines Maya and Valeri. Both have offered assistance, which is not at present required.'

An American said, 'Can you define our present position more closely, sir?'

Cheskin said, 'Certainly. We are proceeding to base under our own auxiliary power. Tankers are withdrawing reserves of diesel fuel, which may not be jettisoned in this area. Civilian personnel will not be evacuated; there is no danger, and the situation is under control.'

Somebody said, 'Can you tell us anything as yet about the Russian encroachment?'

Cheskin turned. He said, 'It is by no means certain an encroachment has taken place. It is possible a computer error was responsible. At the moment this is my personal opinion, and is not for publication. A full-scale investigation will, of course, be held.'

The American came back to the attack. He said, 'This reef, sir. Was it not detectable by radar?'

Cheskin said, 'Under the circumstances, no. It was masked by the bulk of the approaching vehicle. Yes?'

The question was barbed. 'Under the circumstances, I'd say this machine was a write-off. Where do you put the blame?'

Cheskin glanced up tiredly. He said, 'An investigation will be held. Until its findings are known, I cannot answer you.' He paused. He said, 'I am Combine Controller. I will naturally assume such responsibility as may be necessary.'

There were other questions. They tended to pass Harrison by. Finally Cheskin looked at his watch. He said, 'I have to inform you full communications have been restored. You may cable your stories if you wish. Thank you, gentlemen. And ladies.'

There was a rush for the door. Harrison let himself be left behind. At the door he turned. He said, 'Controller.'

'Mr Harrison?'

Harrison said, 'Had the reef not intervened, would you have closed down?'

Cheskin rose, stood hands clasped behind him. He stared down for a time at the ruined deck. Finally he turned. He said, 'I find your question difficult to understand. There would, of course, have been no other choice.'

Harrison said, 'Thank you, sir.'

Cheskin nodded. He said, 'Goodbye, Mr Harrison.'

Harrison walked back to his cabin, stood staring. But the packing was finished. He thought, 'Once more, I'm killing time. It does seem a waste.' He got the Olivetti out, started reworking his notes. He thought, 'While I'm doing this, the thing's still alive.' Finally, he got himself a meal. He had to wait a goodish while; C deck restuarant was still suffering malfunction. Afterwards there was some whisky to finish. He sat and swilled the glass round and thought, 'So life goes on. Habit is a wonderful thing.'

The intercom buzzed. He thumbed the control, said, 'Harrison.'

The speaker said, 'Mr Harrison, this is Sick Bay. We have a Mr Hauser asking for you; are you available?'

He thought, 'I don't know a Mr Hauser.' Then he remembered. He said, 'I'll come at once.'

C deck looked tidier now, but D level was still a shambles. Repair crews were working with cutters; he stepped over a mess of cables, ducked through a bulkhead door.

He nearly ran into her. She said, 'Oh . . . hello, John.'

He smiled. He said, 'All right?'

She said, 'Just about. I got knocked down. I'm bruised all over.'

'How's O'Hara?'

She said, 'Developing. The scoop of the year.'

He said, 'I'm going to see Swissy.'

Her eyes widened. She said, 'I saw it. It was horrible. You mean he's not . . .?'

He said, 'Apparently, he's still kicking. With one foot.'

She said, 'I'll come too.'

Harrison said, 'I don't suppose they'll mind.'

Emergency beds had been set up in the corridors. There was a clanging and clattering of trolleys A nurse met them; a striking girl, dark-haired and high-cheekboned. On her shoulder tabs were neat red stars.

Harrison said, 'A patient was asking for me. Mr Hauser.'

She said, 'Yes.' She smiled. She said, 'I'm sorry. Small English. With me, please.'

She walked ahead, opened a door. She said, 'Doctor say – very short.'

Harrison said, 'Thank you.'

The room was tiny, not much more than a cubicle. Swissy looked very sick. A cage had been rigged over his legs; beside the bed a blood drip was set up.

He said feebly, 'Ah. De love bird.'

Harrison said, 'How are you, Swissy?'

He said, 'Had a foot gone. Christ, when I go t'rough dat t'ing, I t'ink dat's it. No more take de piss out of Bertie.'

Alison said, 'I'm . . . terribly sorry, Swissy.'

He waved a hand. He said, 'I get over it. Same like everyt'ing else.' He closed his eyes, wearily. He said, 'Always a way. Eh? Not so?'

Harrison said, 'Is there anything we can do?'

Swissy said, '*Ya*.' He fumbled beside the bed, held out an envelope. He said, 'Little t'ing. You don't mind?'

Harrison said, 'I don't mind.'

Swissy said, 'Dey fly me out tomorrow. Don' want de kids to know. Tell 'em myself, in a bit. But dey need money.'

Harrison said, 'I'll go and see them.'

Swissy said, 'No, don't matter to see 'em. But send it on. Is in dollar. OK?'

Harrison said, 'OK.'

Swissy said, 'Christ, dat li'l one . . . only twelve, but she know how to spend. Know what she want already.'

Harrison said, 'It'll be done. Get some rest, Swissy.'

Swissy said, 'Ain't got much blowty choice . . . 'Bye, Al'son. Don't do not'ing I wouldn't.'

She said, 'Chow, Swissy.' She walked through the door. Harrison closed it after her.

She leaned on the wall and rubbed her face. He said, 'Are you all right?'

She nodded. She said, 'I just don't like hospitals.'

They walked back the way they had come. He said, 'I'm flying out tomorrow.'

She said, 'Yes. I know.'

He said, 'Meet me for a drink tonight? End-of-term party.'

She said, 'I suppose so . . . Haven't you got a lot to do?'

'It's done. Goldie takes over, anyway.'

She said, 'Swissy's bar. if it's open. About twenty hundred.'

Harrison said, 'OK.'

She said thoughtfully, 'It won't seem the same.'

He said, 'No. It won't.'

He walked back up to B deck. He was surprised, vaguely, to see it was evening already. The combine was heading nearly due west across the miles of stubble. He turned away from the pouring redness. A hundred yards off, a massive recovery tractor paced the crippled machine. A helicopter swooped low, belly lamps winking. He leaned on the rail, watched the slow flowing of the ground. He missed, now, the thunder of the mains; Patsy seemed somehow less than half alive, a crawling red shadow in the dusk.

A tanker moved away, left behind a rich gust of fumes. As the light faded, the torches working on the ruined forward housings sprang into prominence. He watched the white glare shift and flicker, the sparks fall like hot coals. He stayed still a long time, smoking, till the land was wholly dark.

The wind was rising, keening in the rigging. He pushed his jacket sleeve back, looked at his watch. He walked to his cabin, used the dry shaver and washed. He went to the locker, slipped the little charm into his pocket. He thought, 'We must be ships, passing in the night; but elegantly, so elegantly. Nobody gets hurt.'

Halfway to C deck he thought, 'I hope she's stood me up. It's about time.' But he pushed the door open knowing she would be there.

She wasn't *that* kind of girl.

I Lose Medea

The first trouble was the ghosts. You wouldn't think a field of cloth of gold would get itself all that haunted but there they were all right, whole formations of them drifting round like smoke puffs and congregating above the hedgerows. I drove from the gate bumpety-bump, clank, bump, up across the swell of land to where you could see the barrows in the distance and the big stone circles crowning the downs, and the glower low down on the horizon that meant just there was the sea. Then Medea said, 'Stop, this is fine.' I don't know how she could always tell the exact place she wanted to be. I stopped the car and put the engine off and sat a minute thinking, 'We're here. We got here at last.'

But the light looked as if it was nearly ready to fade so I didn't fancy sitting around too long. I got out and unlocked the boot and pulled the lid up and Medea started throwing canvas out on the grass in rolls like big grey sausages. Then there was the holdall with the mallet and the spare hanks of nylon line and all the framing and stuff. Some of the framing was round and some was square, I could never remember at the start just how it all went except there were two big wishbone-shaped pieces that made the tent gables. I found the bits for them and fitted them together and laid them out alongside the rest.

Medea was looking good, she was wearing white stretch pants and a dark blue top and had a kerchief bound through her hair. When she squatted and started pulling the canvas into shape you could see a big half-moon of brown back. She got the tent laid out OK, then she changed her mind and said we were pitching wrong way on the slope or something and started in again turning it all round. This was the thing about Medea, she never had much of a sense of time.

The ground sloped down towards the back of the field and there was a high tousled hedge with a gap in it and a stile, and a couple of trash bins stuck at angles in the grass. I looked across and started feeling a bit annoyed because the smoke puffs were separating above the hedge and quite a few starting to drift our way. Medea got the tent lined up and crawled inside with the ridge-pole and one of the uprights, you could see the canvas writhing round like a sack with a good-looking ferret in it. I'd have nipped in after her but I was getting worried about the ghosts, one or two of them were looking nasty. There was one big grey chap with horns, I could see from his expression he was just looking forward to coming over our way and dropping a hundredweight of fog on top of us which was all we needed. I called to Medea to hurry up a bit and she said something muffled inside the canvas, something about having got the wrong pole. I couldn't see how that could be because she'd got all the sections marked with bits of surgical tape with numbers on them, and tied in bundles with lengths of the nylon cord.

The big chap was certainly extremely nasty but fortunately for us he was none too well organized. He'd got himself caught up on the briars and stuff in the hedge, he'd get one part free then something else would catch and he'd roll over snapping and writhing like a horizontal column of bonfire smoke. But I could see he was making it by degrees and I was getting really mad with that slow old Medea. Thing is, your own Field Spirits take over as soon as you've got something up that looks vaguely like a roof and then you're OK, but till then they're just plain disinterested. You can be anybody's meat, whether you're on their patch or not.

Some of the nasties were fairly close. I broke up a couple of little ones with one of the awning stays and swirled them round a bit on the grass but there were some bigger jobs I didn't fancy tackling on my own. I turned the car round to point at the hedge and put the headlights on to main beam. The big chap flattened and streamed down the other side out of sight, but I knew that wouldn't last for long. I called to Medea to come out. I said, 'I'll get the thing up, you do the other stuff. We're getting surrounded here.'

She crawled out with her jumper pulled half up her back and her hair all tousled. She had a whole bundle of bits in the car, crucifixes, lightning conductors, old cavalry sabres, that sort of thing. She started walking round sticking them in the grass and muttering. She set up an interesting crossfire of emanations, but I couldn't see the effect lasting much longer than the headlights so I humped into the tent and started straightening things out. The tent was one of those with a built in groundsheet which are fine when they're up but can be a nuisance if you don't know for sure what you're doing. I got the upright located and stood up and slipped the ridge pole on top and called to Medea to put the end guy on and a couple of side lines, and after that it wasn't so hectic. With the second upright in place the tent ridge filled out nicely and the Field Spirits there were a pair of them, husky-looking blighters as far as you could see went thundering down past us cracking whips and such and the locals just shredded up and blew. The big chap went really amorphous, the last I saw of him he was streaming off into the valley like a snake of thick white mist. He was mad too, he kept looking back at us with his yellow eyes. Somebody was in for a bad night, but as it wasn't us I didn't worry too much.

I'd got pretty hot and sticky, pitching camp is not a thing I go for though it's usually worth the effort afterwards. Also cloth of gold is great stuff but hell to get pegs into. I bent three all up and had to knock 'em straight again with the mallet, but eventually things got more organized. Medea had unloaded the rest of the stuff from the car, the twin-ring burner and the lamp and the big gas bottle and hanging larder and all that. I'd got the second ridge-pole up and guyed and the tent inner pegged down tight, all we had to do was rig the fly and the bell end and we were there. I lit a cigarette and sat back for a bit to cool off. There was a strip of light now along the top of the downs; the grass shone gold, nearly technicolored. There were a lot of people up there, you could see the priests in their white robes, very distant and sharp and clear. The stones looked good, the lintels dark against the glow, and the incense smoke threading straight up in the still air. Our field was very peaceful now with the ghosts gone, there was a smell of dog roses and hay.

We got started again and rigged the rest of the canvas and I went round and shifted a couple of pegs Medea had put in wrong. Then we got the stuff inside and lit the lamp and it all started looking more like home, beetles and moths blundering in knocking their fool heads against the light. I said, 'I'll get some water,' and Medea said, 'I'll come with you,' so we walked diagonally across the field to where there was a tap on a standpipe and an old enamel bath. There was a notice scrawled on a board saying not to empty detergents into the bath, I suppose because the cattle sometimes used it. The 'S' on the notice was printed the wrong way round, I'd never actually seen that done before. Medea had taken her shoes off, as she walked she kicked up little flurries of embers and dark sparks like jewels. Round the bath the ground was all muddy and churned up and she sloshed through that as well, mud never seemed to stick to her. Not for long, anyway.

While we were filling the water carriers I said, 'We shall have the place to ourselves,' which was a classic case of speaking too soon because a Land Rover came down the farm track nearly at once, towing a great long trailer. The car was full of young Danes, leastways I think they were Danes, they nearly all had fair hair. They all piled out laughing when they saw us and called to help unhitch the trailer because it was too long to swing in through the gate. But I wasn't having any of that. I said to Medea, 'Maybe if they can't get in they'll go off someplace else.' They had a maypole on the trailer, so it looked as if they wanted to be hectic. What with the war starting any minute it didn't seem there was going to be much rest and quiet.

The girls all had hip-length pants and little blouse tops in white and turquoise blue. They got the trailer unhooked and started shoving it about trying to angle it to get it through the gateway. It was a big trailer too, one of those lattice-sided things they used to call a Queen Mary. I took the water carriers from Medea and we walked back to the tent. She said she wanted to get the bed straight and hang our stuff up and get supper on, all of which things she was better at doing by herself. I walked over to see how the Danes were getting on. They were in the far corner of the field by the copse. They'd got the trailer in position and the maypole cleared for lifting. Up close you could see what sort of thing it was, I mean what it was all about. It was garlanded with flowers and green boughs and the tip all painted shiny ochre, lying there against the cloth of gold. They had some transistors stood about, one on the cab roof of the Land Rover, but fortunately the sound wasn't travelling very far.

I said we'd had some trouble with ghosts but they got shooed off and we didn't think they'd be back. They gave me some beer, they had cans and cans of it all strewn about. After I'd drunk it I decided I'd walk on up to the main road and see how the war was getting on.

The light was changing all the time now, which pleased me. The sky had turned a sort of pinky bronze, the sort of colour you get if you hold a candy wrapper up close to your eyes. There was a farmhouse on top of the hill, all little and twisted and built of stone like something in *Snow White*. It had very tall ornate chimney stacks, where the light caught them they burned orange like flames. Somebody had hooked a wire across the farm-track. It had a spring one end to keep it tight and a piece of white rag hung in the middle so you could see it was there. I hoped this meant no other people would come in because I had a proprietary feeling about that field of cloth of gold, having been there several times before. I stepped over the wire and walked on up the track. There was an old outhouse I hadn't really noticed before, it had a vintage Morris motor-car in it which pleased me a lot because I like old machinery. It was a pretty sad-looking Morris though, somebody had dumped a stack of old sacks on the roof and one tyre was flat. I wrote my name and Medea's name in the dust on the bonnet before moving on.

What made the campsite so secluded was the copse on the landward side, beech saplings I think they were. They weren't all that tall, but the lie of the land made it impossible to see much beyond. Once I got to the lane though the first of the castles came rearing back into sight, it wasn't really so far off. It was pretty huge; it always surprised you how big it was, it didn't matter how many times you saw it. There was a slip of moon behind it in the sky, in that light the stone didn't look any more substantial. The whole building looked sort of translucent, as if the light was really pouring through. Some of the windows flamed and reflected like diamonds, others were dark.

There were seven castles really, stretching away in a big curve into the distance, though only the first four were visible; the others were lost in the haze, or occulted one behind the next. The nearest, the big one, was silent though the next in line was working very hard. They had cranes rigged on the battlements and you could see loads of stuff going up and the empty slings swinging back down. That castle was really busy. I think it was prepared for trouble, which it was certainly going to get.

I couldn't see any guns from where I stood so I walked on up to the main road. There was a little wooden structure on the verge like a shop counter standing all on its own where you could buy jam and marmalade sometimes, and pots of cottage-made lemon curd. It was all sold out when I got there though, except for a bunch of flowers which looked pretty sad, and anyway I didn't want them. There was a blue Sellotape tin with some sixpences and florins and ten-shilling pieces in it, so it looked as if they'd had a busy day. I lit a cigarette and wondered where the batteries were, but after a while I saw them down below the road some couple of hundred yards away. There was a gate and nobody seemed to be worrying too much, so I opened it and walked on down. There were a lot of vehicles parked, and a steam traction engine with half-tracks. The guns were big things with angular shields in front of the breeches, I think they were eighteen-pounders. The crews all wore shabby peaked caps and khaki uniforms and queer-looking tightly strapped puttees. They had an officer with them, a captain. He looked harassed and red-faced and kept making notes on a clip board. There was a lot of running about and shouting; a fatigue party was filling sandbags from a big pile of sand dumped to one side of the emplacement, others were farther on down the valley hammering stakes into the ground and stringing coils of barbed wire between. It seemed too there was some trouble with the field telephone; a man with headphones on was cranking a handle and saying, 'Hello, HQ,' but nothing was coming through.

I watched them getting the guns lined up for a time. There were shells stacked about on the grass, big ones with shiny yellow cases. I wanted to see the crews open fire but they didn't seem anywhere near ready so I walked on to the next emplacement, which one of the gunners had said was called the Tudor Lines.

Of the two groups the Tudors seemed the better organized. One party was unloading tall wickerwork cylinders from a cart; another was arranging them as a breastwork in front of the guns, and filling them with earth. The guns were enormous things with ornate brass barrels, all rings and straps and curlicues. The gunners wore dusty brown leather costumes and shoes with big buckles and queer flat shiny leather caps. Behind the emplacement two men were mixing powder in a tub. They were using wooden spades so there wouldn't be a spark, but the whole operation still looked risky to me.

I'd expected some really heavy pieces to be brought to bear and so wasn't too surprised when I saw Mons Meg. A little farther on though they had the Dardanelles Gun, which struck me as a bit unnecessary. They had the breech and barrel shored up on stacks of timber and were trying to align them preparatory to screwing them home. They weren't having too much success, which considering the size of the piece wasn't surprising. The gun captain was standing up on top of the barrel trying to jiggle it into line by stamping on it. I called up to him that what he needed was a jack but he was too busy to listen, so I walked back to the eighteen-pounder lines to see if I could borrow one. They didn't seem altogether keen. I got one eventually from one of the supply trucks, though I didn't really see why I should bother since it was my rest that was going to be disturbed. Anyway I lugged it back across the grass and the Tudors were extremely pleased once they got the hang of it. They lifted the muzzle of the gun into line and a dozen started in with crowbars, ramming them into the sockets on the breech and twisting to get the thread started. But that didn't work too well either, as the thread was corroded through being left out in the weather so many years. I left them chipping away at the screw with cold chisels, and greasing it with butter and lard.

The RA captain was studying the nearest enemy position through a little pair of field glasses. He had longish fair hair that had strayed down outside his cap, and he was looking extremely annoyed. I said, 'What you need are some tanks,' but he just looked blank. Then I had another idea and said, 'I mean Land Ships,' but that didn't please him any better. He jumped down from where he was standing and started waving a revolver and shouting something about breaches of security. The revolver was a nasty-looking Webley .38, so I walked over to the nearest of the gun crews in case he started pointing it at me.

It seemed they'd got the land line working because shortly afterwards the order came through to fire. The first gun went off with a big crash and lurched back some distance from the breastwork of sandbags. One of the crew knocked the breech open; out came the shell case sizzling, in went another shell. This time I stood well back behind the line of flight. I found I could watch the shell in the air quite easily; for some reason it seemed to be making a lot of smoke. It was very accurately aimed; I thought it was going to hit the target dead centre, but at the last instant it veered like a side-winder missile and swerved behind the keep. I was expecting a fairly healthy bang over there, but instead the thing fizzled out nearly with a plop in midair. Or rather it didn't exactly fizzle out; it sort of dwindled to a dot and vanished, and the sky shut behind it. Wherever it had gone, it was obviously not going to do much good. I said to one of the gunners, 'At this rate you'll be here all week,' but he seemed very optimistic, he told me they just hadn't found the range. They set to at once loading the gun again and I walked back the way I had come as nothing else seemed likely to happen.

The Danes had got the maypole set up; they'd built a bon-fire, which was against camp rules, and were making a lot of noise. Dusk was settling, but the flames lit their corner of the

field cheerfully. On the crest of the downs the stones stood sharp
and ragged like teeth, but nobody was moving up there, it all
looked very grey and cold and far away.

Medea had cooked a paella, one of those dried, packeted
things. She said, 'About time too,' when I stepped into the
tent, and started ladling the saffron-coloured rice on to a plate.
She was wearing a big chunky sweater now, I thought how
good she looked. I'd have shut the tent flap because it all looked
bleak and miserable out there and it was worrying me, but I
knew she'd want to see out so I let it be.

We'd got a bottle of wine, a Beaujolais; she'd put it by the
cooker to warm and forgotten it, and it had really got hot. If
you've ever tried drinking hot Beaujolais, it burns your throat
right through. Also all we'd got was plastic cups, which didn't
help the taste, and what with that and the barrage banging
away over the wood I started getting annoyed again, though I'd
nearly got over the business with the ghosts. I said, 'It's wrong
to drink this with paella anyway, you should have got som
white,' and she said if I didn't like it I didn't have to drink it,
then she had a big snuffly thing and I had to go over and comfort
her though I didn't feel very much like it. However I really
enjoyed stroking her, she was really very nice, and afterwards
she finished her paella and we had a cigarette and laughed
about the Beaujolais being so hot. She sat a while with her head
on my shoulder and watched the last of the light drain away over
the downs, then she said, 'I want to go to bed, you shut the
tent flap.'

I took the awning stays down and brought them inside and
started lacing the canvas shut. She looked good getting undressed, with the greenish-yellow light from the lamp making
big shadows on the canvas walls and the moths and bugs all
zooming about. The barrage was still going on, I'd nearly got
used to it; but just as I was putting the light out there was a big
rolling crash louder than the rest, then another, then one you
felt through the ground that made that old field of cloth of gold
really shake and ripple. She said, 'What's that?' and I said,
'The Dardanelles Gun, they must have got it screwed together.'
It didn't look as if we were in for a very peaceful night.

Anyway the noise died down after a time and you could hear birds hunting and the crickets in the grass. I liked it lying there with her in the sleeping bag, feeling how smooth and firm her hips were. We made love several times, she was good to love, she was cool and she didn't get smelly and all that. Finally I got tired, so I rolled over on my side and went to sleep and she tucked in back of me with her arms round me, very comforting.

It didn't last all that long though, because the next thing I remember was her stepping on my ankle which woke me up very sharply. There was a lot of din going on that I couldn't at first place. I sat up and saw she'd lit the lamp and was trying to deal with all these cats, and boy there were some cats. We had cats like Bishop Hatto had rats. They were everywhere, six or eight were jumping up trying to claw the larder down, others were cleaning the bits off the plates we'd forgotten to wash, they were up to all sorts. It was raining too, the drops pattering and slashing on the canvas and the bell end of the tent leaking all over, I suppose where Medea had touched it while she was trying to deal with the cats. I started yelling, 'Get rid of these cats, get rid of these damn cats.' I grabbed for a few myself but it was no good, they just smoked off through your fingers worse than those old ghosts. Then I saw there were some three or four starting to drag the garbage bag out under the tent flap so I shied something at them that turned out to be her handbag, bits and pieces flew all over. Then we really had a row. She had her arms full of cats but you could see she wasn't really trying to push them out, not all that hard. I said, 'They are your damn cats and you could get rid of them if you wanted.' Anyway she started in crying again, really crying; then she started pulling the tent flap undone, she said she'd sleep in the car or outside someplace because I didn't want her either. Then the field guns let fly again over the hill and it was hell in there, I tell you. So I let her go which was a pity, she was only wearing a sweater and nothing below the waist and she looked really nice. I lay back and tried to get some rest in between the ground shaking. I remember thinking, 'She's got to be taught a lesson, she brought those damn cats on purpose.' I was still plenty mad.

I think I dozed for a time; anyway, when I sat up the lamp

was still burning, hanging where she'd left it, and the rain was
thudding down and the tent was empty. I felt really bad about
her, I mean having sent her out in the rain and all. I got up and
put some things on and started calling her, but there was no
answer. Then I remembered she'd said she would go to the
car. I ran out to fetch her but she wasn't there.

I really got upset then. I was mad with myself for going to
sleep, it seemed most heartless under the circumstances. I ran
down to the stile where the ghosts had been and called again
but there was nothing, only the wind. There were some big
trees in the next field, really big, you could hear the wind boom
in the branches. The flashes from the field guns kept lighting the
sky, but they weren't bright enough to see by. Rain was trickling
down my back and I was getting soaked. I looked back up the
field and you could see the lamp on and the light glowing through
the canvas, it all looked homely and warm, it was terrible she
wasn't there.

I went back and put a blanket round my shoulders and sat
shivering, listening to the rain. I must have got really confused
then because I remember thinking I'd sent my cat out in the
dark and it wasn't her fault at all, just me and my bit of bad
temper. But there was nothing to be done, once a cat's gone
it's gone in a big way, as I expect most of you know. I lay on
my side after a bit. I kept thinking, 'Come back, Medea, it's all
right,' and trying to set up a sort of mental beacon for her to
home on if she couldn't see the light. I didn't think I'd sleep,
but eventually I dozed off again.

I was warmer when I opened my eyes. I lay there for a bit
feeling good, thinking about the breakfast we were going to
have; cereals and marmalade and toast, and oatcakes and
Scottish cheese. Then I remembered and sat up feeling terrible.
I went out to the car but there was no sign of Medea, the whole
field was still and empty and the dew all grey on the grass and
rough.

I put the kettle on and made some coffee but I didn't want it,
with her things all scattered about like that it just wasn't the
same. I thought I'd better take the car and go and look for her,
though really I had no idea where to start. I got in anyway and

started the engine and I was just turning round when one of the Danish boys came over shouting and waving his arms. He said a girl had cut her throat in the night and would I come and see. I asked was it Medea, that was how bad I was feeling. He said no it wasn't, but I still had to see.

I looked across to the corner of the field. It was still shadowy there, the ground being low and beneath the spinney. The little tent in which it had happened, being soaking wet, had taken up some rather nasty colour from the groundsheet, which colour was staining upward in fans across the canvas. They had lit lamps inside which made the whole effect somewhat worse, they should have known better. I said, 'I don't want to see a thing like that,' and drove away.

I'd forgotten the wire across the track till I drove into it, giving the car a scrape across the paintwork. Anyway I didn't stop, I was too concerned about Medea. There was no sign of her in the lane, so I drove up to the main road. It was broad and white and empty. There was a Shell filling station to one side, but it was shut. I drove the car to the batteries, turned into the gateway and got out. I stood looking over the gate. They'd had more success than I had expected. The nearest castle was a ruin, great shells of wall pierced and fretted with windows and high doorways, all still and vague in the early light. The other castles were still fighting; I saw some nasty-looking stuff drift over, like soft, dark flak.

The eighteen-pounder emplacement was a mess. The grass had been churned into mud and the guns were filthy, all streaked with black and big chunks of mud sticking to the wheels. There were shell cases scattered everywhere and the crews were sitting about in greatcoats looking huddled and miserable. A man with a bandage round his head was cooking sausages over a stick fire, but they none of them looked as if they wanted to eat.

The captain had got his Blighty one sometime during the night; they had him on a stretcher, tucked round with bright red blankets, and there were a couple of nurses. He was propped up with a greatcoat for a pillow, he had a cigarette in his hand and was shouting something about getting more sandbags, but I didn't like his colour. His cap was off; I saw his hair was grey rather than yellow. I asked him if he'd seen Medea and he said no, nobody had come that way.

I went on to the Tudor Lines but nothing was moving there at all. The fires were out, and the big cannon strewed anyways across the hill. One was cocked up on its carriage pointing at the sky, and the muzzle and barrel all smashed. Round it the grass was black and trampled and there was a smell of burned powder, like fireworks.

They had some little gay-striped tents, each one topped with a pennant, but I didn't feel much like looking inside. I walked back the way I had come. As I passed the captain, he pushed himself up on one elbow. He shouted, 'They were going to send us naval support. They promised us naval support.' Then he started to cry, big tears rolling down his face. I felt very sorry for him, but there was nothing I could do.

I got back into the car and drove off. I thought, I don't know why, that she'd probably gone down to the coast, to one of the bays. Trouble was there were several bays, I had to look into them all. I drove to four but they were all the same, there were stands of gorse and bracken, drystone walls, little farmhouses and barns with tractors parked outside. The sea was pale silver, very cold-looking, and it was still only halfway light.

The fifth bay was big, with cliffs of crumbling grey clay. I drove the car as near the edge as I dared, got out and looked over. I saw her at once, lying down there tiny as a moth. Beyond her the beach was a wide half-moon stretching to the sea. The sea was still, nearly unrippling. There were big mirror-streaks of swell moving in, lazy and calm; and out in the bay a ship of the line was practising at the greatguns. The broadsides rolled out fleecy clouds of smoke; the noise of the barrage came in dim across the water, like thunder a long way off.

I started climbing down the cliff. There were gullies, criss-crossing, and the paths were very slippy. I reached the beach near where a little stream ran out under a plank bridge, soaked itself away across the pebbles. Beside the bridge was an old concrete pillbox. The beach was littered, there were sprags of wire, bits of old dried seaweed and half-bricks and broken

bottles and big boulders that had tumbled down out of the
cliffs. Nearer the water the sand was smoother, firm and grey. I
kept wondering what Medea was doing there anyway because it
was none too warm and she was wearing this little white cotton
bikini, very small. I called her but she didn't answer.

I reached her, squatted down. She was lying on her side, back
turned to the sea and her head on her arm. I touched her ankle.
She was very light, I think she must have been hollow. When I
touched her her whole figure moved, sand and bits of dark grey
shale started trickling into the depression where her hip had
been. I remembered the whole thing then, about snipping her
out of a calendar page and pasting her down so carefully. I was
really upset because it was all my fault, I'd just stopped thinking of her in the round and that had been enough. Though what
with the war and all I suppose it was understandable.

Anyway she was still three-dimensional, which was something. I started moving round her in a rather ungentlemanly
way, being curious to see what she looked like from behind.
Which was my second big mistake because I took my mind off
her again just for a second and it gave her a chance to flatten
right out. She was supported at the back by a framework of
scantling, very neatly made. The wood was new, pinkish
yellow, and two struts were pushed down into the sand to keep
her firm. I started getting really depressed then because Medea
hadn't been the sort of exercise you can do all that often; I
mean, these days even good calendar pages aren't all that easy
to come by.

The frigate seemed to be drifting in closer to the cliffs, I
looked up and she was getting really vast. She was turning
too, showing the black and amber stripes along her side and her
row of gunports. It wasn't a good place to stop but I was still
worried about Medea. I thought for a bit but I couldn't see how
I was going to take her with me, she was too big to go in the
car even with the hood down and naturally being a soft-top
there was no roof-rack. It seemed I was just going to have to
leave her there, which was a great pity on top of all that had
happened. It was raining again, a thin, misty drizzle, I could see
her buckling pretty soon and getting spoiled.

In the end I turned her round so at least she was facing the sea, and propped her with a couple of stones. I ran back the way I had come. As I got to the top of the path there was a boom and the whole cliff shook. I looked back and saw shingle and bits of rock fly up in the air. I was really sorry then, I felt I should have tried to take her with me instead of leaving her to get blown apart. I should have guessed they'd use her as a mark.

I sat in the car for a bit and thought things through. The first problem was the tent, which had of course been hers. Also there were her things, her clothes and all the rest. It seemed probable the whole lot would have vanished, leaving my gear just strewn about on the grass. I sincerely hoped so, as I wasn't relishing the prospect of burning the camp. Killing a pretty woman now and then is all very well but getting rid of her possessions afterwards is quite another thing. However there was plainly only one answer, I had to go and find out. The drizzle had misted the windscreen so that I couldn't see, I started the wipers and drove that damn old car away up the hill.